CANCUN
M O O N

Duane Stanley

◆ FriesenPress

Suite 300 - 990 Fort St
Victoria, BC, V8V 3K2
Canada

www.friesenpress.com

ISBN
978-1-03-911971-0 (Hardcover)
978-1-03-911970-3 (Paperback)
978-1-03-911972-7 (eBook)

1. FICTION, COMING OF AGE

Distributed to the trade by The Ingram Book Company

CANCUN
MOON

Chapter 1

Susan Jenkins is suddenly woken by a faint crackling sound echoing from somewhere in her apartment. Unsure of exactly what the noise is, she slowly and cautiously tiptoes down the darkened hallway to where she can just barely see a slightly familiar, long, brown, crumpling envelope, nosing around frantically, then becoming wedged, tight, into the crack at the bottom of her apartment door.

"Thank God!" she whispers, obviously quite relieved as to what the noise actually is. She immediately relaxes from her rigid, on-guard tiptoe stance, then continues softly, and silently, towards the door. She listens intensely, with her ear pinned against the door, breathless and motionless, anticipating the unknowing, heavy footsteps of her fat, greasy-haired landlord dissipating down the stairs and out the front door of the apartment building.

She reaches down and pulls firmly on the jammed envelope but is unable to retrieve it from her side of the door. Slowly and silently, she opens the door, then quickly swoops down and snatches it up. She swiftly closes and locks the door, all in one motion, then instantly tears the letter open with her sharp fingernail. A silent pause.

"Damn!" She curses softly. Shear frustration races across her face while glaring intensely at the heading of the letter. "Oh no! Do you believe this?" She shrieks, almost in tears, while lightly stomping her foot and quivering the letter. "Damn!" She curses on, accelerating her frustration and anger.

Ring . . . Ring . . .

"Ah!" She screeches while moving towards the house phone and giving the letter one last good shudder above her head.

Ring . . .

"Hello." Susan answers in an abnormally edgy tone.

"Good morning!" Chris greets piercingly.

"Oh, good morning." Susan replies, still revealing an abnormal, quite obvious, slightly edgy tone in her voice.

"Is everything all right?" he questions, genuinely concerned. "You sound a little upset," he adds, in total suspense as to what might have happened.

"I am. I can't believe I just got another rent increase, after all the fixing up I've done around here. Every year I've gotten one!" She persists heatedly, lightly whining, while reading a bit further into the letter, occasionally glancing around her beautified apartment.

"Oh . . . Sorry to hear that." Chris sighs in relief, thanking God that it wasn't something he might have said or done. He wipes his forehead with the back of his hand and sinks back into his old, worn couch. "I know exactly how you feel." he confesses with a deep breath and genuine sigh. "I'm sure I'll be getting another rent increase soon too. Because I just got one last year, one year to the day I moved into this place."

A few seconds of dead silence over the phone.

"Hey, you know what? I've got an idea," Chris suggests, wide-eyed, while leaning forward on the edge of his couch.

"What?" Susan asks curiously.

"Enough of this doom and gloom!" he insists with cheerful persuasion. "How about breakfast on me, at the old Look Out Café? Would that cheer you up a bit?" he asks, while reaching out to the coffee table for his package of cigarettes.

"Oh, I'm sure it probably would." Susan can't deny. She cracks a cute smile and bites her baby fingernail.

"Excellent! What time should I pick you up?" Chris asks sharply as he smoothly draws the last cigarette from the pack using only his lips. He abruptly crumples and fires the empty package across the room, landing it only a few inches from the garbage can, then strikes a wooden match on the side of his faded, tattered blue jeans, and lights up.

"Umm, oh, that's OK. I think I'll just walk down to blow off some of this steam," she says, chuckling nervously while quickly twirling one of the short, fuzzy strings from her sexy, almost see-through pajamas around her finger, back and forth, back and forth.

"All right. See you there about nine-thirty, quarter to ten?" Chris suggests as a big cloud of smoke billows from his lungs.

"Sounds good." Susan replies while checking herself out in the front hall mirror, playfully ruffling up her hair.

"OK, see you soon," he says, dousing his cigarette out in the ashtray.

"Ok, Bye."

"Bye."

Click.

*   *   *

Chris arrives a little early, grabs a booth and the daily newspaper, and orders two coffees while unconsciously flipping right to the classified section, "HOMES FOR RENT." He looks down at the page and whispers to himself. "Two-bedroom heritage home for rent in quiet neighbourhood, $1175 a month."

Seconds later, coffees, ice waters, and menus arrive at the table just as Susan walks in half smiling, sits down, and quickly stirs a cream into her coffee. "It's freezing out there!" she says with shivering shoulders. "I can't believe you can already see your breath in the air, and it's only the end of August." she conveys, while rubbing the palms of her hands together.

Chris just smiles, then reaches out and gently pinches her rosy cheeks before flipping a couple pages.

"Anything interesting in the paper today?" Susan attempts to ask as cheerfully as possible, considering her latest circumstances, while sipping away on her coffee, both hands clutched to the warm cup.

"As a matter of fact, there is." Chris states in an unusually suspenseful tone, then quickly flips back a few pages. "Now, where was that?" he mutters while scrolling his slightly yellowed smoker's fingers up and down the columns of the classified section, "HOMES FOR RENT." "Oh, here it is, two-bedroom heritage home for rent in quiet neighbourhood, $1175 a month." He reads aloud with intent.

"Sounds nice. Are you thinking about moving?" Susan asks while propping herself up a bit in the seat.

"Well, funny thing is, I just flipped the paper open, right to this page. I wasn't even thinking about moving, but after reading this add and you telling me about your rent increase, I just thought of a very interesting idea." He boasts enthusiastically.

"What do you mean?" she asks, displaying her cute, puzzled-eyebrow look while still grasping her warm cup.

"How much is your rent going up to?" he pries, leaning forward on the table.

"Well, $875 a month," she reveals, apprehensively, still looking a little puzzled. "Why do you ask?" She urges on curiously.

"Hmm, well, mines $855 a month right now, but who knows how much it's going to go up to in a couple months when another year is up." He easily predicts the worst-case scenario.

"So, what's your idea?" She digs a little deeper.

"Well, I was thinking," he explains while using his fingers for points of reference to ramble on. "We've known each other about three months now. We get along really well, we like the same kinds of food, we like the same kind of movies." He says enticingly.

"So, what's your idea, silly?" she persists, leaning forward on the table as well, happily expecting the answer.

A silent pause.

"Well, what if we got a place together?" he suggests in a fidgety manner.

Susan appears shocked and slowly leans back in her seat, remaining silent while sipping away on her coffee.

"You could still have your own room, if you wanted," he insists with a slight pitch change in his voice. "And we'd both be saving a lot of money, right off the bat. Just think, right now, with both our places together, we're paying over seventeen hundred a month. Not including utilities." he urges persuasively.

Susan listens intensely, occasionally nodding, but remains silent, seemingly pondering his idea.

"Wait," Chris blurts out with both hands in mid-air. "Before you say anything, let's get on the phone and find out more details about this place. Then maybe we can take a quick drive-by after breakfast to see what it looks like. It would be fun," he insists, while clasping his hands together. "What else do you have to do today?" he asks, suggestively.

"Hmm." Susan contemplates his idea while glancing out the window.

"Well? What do you think?" Chris pries, hoping for a quick answer.

"Sure, why not!" Susan agrees.

"Ah, shoot, my phone is as dead as a doorknob. This thing just won't hold a charge very long anymore. Ever since I dropped it that day." Chris curses in disbelief. "Oh well, I'll just get another one today or tomorrow," he decides, lightly slapping his dead phone down on the table, then quickly stuffs it back in his pocket.

"Oh, right. Nice, looks like I forgot my cell phone at home." Susan suddenly realizes while scrambling through her track top. "I'm a little out of it. Waking up to that letter, ah!" She regretfully reminisces.

"Ah, no worries. I'll be back in two seconds!" he exaggerates, and quickly exits the booth.

Chris marches to the old phone booth just outside the cafe window, which is still in plain sight of Susan sitting at their table. He waves and blows her a kiss, then dials the push-button phone.

Susan responds with a big smile and a wave back. She looks down at the ad and whispers to herself, "Two-bedroom heritage home for rent in quiet neighbourhood, $1175 a month, hmm." She allows her curiosity to get the better of her, then flips a couple of pages.

"Good morning!" the waitress greets cheerfully as she approaches the table.

"Good morning," Susan replies.

"You guys know what you're having today?" she asks, ready to take their orders.

"Not quite yet, thanks," Susan says respectfully. "He just stepped outside there to make a quick call." She politely points out. "He shouldn't be too long though," she concludes with a cheerful smile.

"Oh, that's OK. No problem. Please, take your time," the waitress insists, displaying a genuine smile as she tops off their coffees.

Susan just finishes reading her somewhat optimistic horoscope when Chris heads back into the cafe with a look of excitement plastered across his face. He slides back into the booth, and without a word, quickly rips open a cream and pours it into his coffee. He stirs his coffee rapidly, creating that sometimes unintentional, always familiar, extra loud tingling noise as the spoon hits the inner side of his cup, then immediately takes a big gulp.

"Ah, hot!" he gasps while waving his hand in front of his mouth as if to cool the freshly poured coffee.

"Are you, OK?" Susan asks, leaning forward for a closer look.

Chris frantically grabs his ice water and guzzles it down, hoping to cool the over-the-top burning sensation in his throat. He stares, wide-eyed, with a mouth full of ice and water, silently nodding his head up and down, confirming that he is going to be just fine.

"Wow, I felt a lawsuit coming on," he jokes, just as he catches his breath, and they both have a good laugh.

"So, what did they say?" Susan asks, left in total suspense.

"Well, we can take a look at it around one o'clock this afternoon. And you won't believe this," he says in a deeper-than-normal, long, drawn-out tone of voice.

"What?" Susan asks, intrigued, before taking a noisy sip of coffee.

Chris leans forward on the table with wide eyes and begins rattling off each of the points by tapping his fingers on the table. "It has a fireplace, hardwood floors, a big backyard, and a washer and dryer. And you're allowed to have a pet!" he adds enticingly while reaching across the table and gently squeezing her hand. "You always say you wish you could have a dog. It's in an older part of town called James Bay, right near the water," he elaborates.

"Sounds too good to be true," Susan insists in a sarcastic tone. A silent pause. "It would be a pretty big step for me to move in with anyone right now. I've never lived with anyone before, except for my family of course." She chuckles nervously. "But I must admit, it is a very interesting idea," she says optimistically. "But I would definitely need time to think about something like that, though."

"Hey, look. The sun's coming out," Chris shouts while grinning and pointing out the cafe window. "We'll definitely put the top down on the old convertible today. But we better stop by my place and grab a couple extra sweaters, just in case it gets a little chilly out later in the afternoon."

"Good idea," Susan agrees.

"What would you like for breakfast?" Chris asks promptly while looking up at the specials on the chalkboard, then back to Susan.

"Well, I'm not really that hungry right now," she admits and closes her menu. "Are you?"

"Not really," Chris says, then pushes his menu towards the centre of the table. "Not for breakfast anyway. Wink, wink, nudge, nudge. Just kidding," he jokes, and they both have a good laugh. There's a silent smiling pause between them, except for the soft music playing in the background. "Hey, maybe we should just head into James Bay a little early and have lunch there. Then maybe take a drive around to see what the neighbourhood and town are like," he says excitedly while leaning forward with his wide eyes.

"Sure. Good idea," Susan says, and takes one last sip of her coffee.

Chris reaches in his pocket and pulls out a five-dollar bill and some change for their coffees, and a small tip. "Cool, Let's go!" he says in a mildly panicked tone, half-standing, half-sitting, as they both exit the booth.

"Have a lovely day!" the waitress says, waving from across the cafe.

Chapter 2

S usan grabs a map from the glove compartment just as the electric convertible top slowly eases down. "It's like we're going on some kind of adventure," she says while buckling her seatbelt.

"I know. I can't wait to see this place!" Chris shouts ecstatically, then starts up the car.

"What did you say the name of that place was?" Susan asks, with her cute, puzzled-eyebrow look.

Chris reaches into his left shirt pocket and pulls out a crumpled piece of paper. "Cook Street, three thirteen Cook," he rambles.

"No, the name of the town!" she chuckles.

"Oh, James Bay." He instantly recalls.

"James Bay," Susan repeats slowly as she unfolds the map. "I think I've been there before," she ponders while holding her right hand on her chin. A silent pause. "Yeah! Now, I remember. When I was about six or seven my father and I drove into James Bay to pick up my grandfather from the train station. If I remember correctly, we drove right along the water line, straight into James Bay," she explains as she follows the map with her finger. "Yeah, just drive south for about ten miles, then hang a right onto Ocean Boulevard, and keep driving west for about twenty more miles. According to this map, Cook Street is only about six or seven blocks off of Ocean Boulevard."

"Excellent! It shouldn't take us too long to get there then," Chris states.

"Not really," Susan agrees. "But let's just take our time anyway and enjoy the scenery along the way. Although it was about twenty years ago, I can still remember how beautiful a drive it was along the ocean," she reminisces with a serene look and a calming voice.

Chris pulls the car out of the cafe parking lot, then takes a quick detour down a few back alleys towards his apartment. He quickly clunks upstairs to his apartment while Susan waits in the car, listening to the radio and looking over the map. While upstairs, Chris pulls out his secret stash of marijuana and expertly rolls up a big fat joint. He quickly lights it and cravingly draws in two big puffs. *Cough! Cough!* "This is super strong stuff," he chokes. Now grinning from ear to ear, he quickly butts the joint out on the inside of the kitchen sink. *Cough! Cough!*

He rips open a drawer and fires a couple mints into his mouth hoping Susan won't be able to detect the strong smell of marijuana on his breath. He scurries into his bedroom and grabs a couple sweaters from the bottom drawer of his messy dresser. He locks the apartment door, then runs downstairs and literally jumps right back into the driver's seat without even opening the door.

Susan does a double take at his actions and lightly shakes her head. "Crazy guy," she whispers, totally unaware of why he's acting just a little off the wall.

He starts the car and backs it up recklessly into the alleyway, not really looking where he's going. The car skims an old garbage can, sending the lid spiraling like a top across the pavement where it eventually leans itself up against the very can from where it was shaken. "Oops, oh well. It's empty anyway," is all he can say, and they begin laughing. "What are the chances of doing that again? Time to buy a lotto ticket!" He calculates sarcastically with a grin.

"I couldn't begin to guess," Susan confesses with a smirk.

Chris instantly slams the car into drive and steps down hard on the gas, as if there was no time to waste. "Well, here we go," he states the obvious while leaning forward into the steering wheel with a big kid-like grin plastered across his face. In doing so, he accidentally glances in the rear-view mirror, revealing his noticeably red eyes. "Oh, shit!" he mutters, and slips into his sunglasses.

"What's that?" Susan asks innocently as she folds the map between her legs.

"Oh, nothing. It's all good," he quickly covers while scanning the stereo for the perfect song to play. "It's all good!" he repeats with a grin.

The sun is shining and the air is crisp while the latest hit song, "The Simple Things in Life," whisks them down Ocean Boulevard towards James Bay.

"Was I right about this being a beautiful drive?" Susan asks, stretching her arms way up over her head, simultaneously inhaling a deep breath of cool morning air through her nose, then slowly exhaling out through her mouth. "The salty air is so amazingly refreshing!" she adds while shaking her windblown hair from her lips.

"I can't argue with you there," Chris agrees as he turns and looks right at her. "It's pretty damn nice, if I do say so myself," he adds while reaching over and taking her by the hand. The radio plays on, accommodating the beautiful drive along Ocean Boulevard.

"Look!" Susan points to a sign at the side of the road. "James Bay, 4.6 miles."

"Oh yeah," Chris says while glancing towards the dash. "We better pull into that old gas station just up ahead on the left there. We're getting a little low," he realizes just before pulling into the station.

Ding! Ding!

"Good morning!" the noticeably good-looking attendant greets as he pops his head out from under the hood of an old '47 pickup. He saunters towards their car, wiping the grease from his hands into an already slightly greased rag.

"Good morning!" Chris says while reaching deep into his pocket. "Forty bucks, regular please," he demands assertively and hands the attendant two twenty-dollar bills. "Do you want anything from inside, Susan?" Chris asks as he steps out of the car.

"No thanks," she replies.

"I'll be back in two seconds. I'm just going to grab some cigarettes," he says while spinning around to face her.

"I thought you were going to quit," Susan says in a sarcastic tone while shaking her head.

"I will! I will!" Chris yells back, walking forward, looking backward with a crooked grin as he enters the gas station store.

"Nice car," the attendant remarks as he removes the gas cap and gently eases in the nozzle.

"Thanks. He just got it not too long ago. I think it's been in his family since it was brand new in '67."

"Oh yeah? It sure looks good," he says while thoroughly looking over the car. "Do you want me to check the oil?" the ever-so-charming attendant asks while eagerly walking towards the front of the car.

"No thanks. That's OK," Susan says politely.

The young attendant gently swipes his squeegee across the front window of the car, clearing a strip of soapy suds, when close eye contact takes place between them.

Susan blushes and gently shies away.

"Are you guys from around here?" he asks while looking over the top of the window, trying very hard not to look directly at her tasty lips.

"Not really, we're just checking out an old house for rent in the James Bay area," she says, smiling and pointing to the exact location on the map.

"Oh yeah, Cook Street. That's a really cool area to live in," the attendant explains as he wipes the leftover water drops from the window with a paper towel. "There are huge maple trees all the way up and down both sides of the street, and all the houses are really funky looking. Antique or heritage style, I should say," he clarifies.

"Sounds very nice," Susan says, nodding.

"Yeah, it is. I've lived in James Bay practically all my life. It's sort of a party town, but I mean that in a good way," he continues. "There's a couple small pubs with live music every Friday and Saturday night about ten blocks from the Cook Street area, and there's always a drop-in, sing-along beach party going on somewhere around James Bay in the summertime."

"Cool," Susan says. Chris exits the gas station store with a half sack of beer in one hand, while stuffing two packs of cigarettes in the top pocket of his shirt with the other.

"Hey, Chris!" Susan shouts lightly as he nears the car, seemingly a little nerve racked from the heartfelt connection she just experienced with the attendant. "This guy, sorry, what's your name?" Susan asks politely.

"Brad," the attendant informs.

"Hi, I'm Susan and this is Chris." They nod towards one another.

"Nice to meet you!" echoes amongst them.

"Brad's been telling me a little bit about James Bay," Susan says.

"Oh yeah, do you know of any good places we could have lunch?" Chris asks, as he shuffles back into the car and closes the door.

"Yeah, as a matter of fact, I do," Brad says while plunging the squeegee back into a bucket of soapy water. "Well, actually, there are a few good places in town. The Wild Reel has a lot of different kinds of food, but mostly pasta and seafood dishes. And then there's The Reef Diner. That's a fifties type place, you know, hamburgers, fries, stuff like that. Then there's Rocky Shores Fish & Chips right on Fishermen's Wharf. They've got the best fish and chips anywhere! And the town's not really that big, so you can't really miss them. Anyway, most of the stores and restaurants are right on the main strip," Brad concludes with a big smile.

"Sounds good," Chris says, and starts up the car.

"Thanks for all the info," Susan quickly adds in. "See you! Bye!"

They all wave as the Mustang burns out of the gas station, spitting the occasional rock from its spinning tires as they cross over the gravel shoulder.

"If Brad is any indication of what the people are like in James Bay, it must be a pretty nice place to live," Susan says smiling, then casually glances back towards the old gas station.

"Yeah, you could be right about that," Chris responds in a quiet tone, then turns and looks her straight in the eyes, suddenly sensing the possibility that there might have been some kind of connection made between her and Brad back at the old gas station, but his paranoia is quickly shrugged off by his stoned ego.

Susan takes in a deep breath and leans back into her seat.

A silent pause between them as the radio plays softly.

"Even if we don't end up liking the house, we still will have had a beautiful day driving out along the water!" Susan says while looking toward Chris, smiling gently as she pulls the windblown hair away from her face.

"I can't argue with you there," Chris agrees and accelerates the car another twenty miles per hour.

"I just can't believe we haven't driven down this road more often," Susan states regretfully.

"Well, you never know," Chris says as he turns to her with a smirky grin on his face.

"If we did live out here, how much further do you think we would have to travel to get to work every day?" Susan asks with her puzzled look.

"I'm not quite sure," Chris admits. "Check out the map." He instantly points between her thighs.

"Oh, right." A silent pause. "Well, it looks like the city is about ten or twelve miles north of James Bay, and if we just kept on driving straight right along Ocean Boulevard, it eventually loops us right back into the city."

"Oh, really?" Chris says, as though just scoring a point. "Yeah, so, what you're saying is, if we did live out here, it would probably be even faster for us to get to work every day. Because there's not as many traffic lights along Ocean Boulevard," he states with a childlike, devilish glance she never sees.

"Yeah, you could be right about that," Susan agrees while double-checking the map. "So, basically, when we drive into work from where we live now, we travel west into the city, the same direction as we're travelling right now, but on the opposite side from where we are right now. Well, you know what I mean," she explains, looking for confirmation.

"Sounds about right," Chris agrees in a smart-ass, sarcastic, know-it-all tone, then cranks up the stereo just as "Your Desire" begins playing. They cruise smoothly along Ocean Boulevard, enjoying the sights and sounds as one hit after another plays loudly over the car radio.

"Oh we better slow down. We're getting really close," Susan announces abruptly, instantly releasing herself from the peaceful trance of it all, while simultaneously turning down the radio. "Take the next right onto View Street. Then the first, second, third, fourth, fifth, sixth left onto Cook Street." She double-checks with definite accuracy while following her finger along the windblown map.

Suspense fills the air as the car slowly eases along Cook Street.

"Oh, wow, there it is!" Susan lightly shouts while pointing and leaning forward in her seat.

"Where?" he asks, mistaking her pointing finger's line of fire.

"Right there!" she stresses, pointing to the house, now leaning in a little closer to Chris in hopes of recalibrating his focus. "The blue one! Right there!" She instantly clarifies, jabbing her pointing finger right at it.

"Wow, look at that place!" Chris whisper-shouts as he pulls the car over near the front of the house and shuts off the engine. "Are you sure that's it?" he asks while raising himself from the seat and peering over the top of the windshield.

"Yeah, three thirteen Cook Street you said, right?" Susan double-checks with her cute, sarcastic, puzzled look.

"Yeah, that's definitely it then. Nice place!" Chris states while staring in a comfortable disbelief. "What time have you got?" He asks as he plops himself back down in his seat.

"Eleven twenty-five," she says while displaying her fancy diver's watch right in his face.

"Hmm, we've still got about an hour and a half before we can really take a good look at it," he says, confirming the obvious. "Do you feel like having lunch somewhere now, or should we just wait until after we look at the place?" Chris asks, nodding his head towards the house.

"Well, we might as well go have lunch now," Susan suggests. "Because like that Brad guy said, the town is not really that big. So, I imagine everything is fairly close to here," she adds optimistically.

"Yeah, you're probably right about that," Chris agrees. "What do you feel like having for lunch?" he asks with both hands clutched to the steering wheel.

"How about that fish and chip place, right on Fishermen's Wharf?" she suggests sweetly.

"You got it!" Chris agrees excitedly as he starts up the car, slams it into drive, then steps down hard on the gas pedal, barreling them off towards the centre of town.

"Easy there, Speedy Gonzales. Remember, we've still got plenty of time," Susan sarcastically reconfirms while displaying her watch right in front of him and tapping on the glass face. They both laugh.

Chapter 3

"It's like we've just stepped into some kind of time warp," Chris remarks while glancing from side to side as they quickly pass by the slightly blurred buildings of James Bay. "Everything looks like were still in the 1940s, And the buildings almost look brand new," he adds while nonchalantly checking himself out in the side-view mirror.

"Yeah, they sure do look after this little town, don't they?" Susan agrees. "Look! There's the sign. Rocky Shores Fish & Chips. Turn left, then right, then straight in through there," she happily directs, right through the opened antique gate.

Chris slowly pulls the car into the dusty gravel parking lot and drives right up to the edge of the wharf, which overlooks a crisp, picturesque scene where many rows of high-masted boats are docked.

"Wow! Look at all the fishing boats," Susan says with wide eyes of amazement as they both exit the car.

"Hey, it looks like there's some crab and lobster boats too. Look, see all the traps on the back of those boats?" he shouts excitedly while squinting and pointing.

"Yeah, let's go check it out," Susan encourages.

"FRESH SEAFOOD!" a wiry, old, red-headed fisherman shouts out repeatedly with intent. "FRESH SEAFOOD!"

"Wow. Unreal. It looks like you can even buy fresh seafood right off the boats here too!" she says, seemingly amazed, while shading the sun with one hand and pointing with the other.

"Yeah, you can't get it any fresher than that, that's for sure!" Chris elaborates, then wraps his arm around her shoulders.

"Come on, let's go check it out," she encourages once again as she breaks from his clutches and begins walking swiftly towards the thick wooden ramp that connects the land to a floating maze of wooden pathways down below.

"Wait a sec. Why don't we just go have lunch now and relax in the sun for a while?" Chris suggests in a slightly whiny tone. "Then maybe we can come back down here later this afternoon and pick up something for dinner. You never know, we might just have something to celebrate, right?" He adds with his stoned grin.

"All, right, sounds like a plan," Susan agrees as they both start walking towards the old Rocky Shores Fish & Chip shack.

* * *

"What can I get for you two today?" rumbles the very large, burly fish and chip man as they approach the funky old shack.

"Hmm, I'll definitely have the halibut and chips and a large lemonade," Susan politely orders while reading from the tattered, multicoloured, detachable wooden picture board menu swinging in the wind just above the order window.

"Make that a double order," Chris insists, as he throws two twenty-dollar bills down on the counter.

"Coming right up!" The big Rocky Shores man growls as he dunks a load of fresh cut potatoes into a vat of boiling, crackling oil then hands Chris a ten-dollar bill and some change. "You two just go have a seat over there at one of those old picnic tables and I'll bring it out to you when she's all done up!" shouts the very large gent.

"Oh, thank you." Susan gestures politely with a nod as they turn and walk toward the colourful picnic tables, not too far off in the distance. "Smell that fresh, salty air!" Susan encourages in a long, drawn-out fashion as they approach the picnic tables. She stops dead in her tracks, inhaling a deep breath through her nose, noticeably holding it in for a long moment, then stretches her arms high and wide above her head. She stares at the blue sky where a flock of squawking seagulls fly overhead, then calmly exhales through her mouth. "It's so beautiful out here," she elaborates with a touch of excitement in her voice.

"Can't argue with you there," Chris agrees. They take a seat on the same side of the picnic table, viewing the ocean and the intertwining array of swaying boat masts. "This place is right out of an old movie," Chris remarks as he pulls out a cigarette and quickly lights it.

An uneasy pause erupts between them as Susan must wave her hand in front of her face to avoid the cigarette smoke.

"Oh, sorry about that," he sincerely apologizes. A silent pause. "So, what's been happening at the bank these days?" he asks, squinting from a ray of sun.

"Things are looking pretty good, actually. They're going to be doing some major renovations starting this week coming up. I saw the drawings; it's going to be super modern looking! New everything basically," she elaborates.

"Nice," Chris says.

"Yeah, they're also offering all the employees evening courses to upgrade their computer skills. Even if the course has nothing to do with the bank's computers, we'll still be able to take any course we want, and they'll pay for it," she details excitedly.

"Sounds like a pretty damn nice place to work!"

"Yeah, I guess I'm pretty lucky to have my job. The people I work with are really nice too. How about you? How are things at your job with the new boss and everything?" Susan asks, genuinely interested.

"Oh . . . all right, I guess," Chris replies, unenthusiastically. "Apparently our company is thinking about expanding by splitting the food and drug accounts up into two separate, larger warehouses so they can specialize to the specific customers and become one of the largest competitive warehouse companies around," Chris adds with a touch more enthusiasm as a cloud of smoke billows from his lungs.

"That sounds like pretty good job security to me," Susan encourages.

"Yeah, I guess. I think our contract is up pretty soon too, and that should take me just over the twenty-eight dollar an hour mark. Plus some enhanced benefits too, apparently," he adds with a big grin.

"Good for you," she conveys happily.

"One for you, and one for you!" rumbles the large fish and chip man as he gently rests their overfilled trays of food on the picnic table. "Enjoy!" he shouts and quickly walks back towards the old Fish & Chip shack, wearing his very large, slightly greased, whitish apron that flaps with every motion of the cool breeze, enthusiastic to serve the next customers in line.

"This is fantastic," Chris mumbles while licking his greasy fingertips.

"Hot too," Susan says. "How the heck are you eating it so fast?" she asks while waving her hand in front of her mouth.

"I guess I was hungrier than I thought," Chris confesses as he takes the last few bites, wiping the grease from his face with his crumpled napkin, leaving only a ketchup stain at the bottom of his container. Susan just smiles and shakes her head. "What time have you got now?" Chris asks like an impatient kid.

"We've still got about forty minutes," Susan confirms while looking at her watch. Chris immediately opens a brand-new pack of smokes and stuffs the wrapper into his empty lemonade container. He shakes up the pack, grabs a smoke with his lips, cups his hands, and lights it.

Susan looks at Chris with despair, and it doesn't go unnoticed. A silent pause.

"I promise, if we do end up getting the house together, I'll try to quit smoking, or at least cut back," he insists in a pleading tone.

"All right," Susan says with slight skepticism in her voice.

"I will, I promise," Chris whines.

"You shouldn't just try to quit only because we might live together one day," she stresses in a slightly harsh, convincing tone. "You've got to try quitting just for you. You know it's really not that good for you at all, right? Look what happened to your father." She cracks the emotional hammer down.

There's an uneasy, silent pause between them.

"I'm sorry, I shouldn't have said that," Susan apologizes and puts her hand on his shoulder. "It's just that I care about you," she adds sympathetically.

"I know, I care about you too," Chris assures affectionately as he leans over and kisses her on the lips. "It's just so hard to quit," he insists intensely while looking into her eyes.

Susan breaks the mood with a big smile and a hug, then rises from her seat. "Hey! Let's jump back in the car and check out the rest of the town before heading back to Cook Street," she suggests enthusiastically as she basketball tosses their garbage into the nearby container, then gently cups Chris's face with both hands, anticipating his response.

"Good idea," Chris agrees, now feeling a little more back on track.

They drive around rocking to the songs playing on the radio while taking in the beauty of James Bay. Chris gently grabs Susan's wrist to look at her watch. "It's ten to one," he shouts over the music. "We better start heading back up to Cook!" He then cranks the steering wheel all the way over and does a U-turn in the middle of the main strip.

"Man oh man," Susan mumbles under her breath. "What a crazy driver," she concludes while holding on for dear life.

"What's that?" Chris questions nonchalantly.

"Oh, nothing," she says. "It's just that, I think you must have been a race-car driver in your past life," she adds jokingly, and they both have a good laugh.

*   *   *

Ding! Dong!

The doorbell sounds loudly as Chris presses it. Seconds later, the door opens slowly.

"Hello," greets a tiny elderly woman.

"Hi, I'm Chris, and this is Susan," he politely introduces as they both reach out and shake her hand. "I spoke to you earlier on the phone today, about your house," Chris reminds kindly.

"Yes, of course dear," The old woman remembers. "Please, come in!" she welcomes.

"This is a really beautiful home you have here," Susan compliments.

"Thank you, dear, you're so kind," the old woman says.

"Look at the size of the living room and dining room, they're huge," Chris elaborates as they continue on their tour throughout the old house. "And check out the kitchen," he says excitedly as they walk in from the dining room.

"Very nice," Susan replies. "Everything is so well kept," she adds while admiring the beautifully tiled backsplash behind the counter with the touch of her hand.

"Is that a garage I see back there?" Chris asks while leaning over the kitchen sink and pointing out the window.

"Yes, dear," the sweet old woman replies. "My husband built it just before he passed away last spring," the old woman sadly explains.

"Oh, I'm so sorry," Susan responds sincerely.

"He was a very nice man," the sweet woman remembers as tears slowly fill her eyes.

Ding! Dong!

"Excuse me a moment, dear," the old woman pleads while gently wiping her teary eyes with a small piece of scrunched, tattered tissue paper that looks as if she's been carrying it around all day long.

Ding! Dong! The doorbell rings again.

The sweet old woman suddenly cracks a quivery smile and slowly shuffles herself out of the kitchen to answer the front door.

Another young couple enter the house. Both Chris and Susan can easily hear them express the same genuine excitement about how beautiful the old house is as they did.

"Feel free to look around at the rest of the house," the old woman encourages Chris and Susan in her sweet, soft-spoken tone of voice as she pokes her head around the corner into the kitchen. They both walk down the long hallway.

"Look at the size of the bedrooms!" Susan says in amazement. "And The bathroom! Wow!" she adds with an excited whisper.

"So, what do you think?" Chris asks as he puts his arm around her. "Would you like to live here?" he questions enthusiastically.

"I think it's beautiful!" Susan elaborates. "But I would still like to have a little time to think about it. Like I said, it's a pretty big step for me," she reiterates.

"It's a pretty big step for me too," Chris insists, trying his best to smoothen the idea.

"I know, I know," Susan says, portraying a little frustration.

The other young couple are in the kitchen with the old woman discussing how much they would enjoy living in the old house. The old woman explains to the young couple that Chris and Susan were the first to call so they would be offered to rent the old house first. Chris and Susan can overhear their discussion echoing down the hall.

"What should we do?" Chris asks in a persuasive whisper.

"I just don't know," Susan says, then puts her hands over her face and quietly moans. Chris smiles while staring at her intensely. "I just don't know if we should," Susan pleads with frustration in her voice. "I just hate being under pressure to make such a decision so fast," she elaborates with concern, then spins around and walks to the bedroom window.

"Let's just do it," Chris persuades, now standing directly behind her, reaching out, and softly caressing her shoulders. "It will be great. We'll save so much money and we'll get to spend a lot more time together. And I promise, I'll be extra clean too," he continues to encourage. "You like the house, don't you?" he asks, as if to confirm, knowing darn well that she truly does love it.

"Yeah, but–" Susan spits out just before hearing the old woman shuffling down the hallway.

The old woman enters the master bedroom where Susan and Chris stand face to face, silhouetted by the light of the window, quietly debating. "How are you two making out?" she asks softly with both hands close to her chest, still grasping the tissue.

"Oh, just fine. Thanks," Susan says with a quivering smile.

"It seems the other couple are interested in renting my home, but I let them know that you two were first to inquire," the old woman explains in a sweet trembling voice.

"Yes, we overheard your conversation," Susan willingly admits.

"Well, I guess it's up to us then," Chris anxiously rambles out as he turns to Susan with his head tilted down and his eyes looking up, trying very hard to do his best puppy dog look. There's dead silence in the room, but only for a moment.

"OK!" Susan finally gives in to his idea. "OK," she reconfirms gracefully.

Chris goes into serene shock, and his mouth drops open. "Are you sure?" he asks with both hands gently clasped to her shoulders, smiling away.

"Yes, I'm sure." She nods, still displaying a bit of apprehension in her voice, but it goes unnoticed.

"We'll take it!" Chris blurts out excitedly. "We'll take it!" He immediately reconfirms while wrapping his arm around Susan.

"Fine," the old woman accepts with a smile, then shuffles back down the hallway into the kitchen, turns on the stove for the kettle, and timidly gives the other couple the bad news. Chris and Susan wait a moment for the old woman to break the news to the other couple before entering the kitchen. The young couple seem quite disappointed but take the news well as they totally understand the circumstances about Chris and Susan being first in line to rent her beautiful home.

"That's cool, that's cool, we still have a few more houses to check out anyway. So it's all good!" The young couple spew optimism as they walk down the front steps of the house. "Good luck!" they encourage while waving as they walk down the sidewalk and get into their old two-seater sports car.

"Thanks, same to you," Chris shouts as they all wave goodbye.

"So! When would you two like to move in?" the sweet old woman wastes no time asking as she slowly closes the front door and shuffles towards the kitchen.

"When is it available?" Chris asks as they follow a few steps behind her.

"The end of the upcoming month would be most suitable," the old woman says as she grabs the screeching kettle from the top of the stove and pours it into a nearby teapot. "Would you two like to join me for a cup of tea?" the old woman asks sweetly as she opens the cupboard and optimistically grabs three fine china teacups with saucers.

"Yes, please. Thank you," they both reply.

A pleasant, warm, quiet moment fills the kitchen's atmosphere, as the old woman pours the tea.

"So," Chris breaks the calm, "If we both give our notices today," he calculates, looking for Susan's approval. "We could definitely move in October first. Does that sound all right to you?" he asks, looking directly at Susan as though proposing marriage.

"Sure," she says nervously.

"That will be just fine then," the old woman concludes with a smile. "October first," she repeats for peace of mind. A silent pause while they all sip on their tea. "Would you mind putting a security deposit down on the house today?" the old woman asks in a low, shy voice.

"No problem," Chris says while reaching into his back pocket. "Oh no, looks like I don't have a blank check on me after all, I usually have one in my wallet." He realizes while rifling through it.

"I've got one," Susan speaks up, still displaying a slight touch of uneasiness about the decision her and Chris just made. Her hands shake slightly as she pulls the check book from her wallet. "So, that's half of $1175, correct?" Susan confirms and begins filling in the date on the check.

"That's correct, dear. Just make it out to Joan Bennet," she says, standing before them with her frail hands clasped together around a brand-new piece of tissue paper.

"Well, I guess we should be heading out," Chris suggests as he takes his last sip of tea.

"Yes, I guess we should," Susan agrees, placing her teacup onto the fancy saucer plate. "We've got an awful lot of organizing to do now, don't we, Chris?" she adds, displaying a slightly pale-faced smile. "It's been a real pleasure meeting you, Mrs. Bennet."

They stand up from the kitchen table and shake the sweet old woman's hand.

"It was a real pleasure meeting you two as well. And please, call me Joan," she insists, smiling as they all find their way to the front door.

"We'll be in touch real soon," Chris assures with a single wave as they make their way down the front steps of their-soon-to-be new home. The front door closes slowly. "Wow!" Chris shouts out loud while walking backwards. "We did it!" he boasts with both arms in mid-air.

"I know." Susan slightly stresses. "I still can't believe that we did it," she admits, chuckling nervously while strolling down the sidewalk with her arms crossed and looped tightly through the straps of her purse.

"It's going to be great. You'll see," Chris insists in a convincing tone. "Well, I guess we've got something to celebrate now, don't we?" he announces excitedly then reaches out and gives Susan a big hug and kiss before opening the passenger door for her. "Well, let's head back down to Fishermen's wharf and pick up a couple of those big lobsters you like, and maybe a couple bottles of wine too," Chris suggests. "Then go back to your place and have a nice big celebration steak and lobster dinner. If that's OK with you, of course," he encourages romantically, then starts up the car.

"Sure, why not," Susan agrees then reaches in the back seat of the car and grabs a sweater. "It's getting a little chilly out all of a sudden." She pulls the sweater over her head then cranks up the heater full blast, hoping to instantly warm her legs.

"You're right, it is a little cooler," Chris agrees as he reaches into the back seat, grabs the other sweater, slips it over his head, then vainly checks himself out in the rear-view mirror before slipping into his Mr. Cool sunglasses. Susan clicks on the radio and the hit song "Patience is Golden" begins playing.

"Is that some kind of omen?" she points out while grinning sarcastically, trying to see straight through his dark sunglasses into his soul.

"No, it's just a song, silly, but a good one though." Chris can't deny feeling un-superstitiously amused by the coincidence and turns the radio up a bit louder. "Feeling a little overly superstitious, are we?" he remarks with obvious sarcasm and laughs it up.

Susan just flashes a sharp smile back. The car slowly eases away from the soon-to-be new home while their eyes remain glued on the house until it is out of sight.

"I can't believe we're actually going to be living there together," Chris expresses with amazement. "I just can't wait!" he shouts, then abruptly speeds the car back down towards Ocean Boulevard as the song plays on.

Chapter 4

"My mom and dad are going to go into shock when I tell them the news," Susan stresses with a nervous chuckle.

"When you show them the house and explain that you'll still have your own room and how much money you're going to be saving, I think they'll be totally understanding," Chris says with confidence.

"Yeah, you're probably right about that," Susan agrees. "You're probably right," she repeats with much more optimism in her voice, now displaying relief on her face, more convinced that what they just did wasn't such a bad thing to do after all.

"My mom will be thrilled that we're moving in together," Chris ensures as he reaches over and takes Susan's hand. "I told her a lot about you and she can't wait to meet you." He squeezes her hand a little tighter.

Susan just smiles and leans back in her seat, enjoying the sunshine and music as the cool wind blows through her hair.

"Right on, we're here," Chris announces as he pulls the car into the dusty parking lot of the now extremely busy Fishermen's Wharf. They miraculously luck out finding a parking spot that faces right towards the hypnotic swaying boat masts just as someone is leaving. Susan takes his hand as they walk towards the wooden ramp.

"There sure are a lot more people down here now than there were earlier this morning, eh," Chris states the obvious as he peels off his too-cool sunglasses.

"Yeah, you're not kidding. I can't believe how busy it is down here! Rocky Shores Fish & Chips must make a killing," she says while looking towards the fish and chips shack and its extremely long lineup.

"Yes, it looks like quite the popular little seafood market, that's for sure," Chris agrees.

Hand in hand, they make their way down the wooden ramp that moves with every incoming wave. They stroll along the wharf that almost resembles the atmosphere of an ancient oriental fishing village you might see in a movie.

"All the boats seem to be selling the same stuff," Chris realizes, squinting away from the slightly cloud-ridden sun before slipping on his sunglasses.

"Yeah, you're right. The same prices too. It looks like it, anyway," Susan notices right away as they continue to be taken in by the sights. "Let's go buy our lobster from that red-headed, wiry, old fishermen we first saw earlier this morning," she coaxes while pointing towards the end of the rocking wharf. Chris easily springs for two choice lobsters on ice and hands the fisherman fifty bucks. They continue walking along the wharf, absorbing the magical atmosphere, before slowly climbing back up the ramp and heading back to the car.

"Well, I guess it's back to our old neighbourhoods," Chris chuckles, heavily emphasizing the word "old" as he opens the trunk of his car and fires in their lobsters on ice. "Hmm, we've still got to stop at the beer and wine store, right! Oh, and also pick up some fat, juicy steaks."

"Well, I'm pretty sure we don't need any wine. I keep forgetting, I've still got a brand-new bottle of white wine stuck way in the back of the refrigerator and a bottle of red stashed somewhere in the kitchen cupboards that I got from my mom and dad as a gift last Christmas. Not to mention." She pauses, smiling. "I also have a couple of bacon wrapped filet mignon steaks in the freezer with our names written all over them," she explains.

"No way!" Chris says with optimistic disbelief. "Well, I'll make sure you don't forget the wine tonight," he promises with a devious grin as he lightly screeches the car back onto the main drag.

"I'm sure you won't," Susan says with a smirk, not fully realizing the truth about his secret drinking desires. "You've got beer right here," she says, reaching behind his seat and tapping on the bulky brown paper bag. "Wine goes better with lobster, anyway," Susan quickly admits, sliding her hand up the back of the driver's seat and onto his shoulder, then playfully ruffles up his hair.

"Cool." Chris couldn't agree more, only aiming to protect his sacred stash of beer he habitually keeps on hand behind the driver's seat for when he gets that sudden thirsty urge. "I just can't believe it!" he suddenly shouts out.

"What? The wine?" Susan asks while displaying her puzzled look.

"No! The fact that we're actually going to be living out here, and we'll be able to walk or drive down to Fishermen's Wharf anytime we want!"

"Yeah, you're right," she agrees. "Yeah, it's funny how life is. One day you wake up and your entire world changes without notice, right before your very eyes," she says philosophically.

"What's that?" Chris asks as he reaches over and turns the radio down a bit.

"Oh, nothing. I was just thinking out loud," she says smiling.

"Oh," Chris responds and turns the radio back up.

A few miles pass by. Susan nonchalantly props herself up as they near the old gas station. She immediately spots Brad still working on the same old truck. They speed on by, but thankfully Chris doesn't notice her candid reaction to seeing Brad again, as she slowly leans back in her seat. They remain silent while taking in the sights and listening to the radio all the way back to her apartment.

"You know, even though I'm not thrilled about getting another rent increase, it's still going to be really hard when I actually have to leave this old place," Susan explains as they both clunk up to the top of the stairs and straight into her apartment. "I guess because it's my first home away from home, you know what I mean?" she confesses softly with a bit of sadness in her voice.

"Yeah, I think I know what you mean," Chris says. A silent pause. "Oh! Yeah, you know what we still have to do?" Chris shouts from the bathroom while relieving his bladder.

"What's that?" Susan shouts back.

"Our notices. We've still got to hand in our moving out notices before it's too late," Chris explains.

"Oh yeah. You're right. I'll type them up on my laptop and print them out while dinner's cooking," She assures. "I'm pretty sure we've got until midnight tonight to hand them in anyway, don't we?" Already knowing the answer, Susan continues to gather up the contents for dinner, and temporarily places the plastic bag of live iced lobster into the kitchen sink.

"Yeah, I think you're right. Definitely midnight," Chris confirms.

Flush.

He exits the bathroom, still buttoning up his fly, then walks down the hall and into the kitchen.

"I think I'll let you start the barbecue tonight," Susan insists. "You know what happened last time—*Boom!*" she concludes, smiling away with her arms exploding wide open, and they both burst into laughter.

"No problem," Chris agrees, grinning from ear to ear.

The dinner atmosphere, with all its candlelight and romantic, holiday-style music, takes them late into the evening.

"Oh, I better get going!" Chris abruptly realizes while pointing to the wall clock. "I've still got to drop off my notice in the check box at my place before midnight," he spits out while scrambling to slip into his tight cowboy boots.

"Are you sure you're OK to drive?" Susan asks, noticeably concerned.

"Yeah, I'm just fine," he ensures enthusiastically while professionally concealing a slight stagger, even though he drank most of the two bottles of wine during and after dinner. He grabs both notices from the coffee table and folds them in half, then stuffs his notice into his left shirt pocket.

"You're coming back, right?" she asks while hanging off the door as Chris clunks down the stairs and disappears into the darkness of the stairwell.

"Yeah, of course! I shouldn't be too long," he shouts back while stuffing Susan's moving out notice into her building manager's mail slot. "I'll be right back," he promises as the building door clicks shut.

Chris jumps into his car, starts it up, then slams it into gear. He wastes no time reaching behind the driver's seat and pulling out one of the six twist-top imported beers he bought from the old gas station earlier this morning. A couple of big swigs and the beer is gone. He fires the empty bottle out of his car, sending it smashing into the street. "Oops," he jokes sarcastically to himself, then quickly reaches back behind the car seat, grabs another beer, and cracks it open. His true colours are really shining through.

Three miles down the road he hears a *Honk! Honk! Honk!* "Hey, Chris!"

A group of his friends shout out from their car window as they pull up beside him at a red light. "What's happening tonight, man?" one of them shouts out.

"Oh, not much, not much," Chris says, as he takes a big swig of beer. "Just hanging out with Susan, not to mention, we're moving in together at the end of the month!" he boasts while smirking away, then takes another swig of beer.

"What a lucky guy!" a few of his friends blurt out. Chris just smiles.

"Hey, guys, feel like smoking a couple numbers back at my joint?" Chris invites with a devilish grin on his face. "No pun intended," he adds in while laughing.

"Sure, right on, man!" they all shout back as a few of the guys hang halfway out the car window with their thumbs up, laughing hysterically.

The light turns green. Chris slams down hard on the gas pedal, bolting off the line with screeching tires. His friends do the same, but they quickly pass by him in their big boat of a car, speeding away as if they were in some kind of amateur drag race. Chris leans his head way back and takes a long swig of beer, not realizing that when he does, the wind of his sped-up car blows his "Moving Out Notice" right from the top of his shirt pocket and into the streets.

Two and a half hours of loud music, drinking beer, and smoking pot back at his place passes by very quickly. By the time Chris arrives back at Susan's, he has devoured about nine beers and is now finding it a little harder to hide his sluggish drunkenness. He puts up the convertible roof then quickly runs up the stairs.

Clunk, Clunk, Clunk, Clunk, Clunk.

Knock, Knock, Knock!

He pounds on Susan's door, totally unaware of how loud he is actually knocking because of the drunken state he is in. A sleepy-eyed neighbour peaks out their door, shakes their head, then mumbles something derogatory before quickly closing their door.

"What took you so long? I was fast asleep," Susan asks calmly while standing in the doorway, wearing only her low-cut nighty.

"Well," Chris attempts to explain, with more than just a slight slur attached.

Susan now stands partially bent over, shivering away with one hand between her thighs and her other hand holding the door half open, squinting from the bright lights shining in from the hallway.

"Come in," she whispers as she opens the door a little wider, waving her hand inward. "Come in," she begs sweetly.

Chris slowly staggers into her darkened apartment, which is just dark enough to hide his staggering motion, but not quite enough to hide his overwhelming beer breath.

"Whew!" she says while waving her hand in front of her face, then quickly steps backward in hopes of ridding herself of his strong beer breath. "What took you so long?" she asks in a not-too-terribly-concerned tone.

"Oh, I ran into a couple old friends at a stop light on the way home," he explains with an underlying slur while slightly swaying back and forth. "We all went back to my place and had a couple beers to celebrate us moving in together!" He instantly conjures up a story with a potentially true reason for him to be drinking so much. "Sorry about that," he drunkenly apologizes and takes her by the hand.

"Oh, that's OK," Susan says, still half asleep. "I'm going to go back to bed now, you don't mind, do you?" she questions with a big yawn.

"No, not at all," Chris says with a slight slur and a swagger as he snatches up the TV remote from the coffee table, clicks it on, then slouches down on the couch and slowly fidgets himself into an almost laying position.

"Oh yeah, I wouldn't mind getting a good head start on the packing in the morning," she explains in a yawning voice while stretching her arms up way over her head. "I think I need to weed out a few things that I don't really need anymore, and maybe take some stuff down to the Salvation Army," she informs with another yawn.

"Sounds good, me too," Chris mumbles back.

"OK, good night, Chris," she acknowledges sweetly, then softly kisses him on the forehead and scurries off to bed.

"Good night, Susan," Chris mumbles back, seemingly unheard as he drifts off into a deep snoring sleep while the television flickers on throughout the night.

Chapter 5

The next morning is cloudy and chilly enough to see your breath in the air.

"Good morning," Susan lightly shouts as she enters the living room, turns off the TV, and swiftly pulls up the noisy blinds.

Chris is instantly startled awake and jerks himself up into a sitting position on the edge the couch. "What? What?" He blurts out loud in a groaning, yawning tone while holding his hand in front of his eyes, squinting from the morning light, seemingly not fully aware of exactly where he is for a moment.

"I think I'm going to go over to my mom and dad's house right now and break the news to them as gently as I can," Susan says while giggling nervously and pulling her sweater over her head. She slips into her shoes. "Then I'm going to come back here and start getting organized. I remember just how much work it was when I first moved into this place a few years ago, and I'm sure I've got twice as much stuff in here since then!" She laughs while rattling her keys. "Sorry about rushing you out of here."

"No worries," Chris groans, then slowly raises his stiff body from the couch and heads towards the door.

"It's just that I want to break the news to my mom and dad in person instead of over the phone, you know what I mean," she explains in her sweetest voice. "Not to mention, they have a big pile of boxes in their garage," she expresses happily before locking her apartment door.

"Yeah, of course," Chris agrees, still a bit out of it, as they both clunk down the stairs and out the front door of her apartment building.

"Oh yeah, don't forget. You promised to make me dinner tonight," she shouts while rolling her old VW window all the way down.

"Oh yeah," Chris shouts back as he pulls his car away. "OK, see you soon," he promises while waving out his car window. He races straight back to his place, takes a big puff off an old roach he finds in the ashtray from the night before, then immediately crawls into his messy bed.

Susan casually breaks the news to her mom and dad about her and Chris moving in together at the end of the month.

"Are you sure it's going to be all right? Have you thought it over enough? You haven't really known each other all that long." Both her parents stress some legitimate emotional concerns.

"It will be great. Mom, Dad, you'll see, I'll be closer to work and I'll be saving lots of money every month, and I'll still have my own room. You're going to love the place, I promise. It's beautiful," Susan stresses with a big smile as she takes her mother's hand.

"Ok, sweetheart. We're happy if you're happy. We love you very much and stand behind your decision," Mrs. Jenkins accepts unconditionally.

"So, when do we get to meet this young man?" Mr. Jenkins asks firmly, still sounding quite concerned, as he stands up and gives her a big hug.

Chris is woken several hours later by the phone ringing loudly beside his cluttered bedside table.

"Well, it looks like you're off the hook this time," Susan says in a happy, energetic tone before Chris even has a chance to say hello.

"What do you mean?" he asks in a low, groggy, sleepy tone.

"Dinner tonight," she says. "You don't have to cook me dinner tonight. We've just been invited to my mom and dad's for a big Sunday dinner. How does that sound?"

"Sure," Chris grumbles as he sits up on the edge of his bed, rubbing the sleep from his eyes while yawning noisily. "Oh, I was just thinking about what to make us for dinner tonight too," he smoothly rambles out some untruth. "Perfect then. What time should I be there?" He stretches one arm up way over his head, occasionally yawning, but his yawns go unnoticed as the family dog barks loudly in Susan's background.

"Oh, around six o'clock," Susan says.

"OK, Sounds good," he accepts as he stands up and scratches himself, then walks over and swishes the dusty drapes away from his bedroom window.

"Oh, by the way," Susan says with a touch of suspenseful enthusiasm in her voice.

"What?" Chris asks as he slowly walks down the hallway into the kitchen, opens the drawer to his secret marijuana stash, and quickly lights one of the many roaches he has accumulated in a little wooden box.

"My mom and dad took the news quite well about us getting the house together," Susan happily reports. "I just explained to them about us having our own rooms." She laughs. "And that seemed to relieve a great stress off their minds."

"You mean they didn't want to visualize us sleeping together," Chris says, in a witty, sarcastic tone, and they both have a good laugh. "Excellent! I told you," he blurts out, then silently re-lights the roach, and takes another quick puff. "OK, I'll see you there later on. Oh, wait, where is *there* anyway?" he inquires with a little stoned sarcasm attached while exhaling a big cloud of pot smoke towards the ceiling.

"Oh, right, OK, yeah, I totally forgot, you've never been here before!" She chuckles. "The address is 1429 Rochester drive. It's in the Heritage Woods area, you know the area, right?"

"Yeah, of course, I think so, no worries. I've got my trusty little GPS on my freshly charged cell phone anyway," he says looking a little crinkle-faced while quickly scribbling down the address on the inside of some rolling papers.

"OK, sweetie," she says softly, and with an excited, "Bye for now," hangs up.

"Bye, see you in a bit," Chris just manages to squeeze in, then hangs up. "Holy shit! Meet the parents night in two-and-a-half hours," he says nervously to himself while looking right at the stove clock. He takes one more big puff from the roach and heads for the shower.

The dinner moves along smoothly, with light discussions of the weather and current events. Most of the attention is focused on Susan's younger brother Roy, who seems to be conducting a well-rehearsed ritual of hand feeding the family dog, who sits silently drooling under the dining room table. Both are trying very hard not to get caught at it, even though it's quite obvious.

"Well, I guess it's going to be an early evening for everyone tonight," Mr. Jenkins sighs while rubbing his hands around his full stomach. "Yup, I guess it's back to the old Monday morning grind tomorrow," he adds in while yawning, as if to signal to everyone that all he wants to do now is go to sleep after their big dinner.

"You had to remind us, didn't you, Mr. Jenkins?" Chris says sarcastically and everyone laughs. There's a brief silence in the room, except for the dog that is still under the dining room table, licking his chops from the last handout he just got from Roy.

"Thanks, Mom. That was a really nice dinner and excellent homemade apple pie too. Always the best!" Susan conveys, smiling as she sarcastically dabs the corners of her mouth with her napkin, then stands up and walks around to the opposite side of the very large dining room table and gives her mother a big hug.

"Thank you," her mother says, hugging Susan back. "I must give you the recipe one of these days," Mrs. Jenkins promises as she gets up and begins clearing the dining room table.

"Oh, OK. Thanks, Mom. And you too, Dad."

"You're very welcome. Any time," her father says. "But you know darn well your mother is the only gourmet chef around here!" he willfully admits, and they all laugh.

"I'll give you a hand, Mom," Susan says, and begins stacking the dishes.

"Oh, can I have one more piece of pie and ice cream? Please!" Roy quickly speaks up as the pie is about to leave the table.

"Yes, of course, dear," his mother says. "Would anyone else like another piece of apple pie and ice cream?" she graciously inquires.

"Yes, please!" Chris politely speaks up. "Thank you very much!" he adds, just as Mrs. Jenkins places another huge piece of pie and ice cream on his plate.

Susan's father comically starts explaining how sleepy you can get after having such a big meal not too long after Chris finishes his second piece of pie.

"Yeah, like, it's really hard to tell what you are hinting at, Dad!" Susan sarcastically points out as they all laugh.

"Am I that obvious?" he blurts out, yawning while turning a couple shades of red.

Everyone laughs loudly as they exit the dining room and enter the living room to have a seat.

"Your father worked really hard all day in the backyard, pruning and wrapping the trees. That's probably why he's so sleepy tonight," Mrs. Jenkins explains as she moves towards the fireplace. "Not to mention all that fresh air!" She slides the fireplace screen back and jabs at the red-hot embers with a long fire poker.

A silent serenity is in the air as everyone focuses on Mrs. Jenkins strategically placing a small log on top of the embers, remaining mesmerized as it quickly crackles into flames.

"Well, I guess we should probably head home anyway," Susan suggests realistically as she looks to the clock on the mantel that is sporadically lit up by the flickering fire.

"It's nine o'clock already. Time flies when you're having fun!" Chris throws in a cliché and everyone agrees, laughing lightly.

There's a brief silence in the room, except for the peaceful sound of the crackling fire.

Poof, Poof. Just then, the dog farts, totally breaking the serenity.

"Roy!" Mrs. Jenkins rolls off her tongue. "That's why we don't feed the dog people food, sweetie," she lightly scolds.

"OK, Mom. Sorry, Rex," Roy accepts sadly and pets Rex on the head.

"Well, that was another amazing dinner, Mom!" Susan compliments, instantly lightening Roy's scolding as she stands up from the couch and starts walking towards the front door where everyone slowly gathers.

"Thanks again! Mr. Jenkins, Mrs. Jenkins, Roy, nice to finally meet everyone," Chris says politely as he reaches out and shakes their hands.

"You're very welcome! And nice to finally meet you as well," They reply graciously.

"And you too, Rex!" Chris adds sarcastically as he slowly walks down the front steps sideways while holding onto the railing, waiting for Susan to catch up.

"Good night, Roy!" Susan says while patting him on the head before joining Chris. They walk down the pathway towards their cars, then turn and wave as they near the end of the path. Roy waves back excitedly with Rex at his side.

"Good night! Drive carefully!" Mr. and Mrs. Jenkins shout out simultaneously, still waving away.

"Good night, everyone!" Susan shouts and blows them all a kiss. Chris and Susan give each other a big hug and kiss before jumping in their own cars and driving back to their own apartments to prepare for the start of a hectic new work week.

Chapter 6

It's been a very busy month for both Susan and Chris, not only with their full-time jobs, but all the packing and cleaning that has been taking place every day after work. Each day of the month passes by like the blink of an eye and it's finally moving day. Chris borrowed a big truck from his supervisor for only the price of the gas. Susan, Chris, and Roy, along with many of their friends, make the loading and unloading move along smoothly.

"That's about it!" Chris announces as the last few boxes come in from the truck.

"Wow, we must have done that in record time," Susan calculates while looking at her watch. "Phew! Thank you so much for all your help, everyone!" she says while wiping the sweat from her forehead with her forearm.

"We couldn't have done it without you guys. Thank you!" Chris shouts appreciatively before flipping up the squeaky lid of the cooler. "Don't be shy," he insists, then pulls out two six-packs of beer and begins passing them around to everyone except Roy, who gets handed one of the few Dr. Peppers buried in the ice at the bottom of the cooler.

"Hey, you know what, Chris?" Susan says excitedly as she rips her can of beer open.

"What's that, sweetie?" he asks, totally focused on what she has to say.

"Why don't we have a housewarming party next weekend? It's a long weekend too, we get Monday off," she encourages, anticipating his response.

"That sounds like an excellent idea to me," he agrees. "Cheers everyone!" Chris toasts, raising his beer in mid-air then guzzling it halfway down.

"He'll do anything if there's beer involved," one of Chris's long-time friends admits, in a truthful sarcastic tone. They all laugh.

"Cool!" Roy expresses excitedly. "Can I come too?" he asks wide-eyed and pitchy.

"Sure, why not," Susan agrees, patting him on the head. "I imagine Mom and Dad are going to want to come and see the house too, right?" Susan says while looking down at Roy.

"Ah, Rats! Mom and Dad?" Roy speaks up loudly with a big sigh, really only hoping to hang out with his big sister and all her cool friends without having the parents around.

"It shouldn't take us that long to get organized around here either," Susan predicts and begins ripping open boxes labelled "Kitchen" and quickly unloading them into various cupboards. "Seems like this place is way bigger than both our old places put together," she realizes, easily fitting everything into the cupboards before moving on to the next box labelled "Pantry."

"Sure glad we labelled all those suckers; makes life a lot easier," Chris points out as he makes his way into the living room and begins shuffling all the furniture around with a little help from his friends. An hour and a half later. Susan and her friends finish putting everything away in the kitchen.

"Thank you so much, everyone, for helping us out!" Susan expresses, hugging all her friends.

"Yes, thanks, guys, for showing up!" Chris repeats, reaching out to shake everyone's hands.

Most reply, "No worries, anytime!" then slowly head on their way.

"Oh, and thank you very much, Tammy, for taking my little Roy home," Susan says as Roy jumps into the front seat of Tammy's cool little convertible sports car.

"Anytime!" Tammy obliges and waves.

"Well, here we are. Alone at last in our new home," Susan says as they plunk themselves down on the couch for a quick cuddle and snack break before getting right back at it.

With Susan's expertise on "House and Garden" and Chris's muscle, their new home comes together rather nicely as they continue unpacking and organizing for the duration of the weekend.

Monday comes too soon when their alarm goes off and another busy work week flashes on by.

It's Friday night.

Chris walks into the house with some Chinese takeout just as Susan is igniting the fireplace.

"Oh, wow. Mmm, I'm starved!" she admits.

"Oh, nice. Where did you get the wood?" he asks, a little crinkle-faced.

"There's a big stack alongside the garage," she explains while pointing in the general direction.

They enjoy one of their few peaceful, romantic, candlelit dinners that ends up in the master bedroom, which they have decided to both call their own. They attempt to make love but quickly fall asleep, exhausted from all the final touches of unpacking and organizing they have been doing throughout the work week in preparation for their housewarming party tomorrow night.

They wake up late the next morning to a beautiful, crisp sunny Saturday morning, both feeling refreshed.

"Listen," Susan coaxes as she props herself up on the side of the bed before tiptoeing towards the bedroom window.

"What?" Chris asks, and quickly sits up on the side of the bed.

"The birds!" she whispers softly while peeking out the window through a slit in the drapes. "Come on. Quickly! You've got to see this! Wow, look at all the birds," she reveals upon opening the drapes a little wider.

Chris slowly approaches the window and suddenly all the birds fly away. "I don't look that bad, do I?" he says sarcastically, and they both break into laughter.

Susan walks into the bathroom, turns on the shower, drops her nightie onto the floor, and steps in. She leans her head back under the warm shower with her eyes closed, washing her hair and humming the song "Can't Picture Myself." Chris quietly sneaks into the shower unnoticed.

"Ah!" she screams in a high-pitched voice as she opens her eyes. "You scared the heck out of me!" She lightly smacks him on the backside.

Chris pulls Susan in close and begins kissing her passionately. They make out in the shower until the water becomes lukewarm.

"At least we know how long the hot water lasts around here," she says jokingly as they step out of the shower, chuckling away.

They quickly towel off and slip into their robes, then walk down the hallway into the kitchen.

"Everything is pretty much done around here. Except for the food and stuff we need for the party tonight," Chris says while looking into their somewhat bare refrigerator.

Susan pokes her head inside the refrigerator. "Yeah, the only thing we have left in here is this lovely leftover Chinese takeout dinner you brought home last night," she confirms, expressing thanks, and kisses him on the lips. "This will be a good lunch for us today," she says, then spins around on one foot and closes the refrigerator door with the other. "Well, we better get moving, lots to get! Lots to do!" she says coaxingly as they walk down the hallway, into the bedroom, and playfully make the bed together before getting dressed for the day.

"It sure is nice having our own garage to park in, eh," Chris remarks as he slowly backs his car out into the laneway, then pushes the remote and closes the double-sized garage door.

They arrive at the fairly busy "Urban Fair" food market just west of James Bay, only a short distance off the highway. Chris has miraculously picked them out a wobbly-wheeled shopping cart.

"Nice one," Susan compliments sarcastically.

"It was the last cart out there, I swear!" Chris chuckles, seemingly a little embarrassed.

Susan zips the wobbly cart up and down the aisles while Chris loads it up with just about one of everything, occasionally throwing something right at her to catch and put into the cart.

"We've almost got everything we need, except for the beer and wine," Chris stresses just before disappearing around the corner of the aisle.

Susan continues browsing, then suddenly stops at the end of an aisle and begins filling in their names and their new address. "Win an All-Inclusive Trip for Two to One of Three Five-Star Mexican Destinations. As well as an array of other extravagant prizes!" is colourfully written on the large display and entry box. Chris walks the aisles, searching for Susan, and finds her a few aisles over from where he left her before he went gallivanting off to look for the beer and wine. Susan just finishes filling in the ticket as Chris approaches.

"What the heck are you filling out?" he asks sharply with a scrunched-up face.

"A chance to win a trip to Mexico and a bunch of other stuff too," she says with optimism.

"Oh yeah, yeah, sure!" Chris blurts out pessimistically while nodding his head up and down. "You know what they do with all those names, addresses, and phone numbers, don't you?" He stresses in a know-it-all tone of voice. "They sell them to all the companies that send out junk mail and do telemarketing," he states.

"Oh well," Susan says with a big smile. "You never know, though," she adds as she folds the ticket in half and stuffs it into the entry box.

"I found the beer and wine, way over in the corner there," Chris informs excitedly while pointing and walking a few steps ahead of her. "This way," he directs, waving his arm as if wanting her to come even faster.

"That should just about do it! Don't you think?" Susan suggests while chuckling nervously, watching closely as Chris loads the shopping cart with an overabundance of beer and wine.

"Now that should just about do it!" he concludes with a big smirk on his face while safely fitting two more six-packs of beer on top of the pile and even more underneath. "All-righty then." He snickers proudly.

"Well, it would be pretty hard to fit anything else in here now, I'd say!" She exclaims with a smile as they make their way towards the busy check-out lines.

"That was pretty expensive, wow!" Susan expresses while looking over the receipt.

"Yeah, but look at it this way," Chris says optimistically while unloading the groceries from the shopping cart into the trunk of his car. "This party isn't really costing us anything, if you think about it."

"Why do you say that?" Susan asks, handing him up the last bit of stuff from under the cart.

"Well, we're not really getting all this stuff for free," he admits, in a lower tone of voice. "It's just that our rent used to be almost $900 a month each, and now it's only about $600 a month each," he concludes as he closes the trunk of the car.

"Since we're on the subject of money," Susan reminds him as she gets in the car and closes the door. "I think you still owe me half of the security deposit."

"Oh, I totally forgot!" He reaches into his pocket and pulls out a stack of cash.

"You don't have to give it to me right now," she assures as she buckles up her seat belt.

"Oh, no. That's OK!" Chris says. "I just got paid Friday." He peels off three hundred-dollar bills and hands them off to her. "I better pay you now while I've still got the money in my pocket," he adds with a chuckle.

"Thank you," Susan says and stuffs the cash into her purse.

"I still can't believe we live there!" Susan expresses excitedly as they drive by the front of the house, then continue back down the alleyway and into the garage.

"Yeah, we got pretty lucky, that's for sure!" Chris agrees as he opens the trunk and overloads his arms up with groceries.

Susan grabs a load and follows right behind him.

"I'm so glad you like it, I definitely do too! And the price we're paying for rent is fantastic for what we've got," he adds as they lug the groceries up the back stairs and into the kitchen. "I'll go get the rest of the stuff," he says while setting the groceries down onto the countertop, then quickly runs back downstairs into the garage.

He pushes the remote button and closes the garage door, then reaches over the top of the driver's side door and pushes in the ashtray lighter. He reaches deep into his pocket and pulls out a small plastic bag containing a fat, crumpled joint. He quickly straightens it, puts it to his lips, and lights it as the lighter pops out. He takes in a couple good, long drags, then reaches into the console between the two front seats, snatches up a couple breath mints, fires them into his mouth, and begins chewing rapidly. He secretly wraps the rest of the joint in the tinfoil from his cigarette pack, then sticks it in the ashtray. He immediately checks his breath out, blowing into his cupped hands, before nonchalantly proceeding to grab more goodies from the open trunk of his car.

He scurries out of the garage, up the stairs, and back into the kitchen where Susan has slowly been putting things away.

"A couple more loads after this one." Chris notifies with stoned enthusiasm before literally running back into the garage a few more times. He grabs the last few things from the trunk then slams it closed using only his head and races back into the house. "That's about it!" he announces energetically, clunking the bags down on the counter.

"Oh good!" Susan says happily with her big, beautiful smile, totally unaware of what he has just been up to, thanks to the freshly chewed breath mints.

Chapter 7

The night closes in quickly with a multicoloured sunset filling the sky. Susan is in the kitchen slaving over a hot stove, preparing many appetizers for their guests, and has baked five apple pies while following her mother's famous recipe. Chris is hiding out downstairs in the basement with the music cranked, putzing around with some of his ancient memorabilia that he had packed away in the storage at his old place, frequently indulging himself with more than just a few of the alcoholic beverages they purchased for their housewarming party. Music rocks on with songs from the seventies and eighties.

Ding! Dong!

"Ah, someone's here!" Susan shouts down the stairs and quickly lights the last of the several candles that are scattered throughout the house.

"I'll get it!" Chris shouts as he runs up the stairs and answers the front door. "Hi!" he greets with a five-beer, yet undetectable, ever-so-slight sway. "Come on in!" he says, waving his arm inward. "Susan!" Chris yells out. "Your mom and dad and brother are here!" he announces.

"Coming," she shouts back as she whisks out of the kitchen and heads straight for the front door. "Hi, Mom, Dad, Roy!" she greets excitedly, giving them all a big hug. "Thanks for coming!" she says happily while patting Roy on the head. "So, what do you think?" she asks, seemingly looking for immediate approval, while spinning around the living room with her arms in mid-air.

"Very nice place!" Mrs. Jenkins replies.

"Very nice!" Mr. Jenkins agrees.

"I told you!" Roy explains, as if there was some concern as to the state of the house from her parents.

The front door closes, but only for a few minutes, then the doorbell chimes again and again.

Ding! Dong!

More and more people arrive, and eventually there are quite a few more guests than Susan discretely cared to expect.

Everyone is having a great time, laughing and mingling in small groups all around the house. Susan walks into the loud, crowded kitchen party, where most of the people have gathered. Chris is barely standing, leaning against the counter, with a big, crazy grin on his face.

"Why is it that house parties always end up in the kitchen?" Susan asks sarcastically over the loud music, and everyone laughs.

"Cheers, everyone. To our new place, and good friends," she toasts everyone with her glass of red wine. "Hmm, there seems to be enough food for everyone," she observes while looking at Chris, then takes a bite of cheese and pickle. "But it looks like we're almost out of beer. And it's only nine forty-five," she immediately discovers upon looking at her watch and opening the refrigerator door a little wider for Chris to see as well.

"No, way, we can't be!" he slurs, slightly swaying back and forth, acting surprised as he pokes his head a bit further inside the refrigerator.

"Your friends seem to like beer just as much as you do, I'd say," Susan adds laughing, not truly recognizing the extent of Chris's or his party-animal friends' notorious drinking habits.

"I better go get some more!" Chris says, as he reaches into his pants pocket and pulls out his car keys.

"You can't drive, silly!" Susan demands and gently pries the keys from his clammy hands. "I'll just quickly run down to the pub and pick up some more cold beer for everyone," she says, only wanting to be the perfect host.

"Hey, cool. Here! I'll chip in."

"Me too!" Two of their parched guests insist and both hand her a twenty-dollar bill.

"Oh, thank you!" she obliges.

"All right!" Chris blurts out excitedly, with two thumbs up in mid-air, slightly swaying back and forth. "Take my car!" he insists. "Take my car!" he immediately repeats, as if he never said it the first time.

Susan grabs her coat from the front hall closet, then informs her parents that she must step out for a quick moment. Mrs. Jenkins checks her watch then looks down at Roy, who seems to be having a really hard time staying awake, literally falling in and out of sleep while standing on his feet.

"We should head home anyway and put Roy to bed." Mrs. Jenkins kindly suggests with a big smile while pulling him in close. "We just wanted to come over and see your new place, anyway," she confesses with a smile. "You kids have fun." She gently holds the side of Susan's head and kisses her on the cheek.

"It's a very nice place!" Mr. Jenkins adds and gives Susan a big hug.

"Thanks, Dad! Thanks, Mom! Bye sleepy head!" Susan conveys her love, gently messing Roy's hair up along with his usual pat on the head.

"Good night everyone!" Mr. and Mrs. Jenkins shout out as they exit the front door.

"Good night!" everyone who is near the front door replies.

"Nice to see you guys again. And thanks for coming, Mr. And Mrs. Jenkins. You too, Roy!" Chris shouts, waving from across the room where he stands partially supported by the inside of the living and dining room doorframe, coincidentally swaying to the beat of the music.

"See you in a bit," Susan shouts directly to Chris, then follows steps behind her parents as they slowly continue down the front stairs towards their car. Susan reaches out and gives her father another big hug.

"Good night, Dad, Mom. Thank you so much for coming!" Susan conveys with upmost sincerity.

"Thanks for inviting us!" Mr. and Mrs. Jenkins reply with settled hearts. Roy slowly crawls into the back seat of their car, curls up into a ball, and instantly falls into a deep sleep.

"Goodbye. Good night," Susan shouts out as their car slowly drives away and disappears into the darkness.

Susan moves quickly down the side of the house and into the garage, jumps into Chris's car, pushes the remote, and starts up the car. "Hmm, where should I go to get the beer?" She asks out loud as she backs the car out of the garage and zooms off towards James Bay.

Susan pulls Chris's car into an almost full parking lot at "The Wild Reel." She quickly exits the car and heads into the very crowded and very loud pub. There's a live band playing on the stage and many people are dancing and having a good time. She approaches the bartender and orders one twenty-four pack of beer and three bottles of wine, then turns around and looks towards the stage. "What the . . . I can't believe it." She remembers as her eyes widen. "It's Brad, the guy from the gas station."

Brad sees her the second she turns around. He smiles and nods to let her know that he recognizes her while continuing to sing and play his guitar. The song ends moments later. "Good set!" Brad congratulates all his band mates as he slips his guitar strap over his head and hands the guitar off to one of his roadie band members. "Back in five!" He jumps off the stage.

Brad quickly weaves a path through the dispersing, over-crowded dance floor towards Susan. "Nice to see you again," he says while reaching and shaking her hand.

"It's nice to see you again too!" Susan says with a sturdy handshake back, along with her incredible smile.

"So, it looks like you guys did end up moving out here, after all," he congratulates, with a big grin.

"Yeah, we just moved in last week," she says. "As a matter of fact, I invited my parents and a few of our friends over for a little housewarming party tonight, but quite a few more people showed up than we expected," she adds, unable to control her beautiful, big, white smile. "So, I'm just picking up a bit more beer and wine for our guests. You're welcome to drop by, if you'd like." Susan wastes no time inviting while smiling away.

"I'd love to," Brad says. "But I won't be out of here until at least 2 a.m. Thanks for the offer though. Maybe next time," he suggests with confidence.

"You play here a lot?" Susan asks sweetly.

"Yeah, we usually play here every Friday and Saturday night, from about eight until 1:30 or 2 a.m.," he says, glancing towards the stage. "But since this is a long weekend, they want us to play Sunday night as well. But I don't mind though, I love to sing, And I get paid for it, so it's even better," he adds, laughing. "You should come down and check us out one of these weekends."

"I might just do that," Susan says sincerely.

The band is just concluding an instrumental. "Oh, I better get back up there or the band is going to fire me!" Brad says jokingly with a big grin, then reaches out to shake her hand once again. "It was really nice seeing you," he admits before gently letting go of her hand. Susan watches hypnotically as Brad moves quickly across the dance floor, jumps back up on the stage, grabs his guitar, and smoothly slips it on. "One, Two, One, Two, Three, Four," Brad directs loudly, and the band rips into one of their original songs.

He nods in Susan's direction, as if to say good night, without missing a beat. Susan smiles back, then spins around and pays the bartender. She grabs the beer and wine from the top of the bar and dawdles towards the door, barely interrupting eye contact with Brad, who sings intensely on stage. She seemingly floats right out through the pub door while her heart pounds even more than the first time they met at the gas station.

"I can't believe I feel this way! I'm with Chris," she emotionally reprimands herself while looking in the rear-view mirror, then snaps out of it, starts the car, and heads for home.

Meanwhile, back at the party, people are still having a great time mingling around and sipping on the small trickle of wine that's left, while slowly devouring the rest of the food. Susan pulls into the garage and remotes it closed. She quickly grabs the beer and wine from the passenger's side, exits the garage, and continues toward the back stairs. Chris and a group of his friends are huddled around in a circle, drinking the last of the beer while passing around what smells like a marijuana joint.

"Susan's back!" one of Chris's friends whispers as he painfully cups the smouldering joint in his hand. They all immediately light up a cigarette and pretend there never was a joint being passed around.

"Look who's back with more refreshments!" Chris dramatically emphasizes, hoping to break the ice of suspicion, while slightly swaying back and forth, practically slurring every word as he grabs the beer from Susan's hands and kisses her on the left side of her cheek. Everyone chuckles nervously as the circle breaks up and they all head back up the stairs into the overcrowded kitchen party.

The beer and wine go down rather quickly with Chris and a bunch of his friends, along with some new arrivals, kicking it back like it was the last booze on Earth. The party eases down just after midnight, which is about the exact time the rest of the food and alcohol has been completely devoured by Chris and his stoned, crazed, munchie-driven clan, who seem to have been only thinking of themselves.

"Good night!" Susan waves, set on maintaining the image of a good host as their last three guests walk out the front door and down the sidewalk towards their cars. "Good night, thanks for coming!" She secretly regrets their presence before closing and locking the door.

"What a nightmare," she says under her breath, then races across the living room and turns the stereo down. Chris is totally wasted, slouching in a chair while uncontrollably bobbling his head all around.

"Where did everyone go?" he mumbles while scanning the room, seemingly surprised by the silence. He struggles to pull himself up out of the chair, but eventually gets up after a few sloppy attempts.

"Party's over!" Susan says in an unusually sharp tone.

Chris is right out of it and oblivious to what she has just said. He staggers down the hallway into the bedroom and falls face down and crossways onto their bed. Susan follows not far behind, hoping to get some kind of apology for the way he and his so-called friends carried on this evening. She tries to wake him up by lightly shouting and shaking him, but he's definitely down for the count.

"Chris! Wake up! Wake up! You're taking up the whole bed." A silent pause. "Ah . . . Shoot." Susan screeches while attempting to move him into a normal sleeping position, but he just cannot be budged. After completely shutting the house down, she gives one last attempt to wake Chris, but fails miserably, and quickly sets up camp in the second bedroom where most of her stuff is anyway.

Chapter 8

Susan is woken early in the morning by the sound of rain hitting hard against her bedroom window. "Ah!" She yawns loud and long, with her arms stretched out touching the headboard while her tippy toes reach for the end of the bed. "Time to get up," she decides, now sitting up on the edge of her bed, yawning uncontrollably while reaching towards the ceiling. She shuffles over to the bedroom window and pulls back the drapes. "Ew, it's miserable out today!" she says while slipping into her white, fluffy, terry towel robe. She quickly makes the bed, walks out of the bedroom, and immediately begins waving her hand in front of her face as she enters the smelly, disastrous mess that seems to be throughout the entire house. There are beer bottles, beer cans, wine bottles, dirty dishes, and cigarette butts everywhere, even though there wasn't supposed to be any smoking in the house. Without hesitation, she cleans the place from top to bottom while her favourite thirties and forties music plays softly in the background.

She pokes her head into their stale-beer-breath bedroom to see if Chris has woken up yet, but by the looks of it, he hasn't moved a single inch the entire night. Even all the loud clinking and clanking noises Susan has been making while cleaning the house hasn't seemed to startle him in the least.

"Get up, stinky!" she shouts without sarcasm while standing over him. He still doesn't move in the slightest. A loud snore and the strong smell of an old brewery radiates throughout the bedroom. She moves from room to room, opening all the windows just enough to let in some fresh air, but not quite enough to allow the hard-hitting rain to come pouring in as well, hoping to rid the entire house of its stale beer smell, all the while periodically waving her hand in front of her face. "I've got to get out of this stinky house, right now!" she decides. She grabs a pen and paper from the kitchen drawer and scribbles down a note.

Good morning! See you in a while, I've just gone into town to cash in the beer cans and bottles, I shouldn't be too long! Susan, XO.

She grabs her coat and umbrella from the front hall closet, then runs back and forth from the house to the garage, more than just a few times, carrying the many boxes and bags of empties, strategically placing them tightly into the trunk of her car before heading off towards town.

Thunder rumbles and lightning fills the sky as she drives around searching for a place to take the empties. The rain falls hard, noisily pelting all over her car like the sound of popcorn popping. The windshield wipers can barely keep up to the pounding rain, making it very difficult for her to see. She pulls up in front of an old heritage-style corner store, jumps out, and quickly runs inside to avoid getting completely soaked from the heavy downpour.

"Good morning!" she greets while smiling with a slight shiver.

"Good morning!" the grandfather and grandson storekeepers reply.

"She's really coming down out there today, that's for sure," the grandfather figure insists with gravel in his voice.

"You're not kidding," Susan says as water drips from the tip of her nose onto the wide planked floor.

"What can we help you with today?" the grandson inquires shyly while pushing a two-wheel dolly cart down an aisle towards the back storage room.

"Well, I've got a bunch of empty beer bottles and beer cans, and I was wondering if you knew of a place where I could cash them in," Susan explains while blowing warm air into her clasped hands.

"Oh, yes, there is one place I know of," the old storekeeper remembers while holding his left hand on his chin. "It's a few miles from here, but I'm not quite sure if they're even open today, being that it's a holiday weekend and all. Yeah, I'm pretty sure it's in back of the old gas station, just up the highway," he explains while pointing in the general direction as he walks behind the till.

"Oh, I think I know the one you mean! 'Gas to Go,'" Susan suddenly recalls with her cute, puzzled-eyebrow look.

"Yeah, that's the one," the old storekeeper confirms.

"Yeah, I know exactly where that is. Thank you so much! Have a great day," Susan relays sincerely while exiting the store and heading right back out into the storm.

She closes the big old front door, then scurries towards her car.

Honk! Honk! Honk! Sounds the horn of a slightly familiar old pickup truck passing by the front of the old store.

"Oh my God! It's Brad," Susan says under her breath and stops dead in her tracks.

Brad's truck immediately slows down and pulls over to the side of the road about thirty feet up ahead. You can just barely see Brad's smiling face through the oval rear cab window of the truck as he slowly backs it up and parks it right in front of her car. Susan stands motionless on the sidewalk between the old store and her car while the rain rivets her body. She stares, smiling, becoming almost trancelike, seemingly oblivious to just how soaked she is actually becoming, while watching Brad's every move as he steps out of his truck.

"Unreal!" Brad shouts excitedly, as he walk-runs towards her with his coat up over his head.

Lightning flashes.

"Well, hello," Susan greets with a massive grin. "We sure seem to bump into each other a lot these days, don't we," she says, giggling nervously.

Thunder booms.

"Wow! Where's your umbrella on a day like this?" Brad inquires while scrunching his face from the heavy downpour.

"I've got one right here!" she instantly realizes, and quickly sidesteps to her car, grabs the umbrella from the backseat, and pops it up over them. They stand huddled together under her umbrella, face to smiling face, in a sweet moment of silence, both seemingly very shy.

Lightning flashes.

"So, how are things going?" Brad asks genuinely, with his hands cupped to his mouth, blowing his warm breath into them.

Thunder booms.

"Good! Good!" Susan says. "How did the singing go last night?" she asks, still smiling away.

"Pretty good actually. We recorded a few of our newer songs at the end of the night, just for copyrighting purposes, you know. So no one steals them," Brad jokes, then reaches to steady the windblown umbrella.

"Cool," Susan says. "I'd like to hear them sometime."

"Sure, I should have a copy in the next day or so. I'm just getting them bounced over onto CD. I'll give you a copy next time we bump into each other, which I'm sure we will again soon, one of these days," Brad reassures positively.

"Cool! Thanks. Can't wait to hear it," Susan says with a glowing smile.

"So, what brings you into town today?" Brad asks while lightly marching on the spot.

"Oh, I've got a trunk load of beer bottles and beer cans I have to get rid of from the party last night," she explains in a please-save-me tone of voice while pointing to the trunk of her car.

"Oh yeah! The party! How did it go last night?" Brad asks excitedly.

"All right, I guess. A lot more people showed up than we expected, that's for sure!" Susan stresses, hiding her true thoughts about the evening.

"That's how parties usually go these days," Brad suggests lightly before quickly changing the subject. "So where were you planning on taking all those empties?" he asks while grinning and looking to the trunk of her car.

"Well, I just heard of a place up the highway a bit," she admits, smiling away with her head turned slightly sideways, fully aware of exactly where the place is that will take the empties. "But I'm not sure if they're open today."

"Where exactly do you mean?" Brad asks, an eyebrow raised knowingly. "I've lived in this town most my life and I only know of one place near town that will take the empties. Especially on a holiday long weekend!"

A silent pause as they stare at each other.

"Oh, you mean my grandparents' old gas station where we first met," Brad finally admits while grinning from ear to ear.

Lightning flashes.

"Yeah, I'm pretty sure that's the place they told me about in the store there," Susan admits with a big smile, still playing along with the game as she turns and looks towards the store.

Thunder booms.

"I was just heading down there myself," Brad confesses as he reaches out to steady the windblown umbrella once again. "My younger brother is covering for me this morning, because we played so late last night. He doesn't seem to need as much sleep as I do," Brad admits with a smirk as he pulls his hand out of his coat pocket and looks at his wristwatch.

Lightning flashes.

Thunder booms.

"Oh, we better get going! Follow me," Brad shouts enthusiastically as he side-step runs to his truck, then smoothly jumps in and starts it up.

Susan closes her umbrella, shakes it a few times, then throws it onto the floor in the back seat and starts up her car. She follows very close behind Brad's truck all the way to the old gas station while the rain continues teeming down. Brad steps out of his truck and quickly runs inside the garage. He pulls down on the chain and opens the overhead garage door. "Come on in," he cheerfully directs with a smile and an inward hand motion, insisting she drive her car straight inside the old garage.

"Wow, what a crazy storm!" Susan lightly shouts as she steps out of her car onto the spotless floor of the old garage.

"You're not kidding," Brad agrees while warming his hands together. "I think the storm must have followed us all the way down here, if you know what I mean," he suggests sarcastically with a shimmering grin, then immediately walks over and pulls down on the chain, closing the large, slightly foggy, checkered-glass, overhead garage door.

They both break into light laughter.

"Oh, this is my younger brother Shawn. Shawn, this is a new friend of mine, Susan."

"Nice to meet you," they express while shaking hands.

"Susan apparently has a trunk full of empties for us," Brad divulges, then walks over and clicks on the overhead heater.

"Wow! This place is spotless," Susan conveys with amazement while looking all around. "Who's the neat freak?" she asks with a touch of sarcasm.

"Well, we all are," Brad replies.

Shawn secretly points at Brad for only Susan to see.

"We have to keep it relatively spotless because we practice in here, and besides that, I hate grease on my guitar," he admits jokingly and they all chuckle. "Excellent acoustics in here too, you know," he adds with his irresistible smile, now looking straight into Susan's eyes, reminding her of the very first time they met.

"Hmm. Oh, cool," she says with a gulp and a slight heart flutter. "Do you play as well, Shawn?" She asks while nervously rattling the car keys out of her coat pocket, then walks around to the front of her car.

"Shawn is our timekeeper," Brad says, pointing to the stack of cases over in the corner.

Squeak, sounds the trunk hinges on Susan's car as she lifts it open.

Brad immediately walks over with some lubricant and sprays the squeaky hinges.

"Oh, thank you," Susan says. "You're the, what?" she asks, seemingly puzzled.

"The timekeeper," Shawn says smiling.

"The drummer," Brad immediately clarifies.

"OH, yeah, now I get it!" Susan chuckles.

"That should do it!" Brad says, spraying the hinge once again. "Any more squeaks?" he inquires comically while holding the can up in mid-air, ready to spray anything with a squeak.

"Not that I know of!" Susan jokes, and they all laugh.

"You sure saved up a lot of empties," Brad says as he moves in for a closer look. "Give us a hand here, Shawn."

Ding! Ding!

"Oh, I'll get that," Shawn insists while walking swiftly out to service a gas customer.

"Well . . ." Susan sighs. A silent pause between them.

"Is this all from last night?" Brad asks in awe.

"Yes," Susan says with a funny smile.

You certainly did have a lot of people over last night!" he says, and they both laugh. "Yes, quite the party," she admits, never revealing any of the disastrous details. They both reach down into the trunk and pull out a big bag of empties each.

"Follow me," Brad guides while walking towards the back of the garage, then through a swinging door into a large storage room half full of empties. "Just put them in the middle of the floor here," Brad directs with a smile before they head back for a few more loads. "Well, let's see, hmm, five, ten, eighteen, thirty-two, forty-three, forty-eight, fifty-seven, sixty-two. Yup, sixty-two eighty-five," Brad confirms.

"Wow. You sure can add fast," Susan says with amazement. "We sure could use your talents down at the bank where I work." They both laugh.

"So, what's up for the rest of your day?" Brad asks while stacking Susan's empties amongst the existing empties.

"Well, not sure yet. Maybe head into town and do a little grocery shopping," she decides with her warm smile. "Our guests ate just about everything in the entire house last night," she adds with her arms way out to her sides. A silent pause. "Well, it sure was nice bumping into you again," Susan expresses sincerely and reaches out to shake his hand.

"The pleasure is all mine," Brad says genuinely while gently shaking her hand. "Oh yeah! Your money!" Brad remembers and races over to the cash register and back again.

"Thank you very much! You saved the day!" Susan says as she steps back into her car.

"You are more than welcome." Brad replies kindly, and begins pulling down on the long looping chain, opening the overhead garage door. They both exchange big smiles and a wave as she slowly backs her car out of the garage and back out into the dark, wet, stormy day.

Susan cautiously drives back down the highway towards James Bay and picks up a few things from the "Urban Market." The rain continues to fall frantically, pounding down onto the windshield of her car, to the point where the wipers can barely keep up, causing the windshield to become quite blurry and very difficult to see out of. Even the lines on the road have become a blur. She leans forward, hoping to see out the window a little better while tapping her hands and fingers on the steering wheel along to the beat of the song "Nobody Told Me" coincidentally playing over the radio.

She pulls her car into the garage and quickly walk-runs into their silent house that still smells like a hundred-year-old brewery, then purposely crashes the groceries down loudly onto the kitchen counter.

Ten seconds pass by.

"I heard a bang!" Chris explains with a scrunched face while yawning as he enters a few feet into the kitchen, appearing rather groggy-eyed with his hair sticking up everywhere. "Well, it's about time you got up!" Susan delivers in a tone he's never heard before.

"Well, I'm not really up yet," Chris conveys while rubbing his eyes with clenched fists. "I've got a really bad headache," he dramatizes while holding both hands over his forehead.

"Hmm, I wonder why?" Susan asks in a harsh, sarcastic tone. "Things got a little out of hand last night, don't you think?" she suggests sharply. "I didn't know you smoked pot!" She stares directly at him.

"What do you mean?" Chris asks defensively as guilt riddles throughout his entire body.

"I saw you guys last night. In the back yard!" she emphatically points out while putting the groceries away.

"Oh, that. I just tried a bit, but it didn't do anything for me though," he explains without looking at her.

"I'm surprised you can even remember anything, considering the state you were in last night!" she adds with one last dig of disappointment.

Chris stumbles back into their bedroom yawning loudly, mumbling something in his defence about smoking pot.

"What's that?" Susan questions his muttering tone.

"Oh, nothing, just this pounding headache," he falsely reiterates as he flips the blankets back and quickly crawls back into bed.

"What the!" Susan blurts out as she enters the stale beer-breath bedroom. "You're going back to bed?" she asks, high-pitched, disappointment clearly written on her face.

"I'm still a little sleepy," Chris grumbles in a long, drawn-out fashion.

Susan quickly walks over to the bedroom window and whisks the blinds up as high as they go, then pushes hard, opening the window a bit more. The wind-forced rain pours down frantically, hitting even louder than before against the newly-increased angle of the window.

"I can't stand the reek in here! Yuck!" she says sharply while waving both hands in front of her face. "You can't be serious," Susan questions in a snappy tone while standing at the side of the bed with both hands on her hips, now leaning over him as he lays face down in the pillow.

"I told you! I'm not feeling so good today," he whines. "I've just got to sleep a little longer, OK," he demands strongly and gravelly while agonizingly pulling the covers up over his aching head. Chris instantly drifts off into a deep snoring sleep once again.

"Unbelievable!" Susan whispers. "Unbelievable!" she says once again before exiting the bedroom and closing the door.

I think I'm just going to take all the boxes back to Mom and Dad's house, this smell is just too much. Hopefully it will be gone by the time I get back! Susan zips over to her parents' home and quickly stacks the boxes in their garage.

"Thanks, Dad! See you soon, Mom, Roy!" she promises and immediately jumps back in her car and heads off down the road.

Mr. and Mrs. Jenkins just look at each other and shrug their shoulders. "She's one busy girl!" Mr. Jenkins mentions, lightening the mood.

Ring . . . Ring . . . Susan's cell beckons.

"Hello," she answers over the speaker phone.

"Hi, Susan, what are you up to today?" Tammy asks curiously.

"Oh, hello, Tammy! Oh, not much, just catching up on a few things," Susan says, not revealing much about anything going on at home.

"Do you and Chris want to come by my place this afternoon? I'm having a few friends over." A short pause.

"Sure, I'll definitely come by, but Chris is not feeling so hot today."

"Ok, sounds good to me. Come by anytime you want," Tammy says excitedly.

"Ok see you soon!" Susan says with a smile. "Bye!"

"Bye!"

Susan decides to take a long trip down memory lane and eventually ends up back at her old place. She parks her car in front of her old building and stares up at the window where she once called home. Tears fill her eyes but are swiftly wiped away when she sees her old, fat, greasy-haired landlord exiting the building. She immediately starts the car and heads for Tammy's place.

Buzz, Buzz.

"Hi, Tammy. It's Susan."

Tammy opens the door and immediately embraces Susan.

"Well, hello stranger! Quite the party last night!" Cathy remembers with a sigh.

"Yes, quite the party," Angela, Sherry, and Jenifer all concur while hugging Susan.

"Yeah, it was definitely a little on the crazy side, that's for sure," Susan embarrassingly admits, but not another word is mentioned about it out of total respect for Susan.

The girls all sit around Tammy's kitchen table, sipping away on wine and playing various board games while music from their school days rocks them deep into the early morning.

"Wow, it's 4:45 a.m. already! Holy, do you believe it?" Angela announces.

"Geez, we must have been picked up by aliens or something!" Jenifer jokes and they all burst into laughter.

"So nice to get together with you guys. Thanks so much for coming over!" Tammy expresses her love to her lifelong friends as they are walking out the door.

Susan pulls her car into the garage and looks down at her big, old diver's watch. "Wow 5:50 a.m. I haven't stayed up this late in a long time, and I'm not even tired yet. Weird," she admits and runs up the back stairs and into their freshly aired-out house.

"What a relief!" she whispers. "No more stinky house, yay!" she realizes ecstatically, then takes another deep breath in through her nose, just to be sure. "Ah, beautiful," she says, then quickly runs around the house closing all the windows while grinning from ear to ear.

Upon entering their bedroom, she discovers Chris still laying there like a sack of snoring potatoes. "Wow, never seen anything like it," she stresses in disbelief. She shakes her head, closes the door, and heads for the living room.

She selects a book from her antique corner-shelf unit and tosses it onto the seat of her big, old wing-back chair. She quickly moves toward the fireplace and grabs the pack of long wooden matches from the top of the mantel, kneels down, and slides the fire screen open. She strategically tosses in a couple of logs, some kindling, and some crumpled newspaper, strikes the wooden match across the brick face, and lights the newspaper in several places before gently closing the screen. She slowly sits back in the comfort of her big, old wing-back chair, sighs with relief, and begins reading her book. It doesn't take long before she dozes off into a deep sleep while the crackling fire warms her bare feet. She drifts off into a realistic dream. *Brad is smiling, walking in slow motion towards her from across the dance floor. He leans in, as if to kiss her on the lips.*

Ring . . . Ring . . .

Susan is abruptly woken by the cordless telephone ringing on the end table right next to her. The time seems to have unknowingly just flashed on by. "Wow, what a haunting dream!" she whispers. "What time is it?" she asks out loud, puzzled, while looking up at the old clock on the mantel that her grandfather left her when he passed away.

Ring . . .

"Seven o'clock, hmm." A bit confused, she quickly draws the blinds open. "Dark!" she says, not really sure if it's seven o'clock in the morning, or seven o'clock at night. "Is it morning already? It can't be!" she questions out loud into the fifth ring. "Wow! I think it's Tuesday already, I must have slept at least twenty hours!" She underestimates and picks up the telephone, just as the answering machine kicks in. "Hello!" she greets softly.

"Good morning! Is Chris in please?" a man with direct authority questions politely on the other end of the line, instantly confirming that it is, in fact, Tuesday morning.

"Good morning!" Susan replies and clicks off the answering machine. "No, sorry. He's not in. He's working today. Can I take a message?" she asks, then quickly rises from the chair and scurries down the hall toward their bedroom, just to confirm what she has just told the man on the telephone.

"This is Chris's supervisor. I was just a little concerned because he hasn't shown up to work yet."

"Oh, really?" Susan says just as she opens their bedroom door. Chris is still laying in the unmoved position from the day before.

She thinks fast and covers for Chris. "Oh, you know what. He wasn't feeling very well at all last night, maybe he's still home. I'll just see if he's in his room, please hold on for a second, I'll go check," she pleads gently before holding the phone tight to her chest to block her voice out.

"Chris!" Susan lightly shrieks while shaking him. Chris sits up quickly.

"What! What!" he shouts, a little dazed.

"It's your boss on the phone. You're late for work," she announces.

"Oh, shit!" Chris curses.

"I told him you weren't feeling well," Susan explains before handing him the phone.

"Hello . . . sorry about that, sir. I guess I just slept in. I wasn't feeling so hot the last couple days, but I feel a little better now! I should be into work within the hour."

"Are you sure?" his boss asks sincerely.

"Yes, I feel much better now," Chris confirms nervously. "I'll see you in about forty-five minutes," Chris reassures.

"Sure, sounds good, see you shortly then," his boss says with a crinkled, slightly puzzled, smirky grin on his face. They both hang up the phone.

"Thank you, sweetie," Chris says as he reaches out and gives her a big hug.

"Wow, super bad breath!" she announces while waving her hand in front of her forgiving, smiling face, then turns her head and gently pushes him away.

Chris quickly strips down in their bedroom then walks into the bathroom, turns on the shower, and jumps in.

"Well, I might as well get ready for work too!" she says while prepping the coffee maker and gathering up a few things from the fridge. She shuffles down the hall and into the bathroom, grabs a fresh towel, then gently strips off her nightie and drops it on the floor.

"We'll talk about our crazy party later," she says as she steps into the hot, steamy shower with him.

"Talk about what? What do you mean?" Chris questions with a blank, confused look on his face.

"You mean you don't remember the party?" Susan asks, more than a little shocked.

"Yeah, it was fun, wasn't it?" Chris recollects, totally unaware of what she is getting at as he stands there displaying a puzzled, slightly irritated look on his face.

"Well, you've pretty much been out to lunch for the past two days now. Like I said, we'll talk after work. OK, you've got to get going and so do I," she explains with a soap-covered smile.

"Oh, OK, if you insist," Chris says with a smirk as he steps out of the shower. He quickly dries himself off while peering into the partially steamed bathroom mirror as if looking for the answer to what Susan is thinking. "Huh!" he grunts to himself as he frantically brushes his stinky breath away.

He exits the bathroom, enters his bedroom, and quickly dresses for work. Chris suddenly pokes his head into the shower and startles Susan, gently kissing her steamy lips. "Your breath is much better now!" she assures with her all-too-forgiving smile. "Have a nice day!"

Chris exits the bathroom and flies down the hall into the kitchen. "You too, Susan!" he yells back while grabbing one of the two mismatched, see-through plastic bag lunches from the countertop that Susan apparently threw together during all the panic. He quickly pours an oversized, cream-dowsed coffee.

"Bye, thanks for making my lunch!" he yells out as he opens the back door.

"Bye! You're welcome!" Susan shouts back.

Chris bolts down the back stairs and shuffles along the path, all the while trying very hard not to spill a drop of his coffee or trip over his untied boot laces as he cautiously glides through the side door of the garage, jumps into his car, pushes the garage-door remote, starts the engine, and heads for work.

Chapter 9

Work is going well for Susan as usual, but for Chris, there seems to be some silent and verbal tension in and around the entire workplace. All the employees have just been informed that the company may be downsizing, and that many people may be permanently laid off as a result. Rumours of complete shutdown are also spreading like wildfire, causing anger, stress, and panic to all levels of employment throughout the warehouse.

Chris usually arrives home from work about an hour and a half before Susan. He enters the house with a six-pack of cold beer under his arm and is clearly distressed about the situation at his workplace, giving him a good reason to indulge. He rips open the case, snatches up a beer, twists off the top, and takes a hard half-beer guzzle, then suddenly flies down the stairs into the basement, bee-lining it straight to his secret marijuana stash, and pulls out one of the many pre-rolled joints. He excitedly races back up the stairs and into the living room, cranks up the stereo, then speedily walks into the kitchen and out onto the back deck, all the while taking in a long finishing swig of beer.

He clunks the empty beer bottle down on the ledge then quickly sparks up the joint with a now-more-than-ever-completely-legitimate attempt to calm his nerves by becoming further stoned and intoxicated. "I can't believe it! After all these years, I might be losing my job. Jesus!" He then draws in a huge hit from the joint.

Cough, cough, as he exhales a big cloud of smoke.

The wind suddenly picks up, followed shortly by the odd sprinkle of rain. "Brrr, it's a little chillier than usual out tonight," Chris mumbles to himself with shivering shoulders.

Ding! Dong!

"The doorbell! Hmm, who could that be? I wonder." He gently dowses the joint in a planter box. He enters the kitchen, throws the roach on the table, then moves quickly into the living room and turns down the stereo. He silently proceeds towards the front door and secretly peers through the peephole before swiftly opening the door.

"Hey, how's it going, man?" Chris politely greets the postman.

"I have a registered letter for someone by the name of Chris Baker," the postman explains while looking down at his clipboard.

"That would be me!" Chris boasts, appearing a little red-eyed as he reaches out and abruptly grabs the postman's pen from the top of the clipboard.

"I'll need to see some ID," the postman explains in a fidgety manner while nonchalantly noticing Chris's bloodshot eyes and overwhelming pot and beer breath.

Chris reaches in his back pocket, pulls out his worn, bulky wallet, and removes his ID for the postman to verify. "OK, just sign here and print your name here, if you don't mind." The postman points his finger to the exact locations for signing then quickly looks to his wristwatch.

"So, what is this?" Chris asks with enthusiasm as they switch the pen for the letter.

"No idea!" the postman confesses as he swiftly makes his way down the front stairs and back towards his postal vehicle parked right out front of the house.

"OK, thanks!" Chris blurts out just before closing the door. He stares at the letter with a puzzled look plastered across his face then walks back into the kitchen. He chronically grabs another beer from the case, cracks it open, and immediately takes a big swig before tearing the letter open. "What the fuck!" Chris screams out.

He's just been informed that he owes $855 to his previous landlord for not giving one month's notice before moving out, and that he will get none of his damage deposit back because the place was left in such a disastrous mess.

"What the fuck are they talking about?" he shouts angrily. "I handed that notice in! I know I did!" he continues loudly, trying really hard to visualize the exact moment he placed the letter in the box while squeezing his right hand over his forehead. "Shit! I cannot believe this!" he curses, then quickly guzzles down the beer. "The place wasn't that bad, come on!" he continues, shouting angrily, now with a more-than-ever red crinkled face, as he reads further into the letter. He immediately grabs another beer from the case, cracks it open, then takes in a long swig. He frantically paces back and forth in the kitchen a few times before heading straight out onto the back deck.

"This can't be happening!" he pleads while holding both hands to his forehead, trying even harder to recall if he actually did hand in the letter that Susan typed out for him on that now obvious blur of a night. "I'm sure I handed it in! This is bullshit!" he sharply concludes as he violently crumples the letter up into a ball and angrily fires it down the side of the house amongst some hungry, bushy hedges. "Out of sight, out of mind," he quotes before taking in a long finishing guzzle of his third beer. But who's counting?

He walks into the kitchen, snatches another beer from the case, then smoothly spins around and swoops up the roach from the kitchen table. He sways himself back outside onto the deck, re-lights the joint, and takes in a huge toke.

Cough, cough.

Ring . . . Ring . . .

He quickly buries the burning roach deep into the planter box, then rushes back into the kitchen and picks up the phone. "Hello!" he answers, slightly intoxicated.

"Hi, how's it going?" Susan asks sweetly.

"Oh, not too bad," Chris replies, not revealing the facts of his uneasy state with work and everything. "How are you doing?" he asks, more than happy to hear her voice.

"Oh, pretty good so far," Susan assures. "I'm going to be a little later than usual tonight," she informs.

"Oh, really?" Chris says in a "missing you" tone.

"Yeah. I'm just going to drop by my mom and dad's on the way home from work for a visit. So, go ahead and make yourself something for dinner. Because I'm pretty sure my mom won't let me leave the house without staying for dinner, you know how she is!" Susan explains warmly while lightly laughing.

"OK, sounds good, sweetie," Chris laughs along happily. "Miss you!" he whines, seeking a little more comfort than usual because of his present personal situation.

"I miss you too!" Susan replies sincerely.

"OK, see you soon, honey. Drive carefully." Chris projects his sincerity just before hanging up.

Lightning flashes and thunder booms as rain suddenly pours down fast and hard.

Chris quickly closes the kitchen door. "Wow, holy shit, she's really coming down. Brrr!" he blurts out loud while peering out the window of the kitchen door. He stumbles into the living room while rubbing his hands together. "It's freaking cold, man!" he says as he separates the fireplace screen and begins aggressively stacking some crumpled newspaper, kindling, and a couple small logs onto the grate. He strikes a long wooden match across the bricks and ignites the kindling into a warm crackling fire in a matter of seconds. The music, along with the dancing orange and blue coloured flames, mesmerizes him into a trancelike state as he slowly draws the fireplace screens closed.

Suddenly, he jumps up and races back into the kitchen, only aiming to pursue his indulgence. He rips the beer case open just enough to pull out the two remaining beers and places them deep in the back of the fridge. "Wow! They didn't last long! I should have gotten more. Ah, there's always tomorrow," he mumbles and finishes his fourth beer, all in one swig. He noisily crashes the four empty beer bottles into the case and quickly runs them downstairs into the basement. Seconds later, he comes flying back up the stairs, right into the kitchen. He habitually opens the fridge, stares for a moment, then grabs the beer he swears was staring right back at him. He twists off the cap, takes a big swig, and heads into the living room. He turns the stereo up a little louder, then sits down on the rug in front of the fireplace, comfortably leaning back on the chair's ottoman. He sucks back a few long swigs of his beer while gazing into the fireplace, then quickly doses off into a deep snoring sleep.

Susan pulls her car into the garage, then races down the path, up the back stairs, and into the kitchen, perfectly timed out from the fluctuating downpour of rain that is sporadically accompanied by thunder and lightning. She closes the door and slips off her wet shoes.

"Hey! What? Are you having a party all by yourself?" she shouts over the somewhat loud music, smiling and giggling while moving quickly through the living room, right passed Chris, and turns the stereo way down.

"Ah," Chris groans, stretching his arms way over his head, while sprawled out on the floor in front of the fire, which has now been reduced to only warm, crackling, golden embers. "I didn't hear you come in," he moans sleepily. "What time is it?" he asks while rubbing his eyes.

"Seven thirty-three to be exact," Susan replies, still smiling while looking directly at the old clock on the mantel.

"Holy! I must have dozed off," he realizes while squinting right at the clock, then rises to his feet and stretches out noisily. "So, how was dinner tonight at your mom and dad's?" he asks caringly, then reaches out and gives her a seemingly long-awaited hug.

"Mmm, it was fantastic! Homemade turkey soup with fresh rolls," she expresses with enthusiasm.

"That does sound fantastic!" Chris imagines while licking his lips.

"How about you? What did you have for dinner?" she asks while slipping off her wet coat, then walks over to the front hall closet and hangs it up.

"What's that?" Chris asks, pretending not to hear the question.

"How was your dinner?" Susan asks once again while walking into the kitchen, still smiling away.

"Well, just after you called I had a beer or two, then did some paperwork and I must have fallen asleep until now," Chris fabricates while stiffly following behind her. "It was a pretty hard day at work today too." He slightly whines, avoiding the facts about the situation at his workplace, not to mention the nice bill he just received from his previous landlord.

"Oh, so, you had beer for dinner?" Susan discovers sadly as her sweet smile quickly fades from her face. A puzzled pause. "So where did you find more beer?" she asks inquisitively.

"Oh, I saw them hiding way in the back of the fridge," Chris quickly lies, turning a little red-faced, but Susan doesn't notice. He walks down the hall, into the bathroom, jumps into the shower, and begins brushing his teeth.

"Would you like me to make you something for dinner?" Susan shouts from down the hall. A long silent pause.

Chris suddenly appears, scoops her up in his arms, and heads down the hall into the bedroom. "I think I'll have you for dinner!" he suggests in a big-bad-wolf tone of voice.

"Put me down! Put me down!" Susan screams out while giggling hysterically. They kiss passionately. Susan momentarily breaks up the kiss and smiles. "Nice breath," she whispers, then turns out the bedside table lamp and begins kissing again.

Meanwhile, back at the old gas station, Brad and the rest of the band are practising very hard on a brand-new song that

Brad is writing right on the spot, subconsciously inspired since meeting Susan.

"Excellent lyrics," Shawn encourages. "Where did they come from, Brad?" Shawn inquires in a sarcastic tone, while smirking, yet never revealing to the rest of the band where he suspects the lyrics might have come from.

"Again!" Brad directs with a grin while looking straight at his brother.

"One, Two, Three, four," Shawn shouts out the count while simultaneously hitting his drumsticks together. After a few starts and stops, they magically have a brand-new song to add to their ever-growing repertoire. Everyone in the band is quite optimistic that the song is a hit and should definitely be added to the list of songs to choose from for their new up-and-coming album.

"Excellent practice!" Brad can't help admitting as he gently places his guitar in the case then shuts the PA system down. Everyone agrees ecstatically as they roll all the gear into the back room of the garage. "OK, see you guys Wednesday after work!" Brad reminds.

"Can't wait!" Dave, the bass player, says sharply. Paul, the keyboardist, and the two female backup singers, Jan and Heather, happily concur with Dave's remarks before getting into their vehicles and driving away.

*　*　*

Chris and Susan's lovemaking scene ends comfortably. They lay close together, whispering back and forth about their dreams and aspirations. Chris, still a little intoxicated from earlier in the evening, rambles on into a drifting mumble. Susan slowly rolls over and checks the time. "Wow! Eight forty-seven already?" she says, quite surprised, then slants the clock upward for a double-check. She roles back to see that Chris has quickly dozed off, then quietly sits up on the edge of the bed. She holds her arms close to her naked body as she gently shuffles across their darkened bedroom, grabs her house coat from the closet, and wraps it around her silhouetted body. She quietly scurries down the hall into the bathroom, closes the door, and begins brushing her teeth, then jumps in the shower.

A few moments later, Chris enters the bathroom in his underwear, startling Susan just as she is stepping out of the shower. "Ah," she shrieks loudly, still dripping wet, holding a towel close to her body that just barely covers her unmentionables. "I thought you were fast asleep!" Susan points, then turns around, drops her towel onto the floor, and unrevealingly slips back into her housecoat.

"Well, I was until I had this dream, or should I say nightmare?" he shouts while squirting toothpaste onto his brush. They both laugh. "Yeah, I was leaning way back in the dentist's chair, petrified, totally sweating to death as the dentist came closer and closer to my mouth with that high-pitched, crazy-ass drill." Chris acts out excitedly. "As soon as it touched my tooth, I freaked-out and woke up! Thank God! It was so real. You know that high-pitched whizzing sound it makes?" Chris dramatizes while brushing his teeth a little harder and faster than usual. "I wonder what that dream means," he ponders. "They say dreams have something to do with changes coming up, or something like that," he rambles on.

Susan chuckles loudly while patting him on the head. "I'm sure you'll be all right," she concludes sarcastically, smiling away as she exits the bathroom. She scurries down the hallway and into the bedroom, climbs back into bed, sets the alarm, and turns out the light. Chris is only a minute behind her, and cautiously enters their darkened bedroom, still a bit light-blind from the bathroom's brightness.

He swings his arms out in front of himself, in fear of running into something. "Ouch! What the? You already turned out the light!" he whisper-shrieks after he stubs his toe on one of the bed legs. He is shocked, but truly uninjured, then literally jumps into bed, shuffles over, and snuggles right up to Susan, who is already fast asleep. Moments later, Chris is snoring loudly.

Chapter 10

October flies by like a whispering wind, deep into November. Forecasts have predicted severe winter conditions all over the map. Susan's work renovations have finally been completed and she has just signed up for a few night school computer courses. Chris's work has been holding many in-house meetings with all of its employees over the weeks. The company's managers and supervisors have been trying to convince all the employees that they must take a substantial wage cut if they wish to continue working for the company, claiming that the business is unsustainable with the current wages, and there are solid rumours that clients are seeking cheaper overall rates. Friday morning, November 26th, an announcement comes blaring over the PA. "Good morning, everyone. Please proceed to the shipping dock immediately!"

"Final Meeting!" is the heading at the top of the three-page document being distributed by the supervisors to every employee as they approach the shipping dock area. It has been made very clear by the president of the company, its managers, and shareholders, that voting for the company's request for a wage cut will take place Monday, November 29th, determining the fate of the company and its 189 employees. Each employee must date, sign, and print their names at the bottom of page three, confirming their understanding of the document, then hand it in to a supervisor before returning back to work. "What should we do?" is the main question being whispered on the shipping dock as the last signature is handed in.

"I'll never be able to pay my mortgage, or car payments, not to mention support my wife and kids if we take this kind of a wage cut!" Jimmy the shipper stresses while reading over the document.

"It's only about half of what we're getting now," one of the order picker employees shouts angrily as everyone slowly slumps back to their workstations.

Throughout the day, many long-time work buddies and pals congregate in little secret meetings in and around the entire workplace, expressing the same sort of concerns as Jimmy. The stressful, much less productive than usual workday ends with eighty percent in verbal favour of standing their ground and not giving in to the company's wishes. The other twenty percent, or "goody two shoes" employees, as a few of the other eighty percent put it, do not voice their opinions to anyone, and continue working, as if nothing has changed.

The weekend is back in a flash. Friday night, Chris arrives home, unlocks the door, and enters the house with a six-pack of beer under his arm, all the while appearing slightly panic stricken about the shortage of cash he may have in the up-and-coming future, if he does, in fact, end up losing his job over the wage dispute. After a couple beers, and a stressful head rubbing session of self-deliberation, compiled with the battle of whether or not to tell Susan about anything, he races directly to his secret stash, grabs a joint, and beelines it for the balcony. "I'm not mentioning anything to Susan about this stupid situation going on at work."

Cough, cough!

"That's for sure!" he firmly blurts out during his much-needed, slash mandatory, ever-so-increasing, secret squirrel world of self-induced intoxication. "And I'll definitely never mention nothing about that dam piece of shit, 'Failure to give Notice' charge I keep getting from my old jerky landlord. I'll never pay that lame-ass bill, I swear!" He curses on, remembering crumpling and firing the notice down the side of the house in a fit of rage that now seems to be subconsciously eating away at him. He sucks in a final, long-drawn, finger-burning toke, then squishes its remains deep into the planter box. His subconscious is exposed when he stretches way out, seeing that the crumpled ball of paper still sits there, but is now faded and tattered from the wet-weather conditions, then heads back inside.

Chris slouches around the kitchen table, slurping away on his third beer while tapping his hands and feet to the beat of some old rock 'n roll music playing loudly over the living room stereo. Susan pulls her car into the garage, then quickly scurries toward the house, out of the cold, thick, misty, frozen rain that just seemed to come out of nowhere. She shuffles up the slight, slippery back stairs and slides in through the back door, totally unnoticed, and surprises Chris to his feet.

"Ahh," he shouts loudly, quite startled, and quickly scurries into the living room and turns down the stereo. "I didn't even hear you come in," he stresses in disbelief as he enters back into the kitchen.

"I had one crazy day at work, I tell you!" Susan unusually confesses as she slips out of her wet shoes. "There must be a full moon hiding under those clouds, or something." She hangs up her coat in the front hall closet. A short pause before she walks back into the kitchen. "But, anyway, I'm home now! Thank God," she adds while displaying her cute smile, then reaches out and gives Chris a big hug and kiss.

"Would you like a beer?" he asks suggestively. "Happy hour," he proclaims, and grabs a fresh bottle from the case and holds it up in front of her.

"Sure! Why not, I need one after the nightmare customer I had today!" She chuckles nervously. "To Friday night!" she toasts and clanks their bottles together. "Oh, look!" Susan says while pointing to the blinking answering machine. "We have a message."

"Oh, I didn't even notice," Chris admits with a double take at the blinking light.

"I better check it," Susan insists, and moves quickly to push the answer button. "Oh no! I totally forgot! It's Roy's birthday tomorrow!" The answering machine announces the news. "And I haven't even bought him a birthday gift yet! Shoot!"

"No worries, sweetheart. You can get something in the morning, right?" he assures, softening the situation. "What time is the party at?" he asks before taking a big swig of beer.

"Hmm, it's not until one o'clock," she confirms, replaying the message.

"Oh, lots of time then!" Chris boasts in one of his few, take charge, shining moments.

"Yeah, you're right," Susan agrees, seemingly relieved. "You're coming with me, aren't you?" she asks, hopeful, and takes a sip of beer.

"Ah, shoot, I wish I knew about this a little earlier. I just promised my friend Dave from work I'd give him a hand moving some stuff into his parent's storage tomorrow," he explains sympathetically, then guzzles his beer down.

"Oh, OK," she says with a touch of sadness in her voice. "I understand," she concludes, realizing that it's her own fault for not remembering Roy's birthday anyway.

"So, what would you like to do tonight?" Chris asks as he grabs the last beer from the case and quickly twists off the cap. "Cheers!" he insists, clinking his new beer against her bottle.

"I'm not sure. I'm a little sleepy tonight, actually," she admits. "It's not the nicest night out there either," she reluctantly points out as frozen rain batters noisily against the kitchen windows.

"How about movie night tonight?" Chris happily suggests.

"That's sounds good to me," Susan comfortably agrees. "But what movies do we have to watch?" she asks sweetly.

"None really," Chris admits. "But no worries! We can just buzz down to that one and only DVD store left on the planet and pick up a couple new releases. What's the place called, Oh, yeah, Take-Two DVD," he remembers, now grinning from ear to ear.

"Oh yeah. I saw that place. Cool. Sounds like an excellent idea! But would you mind if I just stay home, ordered a pizza, and got comfortable by the fire while you went down to pick us up a couple movies?" she asks with shivering shoulders.

"Sure!" Chris agrees ecstatically, because now he can make a quick pit stop and grab a few more beers, and maybe even have a quick little puff along the way. "Any particular movies you would like to see?" he asks with a tipsy grin.

"Hmm, yeah, see if they've got that new holiday romantic adventure one, you know the one I mean?" she inquires, questioning sweetly. "Oh! Shoot, are you sure you're OK to drive?" she calls out from down the hall while slipping into her pajamas, totally unaware, that he has consumed five of the six beers he brought home after work, but again, who's really counting. Not to mention the big fat joint he smoked about half an hour ago.

"Sure, I'm fine!" he assures before kissing her on the lips. He silently runs downstairs for a second, then runs back up. "See you in a few!" he promises while exiting the house, knowing all too well that he is legally not OK to be driving. "Yes! Right on!" he whisper-shouts to himself as if his favourite team scores the winning goal. He opens the garage door, jumps into his car, starts it up, turns up the music, and without a moment to spare, lights the big fat joint he just grabbed from his secret downstairs stash.

A couple of rocking, puffing miles down the road, he slows down. "Ah Rats! Slight detour," he mumbles, then cranks the wheel over hard and beelines it straight for the pub, now more determined to get a hold of more beer before hitting the DVD store. His cravings for another beer have become enhanced while indulging on a few good, long puffs from the so-called high-grade marijuana joint, which has now receded to the point where it is burning his fingertips. He abruptly tosses the smouldering roach out the car window. "Shit! Shit! That hurts!" he whines, sucking away on his burning fingers. He pulls the car right up to the pub and decides right there and then that he will definitely grab a couple extra six-packs to cover his, as per usual, six-pack backup behind the driver's seat. He also grabs a couple bottles of wine for Susan, one red, one white, as if to balance out his constant intoxicated conscious, and also because he really loves her. He wastes no time cracking open a beer, and guzzles it right down, then races off towards the DVD rental store.

While in the DVD store, Chris gets a little fresh with the two young attendants when enquiring about the movies they so kindly help him locate. "These are due back in a week, right?" He stops at the door to double check while holding the DVDs in mid-air.

"That's right!" Both girls confirm just before he exits the store. He jumps into the car, starts it up, and the music begins blaring. "No time like the present!" he rambles, and cracks open another beer. He flips the ashtray down, throws in some loose change, and spots a less-than-quarter-burnt joint jammed way in the back. "All right!" he shouts excitedly, gently shimmying it out all in one piece. "Heading for home in style," he claims while guzzling and puffing all the way back to Cook Street.

Chris pops a couple breath mints into his mouth just before entering the house. He finds Susan fast asleep, curled up on the couch in front of a warm crackling fire, with soft, jazzy, romantic music playing in the background. He quietly staggers in close to Susan, then places the wine and movies right beside the large, untouched pizza sitting on the coffee table. You can almost see a tear form in his eye as he stares down at her sweet face. "She's so beautiful," he whispers. "How did I ever get her?" he slurs softly, apparently feeling that old fuzzy, trying-to-be-the-good-guy subconscious ruffling him up once again, mainly because of all the white lies he's been telling her lately, along with his secret world of stress, and his ever-increasing need of constant intoxication. With his heart momentarily back to reality, he slowly crouches down onto the floor, leans back against the couch, takes her hand, and stares deep into the brilliant, orange, crackling fire. It doesn't take long before he drifts off into a deep, snoring, drooling sleep.

Chapter 11

Ring . . . Ring . . . Ring . . .

The new day comes quickly when Chris and Susan are startled awake from their all-night slumber in the living room by an earlier-than-usual Saturday morning phone call from Mrs. Jenkins.

"Good morning! I hope I didn't wake you two. I forgot a few things for Roy's birthday party. Would you mind picking them up on the way over today?" Mrs. Jenkins asks in a mild panic-stricken tone.

"Of course, Mom! No problem," Susan replies while rubbing the sleep from her eyes, and quickly jots down her mother's requests. "OK, Mom, I'll see you guys later on this afternoon. Oh, wait! Mom, wish Roy a happy birthday for me, OK?" she requests excitedly.

"Sure will! He'll be happy to hear that when he wakes up," Mrs. Jenkins assures.

"OK, see you. Bye, Mom," Susan conveys lovingly.

"Bye for now," Mrs. Jenkins says and hangs up.

Susan arrives at Roy's already exciting birthday party. A dozen kids are running around wildly throughout the house, playing some kind of on-the-spot, made-up form of monster tag.

"It would have been nice to have all the kids playing outside in the backyard today," Mr. Jenkins hints while smiling and glancing out the living room window at the now half rain half snow falling intensely. "But the weather is not quite cooperating with us today, now is it!" he adds in good spirit, along with a touch of wishful thinking because the boys are behaving like a bunch of out-of-control orangutans.

"Hot dogs and birthday cake in fifteen minutes!" Mrs. Jenkins happily announces to all the children as Susan hands her a grocery bag full of goodies. Susan places a brightly wrapped birthday gift and card amongst the many birthday gifts that are now completely covering the dining room table.

Meanwhile, back at the ranch, Chris seems to have forgotten all of his true-hearted emotions he was experiencing the night before when he was more than just a little under the influence. He heads to Dave's parents' house, apparently to help move some of Dave's stuff into storage. The true nature of the visit is revealed immediately when Chris enters Dave's basement suite. Dave instantly fires a zip-lock bag full of pot right at Chris.

"Check that out, Man!" Dave encourages. "It doesn't get any better than that!" he boasts in a sinister sales pitch, know-it-all tone.

"Where are your parents?" Chris asks, feeling a little nervous to be holding the big bag of BC bud in his hands while looking all around.

"Oh, no worries mate, they're out of town for another two weeks!" Dave confesses deviously.

"Cool!" Chris adds before he unzips the overstuffed bag of pot and takes in a big whiff. "Nice stuff! You got papers?" Chris pleads as he throws Dave 300 bucks. Chris seems to spend a lot more money on his daily curricular activities now that his living expenses are much less since moving in with Susan. Dave and Chris stand by an open window smoking the joint, laughing and coughing.

"Hey! Do you want a beer?" Dave asks as he slides the window shut.

"Twist my freaking proverbial rubber arm," Chris says sarcastically and walks behind Dave towards the fridge. "Holy shit, man!" Chris expresses excitedly when Dave exposes the million beers in his fridge.

Knock! Knock! Knock!

"Hey! Look who it is!" Mike and Danny both direct right at Chris when Dave opens the door. "We haven't seen you very much these days since you moved into that luxury home with that hottie girlfriend of yours, Susan." Mike mentions and they all laugh.

"I'll roll up another one!" Dave says as he walks into another room and grabs a large bud from his very own secret stash. "Birds of a feather flock together, so they say! Anyone want a beer?" he enquires before sealing the deal on the monster joint. "Just help yourself. There's beer in the fridge," Dave directs while sliding the window open and sparking up the freshly rolled joint.

Knock! Knock!

"What the!" Chris shouts, grinning away. "It's a par-tay," he humorously stretches the word out as Jeff and Scott walk in, both ready to start the day off with a bang.

* * *

Roy's birthday party winds down quickly. The last kid has just been picked up by his parents. "So, Roy, do you feel any older?" Susan questions sarcastically, then gives him a big hug.

"I don't think so. I don't feel any different," he innocently replies while displaying a puzzled look on his face, then resumes playing with his many gifts.

"Ok, Mom, Dad, I better get going," Susan lightly announces.

Mrs. Jenkins immediately scurries into the kitchen and cuts a huge corner piece of Roy's birthday cake specially for Chris, who is now enthralled in an overcrowded, loud, animal house-type party in Dave's smoke-filled, beer-infested basement suite.

Back at home, hours pass with no word from Chris.

"Seven o'clock, eight o'clock, nine o'clock. Where is he?" Susan asks out loud, seeming a little puzzled and worried when

there's no answer on his cell phone. After a few more unsuc-
cessful phone calls, she lights a fire and starts watching one of
the DVDs Chris picked up the night before.

Susan's movie is just rolling the credits.

Ring . . . Ring . . .

"Hello?" she answers in a mellow tone, appearing a little sad.

"Well, hello there!" Chris greets in a loud, obviously drunken
tone while smiling and checking out one of the few easy girls
at Dave's place, who seems to want more than just a smile
from Chris.

"Are you still helping your friend move stuff?" she questions sweetly.

"We're just finishing up!" he claims with another bright
white lie, while still making the occasional eye contact with one
of the so-called easy girls.

"Wow, long day!" Susan sympathizes, remembering back to
when they first moved into their place. "Are you going to be OK
to drive home?" she asks, truly concerned along with a touch
of disbelief that he is actually in this drunken state once again,
but doesn't express her true concerns about his seemingly ever-
more-noticeable drinking adventures.

"Sure, why wouldn't I be all right to drive?" he asks, doing his
best to cover up his rambling slurs, then stands up as straight as
he can under his beer-for-breakfast-beer-for-lunch-and-beer-
for-dinner circumstances.

"OK, see you in a while," Susan says while yawning.

"OK, see you soon, bye!" *Click.* Chris just goes back to partying, secretly flirting with the easy girl a while longer. He eventually drags himself out of the party and into his car to get the heck out of there, but not before a long, drunken, slobbering, guilt ridden, good night kiss from the easy girl that takes place down the dark side of Dave's parents' house.

Chris finally arrives home. It's half-past one in the morning and all the gum and mints in the world don't seem to cure his strong, brewery breath tonight. He confirms this repeatedly by waving his hand in front of his mouth and blowing. Susan is in bed, fast asleep. Chris strips down and fumbles into bed beside her, but his presence goes unnoticed. He mumbles off into one of his many famous, drunken, snoring, beer-stinking, deep sleeps.

On Sunday morning, Susan immediately begins working on her extensive computer homework project that is to be handed in by the end of the week. Chris finally wakes up late into the morning then stumbles out to the garage and begins tinkering around with his car, all the while secretly slurping down a few beers and sparking up a couple half-burnt joints he pulled from the car ashtray.

Sunday evening arrives quickly. Susan is making some tomato soup and grilled cheese sandwiches for dinner. By the look on her face, she is not too happy with Chris's escalating drinking habits. They both sit down in front of the coffee table to eat their dinner and begin the other DVD movie. Not a word is spoken between them. Soon the movie is over and it's time for bed. "Brrr, it's a little cooler than usual tonight," Chris hints as he slips under the cool sheets and squirms up close to her warm body. He persuades relentlessly to have more than a little cuddle time, but his idea is quickly shut down. "Is everything all right?" he asks, sensing the cold shoulder.

"I'm a little concerned about your drinking these days, in more ways than one," Susan says strongly without another word.

Chris regrettably gets the hint, sighs, and keeps his distance. Before long, they both fall into a deep sleep.

Monday morning arrives abruptly with that annoying alarm clock blaring away in the background. Susan is much quieter than usual this morning as she showers, does her makeup, and picks out something to wear, all the while seemingly deep in thought. Chris's relentless attempts to humour her does eventually end up softening her obvious edginess, but let's face it, she is more than just a little concerned that Chris may actually have a drinking problem, way beyond her initial comprehension, but decides not to mention anything more about it this morning. Moments later, they're both out the door and off to work.

Chapter 12

December first. Crunch day. The fate of Chris's employment is in the hands of all its employees. One at a time, they walk up and slip their "Final Decision" vote papers into the slot of the locked, gray metal box in the lunchroom, right beside the time clock where they simultaneously punch-in their timecards.

Twenty minutes into the workday.

"Good morning, everyone!" blares over the PA system. A short pause, with a crackling sound. "Everyone is to attend the meeting on the shipping dock at ten o'clock sharp this morning. There you will hear the final vote count determining the fate of the company and all its employees. Thank you for your attention."

Tensions around the workplace have moved from moder-ate to extremely high because they just may be out of a job for real, and that seems to have set in hard with some guys who have families. There is a lot of angry questioning going on with all the employees about what each person will vote. Most of the personnel have been speculating that the company is just bluffing about shutting everything down if they don't take the substantial wage cut as the company strongly suggested. It seems to have been more like a dream rather than reality to the employees, because for the last two hours there has been a serious closed-door video conference going on in the manager's office that has just now revealed the company's unfortunate fate. The vote outcome also emotionally affects some other half a dozen state managers who are in checkered view on the large flat screen monitor.

Ten o'clock comes fast. "Good morning, everyone!" blasts over the PA. "Please proceed to the shipping dock for the ten o'clock meeting." Everyone willingly takes their sweet time assembling to the shipping dock, seemingly afraid to hear the outcome of the final vote. Once everyone is roll-called over the loud, handheld blowhorn by the supervisor, the manager snatches the horn from his hand and doesn't waste any time relaying the devastating outcome of the vote count.

"It was twenty-eight percent for the proposed wage cut, and seventy-two percent against the proposed wage cut." A long, silent pause. Then with a shocked, cold, callous expression on his face, the manager sharply announces the company's fate.

"We regretfully conclude that we will, in fact, be shutting down the company in thirty days. January first, to be exact."

Cursing, swearing, and yelling are just a few of the emotions expressed immediately after the announcement.

"Nice Christmas present!" one guy yells out angrily. A few others follow suit with increased anger and sarcastic out-bursts. Management expected this reaction after this potential vote count, and secretly hired half a dozen security guards who are now standing by in the parking lot in case anything should erupt.

A wicked fight breaks out, all because one guy is in another's path of travel. It's between the skinny guy, "Goody two shoes" Greg, and the so-called tough guy rebel bully, Bill, "Bill Bash You." Goody two shoes never told anyone that he has been training in mixed martial arts ever since he was seven years old. Greg gets into it with Bill, but mostly there's just a lot of fast relaxed punch blocking going on in Greg's favour.

"Why is it that you always seem to go for the violent approach to everything?" Greg humbly asks while looking Bill straight in the eyes. All the while, Greg maintains a stance of full-on guard mode. Bill is more than just a little shocked and embarrassed about his lacking tough guy performance. Seconds later, the security guards are revealed and break-up the scuffle.

The manager grabs the blow horn and makes a screech-ing announcement, hoping to avoid any further outbreaks. "Everyone will be excused from work early today, but you will still be paid for a full day's work." Surprised looks along with an uneasy pause fills the air. "Report back to work at 7 a.m. tomorrow morning!" he demands in the final crackling announcement. Everyone reluctantly leaves the shipping floor and heads outside to their vehicles. The parking lot clears, fast and furious.

Chris's worst nightmare has now come true. "No more job in thirty days!" he shouts and starts up the car. "How am I ever going to pay the rent after that bullshit decision?" he curses as a bead of sweat drips from his brow. He drives recklessly while frantically searching for his favourite pain-relieving substance. He probes his fingers around in the ashtray and finally discovers an old, tinfoil-wrapped half-joint jammed way in the back. He lights it up and meaningfully sucks in a few good, hard puffs until it disintegrates in his fingers. He reaches behind his seat only to find nothing there. "Fuck!" He curses. "I can't believe it! I'm out of fucking beer!"

He then cranks the steering wheel over for a hard left turn, taking an emergency beeline detour right to the beer and wine store. He loads his trunk up with at least a dozen six-packs, except for the half dozen he always handfeeds from behind the driver's seat. "Good, all stocked up!" he deviously announces with a grin and heads for home.

Chris gears up for a job-losing party all by himself. He's in a sad state. You can see terror written all over his face and pain in his glassy eyes. "I can't wait to get home and roll up a big fatty!" he mumbles to himself excitedly. He cranks up the stereo then gradually speeds his car way up past the speed limit, focusing hard on that big fat joint, trying to forget his current situation.

The days of December are flying by, like they always do. Chris finishes another fast-paced work day, punches his time-card, and somberly walks to his car. He starts it up and heads for home. "Holy Shit! Christmas is right around the corner," he suddenly realizes. "I better hurry it up and get Susan a present," he whisper-shouts to himself. "But what can I get her? And Mom too. God! And how much cash will I even have left after my rent is paid in January?" he says with a touch of panic in his voice. "Fuck!" he curses and smacks both hands down hard on the steering wheel, then mumbles out a few numbers, genuinely attempting to calculate exactly what he can really afford for any sort of Christmas presents. "Holy crap city, man! That won't leave very much," he figures frustratedly.

He reaches behind his seat, grabs a beer, cracks it open, looks side to side, then secretly takes in a long guzzle, right in broad daylight. Chris is so used to living in his own little secret world of booze, drugs, lies, and deceit, it's an easy decision for him to not bother mentioning anything to Susan about his job-loss situation, especially since it's so close to Christmas. "Susan really loves Christmas. I couldn't tell her anything about anything right now. It would totally ruin her Christmas," he whispers in a true warm, caring demeanour. "Ah, crap! I'll just put it on my credit card," he concludes with a finishing guzzle of the overly satisfying beer, then immediately reaches around and grabs another one.

A noticeable bout between good and evil flickers in and out of Chris's life. His heart always seems to be in the right place, but it sometimes gets a little clouded by his prevalent intoxication, which undoubtedly, leads him into making the wrong and selfish decisions he doesn't always remember.

Chris pulls his car into the garage, right alongside Susan's car. "Hmm, she's home." He races toward the house, up the back stairs, and into the kitchen. His excessive adventurous drinking sprees are more prevalent at this time of his life than ever before. His job is going down the tubes fast and it's noticeably taking its toll on him.

Susan easily picks up on the slight sway in his step as he walks in the kitchen door. "So, what's been going on with you these days with all the drinking and stuff?" she asks with a shaky smile, realizing that now is probably a good time to bring it up. She easily puts two and two together, replaying the many times he was just a little more than intoxicated.

"What's that?" Chris asks, pretending he didn't hear the question while slipping off his boots and jacket.

"Seriously, I can count beer bottles just as good as anyone else," she says with a strong taste of sarcasm. "And, we seem to be adding up pretty darn fast in the garage these days, don't we?" she reveals while looking him straight in the eye. A silent pause.

"Shit!" Chris shouts in his mind, feeling the emotion of being busted. He always thought the bottles were completely out of sight, out of mind when he leaned the four-by-eight sheet of plywood up against the towering empties.

"So, what's going on exactly?" Susan questions once again, truly concerned. "Have you always drank this much beer?"

she quickly throws another question his way, along with her puzzled-eyebrow look.

"Not really, we've just been doing a lot of extra loading at work these past few weeks and I'm extra thirsty when I get home," he lies. A long silent pause. "Hey, you're home pretty early today," he attempts to redirect the interrogation.

"Yes, I am. The few of us that have been taking the upgrade computer courses got to go home a little earlier today," she happily confesses as her sweet, naïve nature kicks in, allowing her heart to go right along with his stories, but leaves her emotions a little weary.

Chris doesn't drink any less, since being called on it, he just covers his tracks a little better, leaving only a small trace of beer bottles and beer cans lying around. The extra ones get packed in the trunk of his car, and a few occasionally find their way smashed into the streets, whichever comes first, depending on the state he is in and the convenience of where he is. Everything seems to be normal on the surface, but something is still not quite right, and Susan's intuition occasionally reminds her of that. People at her work have been noticing that she is a little quieter than normal these past few days, and she notices that they notice, but she manages to just shrug them off the subject with a warm smile and talk of a white Christmas.

The weather has been running neck and neck all week, right along with Susan's emotions. "Rain and snow are in the forecast for the next several weeks," announces her car radio as she pulls out of the bank parking lot. The first of the Christmas classics

131

begins playing over the radio, then almost like magic, she immediately perks up and is grinning from ear to ear. "Nothing is going to ruin our Christmas!" she insists. "As a matter of fact, I'm going to go get a Christmas tree right this second!" She happily embraces the idea with a bright smile. "And I know exactly where to go, too! That place, my father always took us to get our family Christmas tree." She reminisces, then turns the car radio up a bit louder. She joyfully seizes the moment, humming and singing along with the festive songs playing over the radio as she gleefully makes her way to the Christmas tree place.

Chapter 13

S now begins falling and is more beautiful with the song, "It's Christmas time Again," playing over the car radio. Susan slowly slides her car onto Cook Street, which now looks like an incredible sparkling, colourful winter wonderland. She glides up to the front of their house with one of the largest, bushiest, freshly-snowed-upon Christmas trees ever. It's as big as her car, especially now with the extra snow on it. She unstraps the tree from the car roof, shakes it off, quickly drags it down the ever-increasing snowy pathway, clunks it up the steps, and unlocks the front door, then quickly runs back out to her car and grabs the tree stand she bought along with it.

Chris is downstairs in the basement taking inventory of his marijuana stash and working very hard on his third beer, when he is suddenly startled by the unusual sound of the front door swinging open and crashing against the front hall closet. He pops a mint into his mouth, just for a little breath insurance, and races up the basement stairs, arriving at the front door right in the nick of time to help Susan.

The massive Christmas tree seems to need more than just a little persuasion to get it in through the front door and situated in the living room. She unties the sash and the tree goes into expansion mode.

"What the!" Chris says with amazement.

"I was going to call you, but I wanted it to be a surprise," she reveals.

"It's freaking huge!" He states the obvious. "Weird," he squeaks out.

"What?" Susan asks.

"I was just looking at the Christmas boxes downstairs," he admits. In fact, his beer was sitting right on top of one of them, but of course he doesn't mention that part of it.

"Do you know which one of them has the Christmas star in it?" Susan asks with encouragement.

"I'm not sure. I'll just bring them all up!" Chris obliges with a touch of hyper-ness attached.

"Yeah, good idea!" she agrees. "Hey, only twenty-one days until Christmas!" she calculates excitedly and dials in some Christmas tunes on the stereo.

Chris sprints down the stairs like a little kid and quickly rustles up every box marked "Christmas." He makes a few trips up and down the stairs and back into the living room, finally revealing four large Christmas boxes. They both stabilize the tree into the new stand and make quick work decorating it, then continue displaying the rest of the many Christmas decorations all around the house while under the sweet supervision of Susan, with her passionate eye on "Home and Garden: Christmas Edition." Chris easily goes along with every decoration placement Susan suggests. He seems to love Christmas, almost as much as she does, as is easily portrayed by the ear-to-ear grin, he has plastered all over his face. He begins clipping up a few strings of his father's old Christmas lights onto the existing clips surrounding the front door, foyer, and stair railings at the front of the house. The night has become one of their few romantic evenings together that ends up in a long-awaited "kiss and make up" sex scene.

* * *

"Only one week until Christmas, then another week and no job," a few of his coworkers nervously discuss as they head for their afternoon coffee break.

"Oh yeah, it's payday! Right on. Hope we all get a big Christmas bonus," Chris blurts out sarcastically as he enters the lunchroom where the supervisor is handing out cheques to all the employees. Chris sits down and strategically rips his cheque open. $566.63. "What the fuck!" He shouts out with a confused look on his face. "Garnished wages! What the fuck are they talking about?" he curses once again, upon confirming the amount in the deductions column. He angrily fires the envelope across the lunchroom, coming near to getting it into the garbage pail, and it's quickly trampled by the many employees in the room.

Chris focuses on the bottom of his cheque-stub on the heading marked, "Notice." Yes, the unthinkable has now happened. It turns out, Chris's previous landlord went ahead with legal action against him for the funds he still owed for not submitting the proper thirty-day written notice upon him moving out, and subsequently got a court order to garnish his wages for the total amount owed, leaving Chris with a measly paycheck. "Shit! Shit! Shit!" He curses, heads back to work a little early, and silently finishes up the work week. Chris is beyond pissed off and races all the way home, ranting and raving about needing that money for Christmas presents as well as rent, but little does he know, it's a little too late for that now. "What the fuck can I do about it?" he curses. "Shit, I got that final warning letter in the mail weeks ago but I forgot. Shit!" he blurts out, knowingly lying to himself, smacking down hard on the steering wheel. "I never thought this was going to happen, anyway." He easily trowels over the truth, knowing all too well he did not even bother to open that letter marked "Final Notice," in bright red ink. Instead, he filed it deep in the back of one of his messy dresser drawers, accompanied by a few previous warning letters, which he also received from his ruthless landlord since receiving the original one he reluctantly threw down the side of the house.

He pulls the car into the garage, runs up the back stairs, opens the door, enters the kitchen, and beelines it straight for his dresser drawer. He grabs the stack of envelopes from the drawer and tears open the one labelled "Final Notice," which quickly confirms the cold hard facts of his situation. "I can't believe this!" he shouts out loud to himself. "I'm sure I handed that thing in. I'm sure I did!" he repeats and shakes the notice before stuffing it deep in the back of the drawer with the rest of them.

He sits down on the edge of the bed, a little foggy-headed about the facts, debating with himself whether he did or did not hand in the moving out notice that night in question. "I remember Susan giving me the letter, but I'm a total blank after that," he confesses, then shuts the drawer and heads for the kitchen. "Nothing a big fatty and a few beers can't fix." He opens the fridge, grabs a beer, cracks it open, and heads out to the balcony, then reveals a joint that magically appears from out of his coat pocket and lights it up. Chris seems to need more and more of his secret drug and alcohol enhancing moments with each passing day, just enough to ease his constant cravings and cloud the shitty realities of his rapidly changing life. There really is a big fat cloud of trouble hanging over him, coiled and ready to strike the moment he does, in fact, lose his first job since high school in less than two weeks down the road.

* * *

Management has just posted a letter on the lunchroom board, right beside the time clock. They are requesting for many personnel to work overtime every day until closure, as they must get all inventory out of the building by December 31st. Chris agrees and signs up for the overtime. He arrives at work early every day, prepared with a few pre-rolled joints and, of course, his seemingly endless supply of beer hidden in the trunk of his car that always trickles a six-pack to his secret stash behind the driver's seat. He sweats out a few hard hours of overtime every night, taking advantage of the sudden work crunch, hoping to maximize his spending capabilities for Christmas presents and his other secret unmentionable desires.

He is now even getting stoned every morning before work and on his first coffee break, lunch break, and afternoon coffee break, and seconds after he leaves the parking lot. With Christmas being so close, he ventures out every night immediately after his long day at work, on varying levels of stoned, drunken, and guilt-crazed shopping sprees with his credit card in hand. If it wasn't for the stoned-drunken state he is always in right now, he might just have sense enough to be more truthful to Susan about everything that's been going on, not to mention the sense to be more truthful to himself about everything as well. The problem lies within some obvious keywords, such as stoned and drunken, that keep impeding all things right. His intoxicated state is being kept under wraps quite well these days, at least for the time being, because of their time spent apart from one another due to all of Chris's overtime and all the

Christmas festivities that have been unfolding, such as visiting, shopping, baking, wrapping, and so on, that Susan has happily been taking care of.

Their Christmas tree is decorated amazingly and seems to have accumulated a huge amount of different-sized, brightly coloured, pre-wrapped Christmas presents that Chris has been strategically placing all around the base of the tree each night after work. He also takes a few presents downstairs into the basement and tags them, "From Santa," then piles them up in a secret spot behind some cardboard boxes. His credit cards are also piling up right along with the Christmas presents, but doesn't faze him in the least. "What's that hit song? Oh yeah, "You Can't Take It with You When You're Gone," he sings to himself, hoping to relieve his nerves, then guzzles another beer just to be sure. Christmas cards have been arriving day after day, filling the entire fireplace mantel and table tops around the living room and dining room area, ninety percent of which are all from Susan's relatives and many of her friends. Over this past week, Susan has also been placing Christmas gifts under their tree for everyone in her family, as well as a few gifts she got for Chris, who, like a kid, has been secretly investigating each present with his name on it, feeling the weight and shaking them up a bit, trying to guess what Susan might have got him every chance he gets.

"Christmas Eve is here at last!" Susan expresses joyfully as Chris walks in the door. She swishes across the kitchen floor and gives him a big hug and kiss.

"Wow, I can't believe it, I know. Sorry, they took us right to the wire at work today," he says without a doubt.

"I'm just glad you're home now," Susan expresses in a warm, caring manner, accompanied by another hug and kiss.

"Me too!" Chris says, burps, then quickly turns his face away. Susan laughs. "Excuse me," he pleads nervously, hoping she doesn't detect his beer and pot breath. Chris has already snuck in a few good puffs, along with a couple beers, about twenty minutes earlier while driving home, but easily maintains his stealth mode with the help of a new, more powerful breath mint he was just introduced to by his friend Dave.

"I'm going to get everything organized so we can head out soon." Susan rustles up the plan. "You go get ready. Oh, here. Eat this gingerbread man I got from work today. They're really good!" she encourages.

Chris devours the gingerbread man one Smartie at a time. "Yeah, that was really good!" he agrees and heads for the shower.

"Poor little guy didn't have a chance!" Susan jokes loudly from the kitchen and they both laugh hysterically.

Chris enters the living room looking as fresh as a daisy and is dressed warmly for the cold night.

"Looking good!" Susan compliments.

"Thank you. You always look good!" Chris compliments right back with a hug and kiss. "I already loaded most of the presents into the trunk of my car while you were getting ready, it's just those ones left to take." She points to the two-foot stack sitting on the coffee table. They exit the house, lock the back door, then head for the garage with the last stack of gifts and carefully load them into the trunk of Susan's classic bug.

"Wow, now that's a sack of presents!" Chris shouts with excitement, then jumps into the passenger seat of Susan's car.

"Buckle up!" Susan demands with a smile. "Amazing! It's snowing again, and it's really coming down now," Susan expresses excitedly.

"Yeah, looks like we're totally going to have a white Christmas, after all! Right in the Saint Nick of time," Chris says, unable to resist throwing in a playful spur-of-the-moment cornball joke that leaves them both laughing.

Chris and his mother have been cordially invited to Susan's parents' home for a Christmas Eve celebration. Mr. and Mrs. Jenkins are quite sympathetic to Chris and his mother since the loss of a father and husband to lung cancer not so long ago, especially more so during this time of year.

"Thanks for inviting me and my mom to your parents' house," Chris kindly expresses.

"You're very welcome, and don't worry, I've got your mom's address locked-in on my GPS. We should be there in about twenty-five minutes," she happily assures the exact time and location, then reaches over and holds Chris's hand. Colourful Christmas lights twinkle up and down every street while the song "It's Christmas Time Again" whisks them smoothly along the slick, wintery roads right into that magical Christmas feeling.

"I'm sure your car is way better than mine in the snow, that's for sure." Chris imagines.

"Yeah, it's not bad, is it?" Susan demonstrates while driving over the slick roads with ease.

Chris reminisces about the pain associated with the loss of his father but keeps his teary-eyed emotions under wraps. Occasionally, it hits him extra hard though, especially when he glances up at the small old black-and-white photo of him and his father washing the car that rests inside a clear plastic sleeve attached to the underside of the sun visor of the old '67 Mustang. This will be the first time that Susan will meet Chris's mother, as she was out of town visiting her sister when they had the housewarming party.

"So, who's all going to be there tonight?" Chris asks, and snaps himself out of his sadness.

"Well, let's see," Susan thinks out loud. "At least two sets of my relatives, and a few of our close family friends, and possibly a few neighbours as well." A short pause just as the song "The Twelve Days of Christmas" is ending. "People will drop in and out throughout the evening, I'm sure," Susan explains. "It's always busy at my parents' house this time of the year." She remembers, smiling, "My Uncle Ed will definitely be there. He's the funniest guy you'll ever meet," she warns with a big smile and the nod of her head.

"Cool, can't wait to meet him," Chris says while tapping along with the song "Deck the Halls" that softly plays over the car radio.

"Oh, we're almost there!" Chris notifies, just before the GPS announces the same thing. "Yeah, just turn left at the next street, then take the immediate right . . . There it is. It's the one with the blue icicle lights on it," Chris points out excitedly, then jumps out of the car and beelines it up the slippery pathway towards his mother's house. Chris helps his mother down the increasingly snowy pathway while carrying a few presents under his arm.

"Hello, hello! So nice to finally meet you!" Susan greets sincerely.

"Oh, hello. Nice to meet you too," June reciprocates with joy as she slips into the back seat of Susan's car, and her gifts quickly follow. They're buckled up and are soon on their way.

"So nice to see you, Mom." Chris lovingly reaches into the back seat and takes his mother by the hand. They continue driving through the magical Christmas atmosphere of falling snow, multicoloured lights, and beautiful, festive songs playing over the radio that radiates all the way to Susan's parents' home.

Chris gently helps his mother and her gifts from the back seat of the car, then gathers more gifts from the trunk and stacks them high in Susan's arms. Chris assists his mother and her gifts up the freshly shovelled front steps of Susan's parents' home.

Ding! Dong!

The door instantly flies open with Roy attached to it.

"Come in! Come in!" Roy repeats. Susan hands Roy the tall stack of Christmas presents and he vanishes, placing them all under the Christmas tree.

Chris scurries back out to the car and grabs the rest of the gifts. He's back in a flash with another stack and passes them off into Roy's excited, open arms. "Wow!" Roy stresses with the biggest grin, then heads for the Christmas tree.

Mr. and Mrs. Jenkins approach the door smiling and warmly meet and greet Chris and his sweet, frail mother.

"So nice to meet you both. Thank you so much for having us. Your home is so beautiful," June compliments while shaking their hands.

"So nice to meet you as well," Mr. and Mrs. Jenkins converse genuinely before introducing them to a few relatives that are all sitting in the living room, nibbling on various snacks and sipping away on hot and cold beverages.

Upon entering the living room, there is a big, beautiful, bright, colourful, twinkling Christmas tree and a warm, crackling fire. Christmas oldies from the forties and fifties are playing softly in the background, and many trays of food with every type of selection you can imagine are placed around the room. Every tray is elegantly designed and placed amongst many lit candles all around the coffee table and dining room table, just begging to be sampled—which they are. There's an amazing assortment of differently shaped shortbread cookies, mincemeat tarts, Christmas cake, cheese, pickles, crackers, sausage, veggies with dips, and many types of pop and alcohol drinks too. Chris seems to be portraying his best behaviour in quite some time, mainly because he can now fill his face and curve the cravings that are driven by the pot-smoking munchies syndrome he developed earlier this evening. But there are forty-eight beers in the downstairs rec room fridge that seem to be calling his name, three of which have already been devoured upon the direct order from Mr. Jenkins to "Help yourself." And he does—several times.

Uncle Ed has been unleashing his crazy stand-up comic routine all evening, clowning around with his jokes and impressions of famous movie stars. Everyone is left in hysterics as Uncle Ed exits the living room.

"Your uncle is so funny," Chris can't help mentioning.

"He is funny," June kindly mentions.

"I told you," Susan whispers right in Chris's ear.

The beautiful Christmas Eve gathering is just what June needed and it shows in her smile. Moments later, a decked out "Santa Claus" appears in the dining room.

"Ho! Ho! Ho!" Santa rumbles as he enters. "Merry Christmas!" he greets, overly cheerful, convincing everyone that he is the real deal, standing right before them. Santa reveals a big red sack with an assortment of gifts stashed in it. "Since everyone's been so good this year, I've got presents for every-one!" Santa gleefully announces. "Ho! Ho! Ho!" Santa rumbles out once again.

"This has been a family tradition for years and years at the old Jenkins home," Aunt Sheila reveals as she leans over and shares the facts with June.

"That is so nice," June says with a gratifying smile.

Uncle Ed reappears as Uncle Ed. He walks right up to the large living room front window, draws the curtains back, and reveals the blizzard conditions outside. "Did I mention it was going to be an extremely white Christmas this year," Uncle Ed points out the obvious and chuckles. Everyone slowly approaches the front room window.

"Wow!" is mentioned over and over as many peer out the window to see that the Christmas snow has now drifted into a blinding, twirling, swirling snowstorm.

"It's so thick! It's like snow fog," Uncle Ed jokes, lightening any concerns, and everyone laughs. "But, on a more serious note," he explains while looking down at his watch, "Whoever is planning on driving home tonight might want to get out there now before we're all stuck in here together until the New Year."

They all laugh and agree. "Myself, Sheila, and the kids are the lucky ones. *We* actually get to hang around this luxurious hotel until just after the New Year! If they'll still have us, that is?" Uncle Ed adds with his sarcastic, funny side. More laughter as everyone disperses to put on their coats and boots. Mr. Jenkins jovially takes on the role of Santa Claus and begins making little individual piles of Christmas presents for everyone who is preparing to head out into the blizzard.

"Thank you very much! Merry Christmas!" all the guests express as they exit the house with their gifts in hand and head for their vehicles.

"OK, Mom, Dad, Roy, Uncle Ed, Aunt Sheila, best neighbours ever, we better head out too," Susan decides while looking out the window.

"OK, sweetie," Mr. and Mrs. Jenkins reply with complete understanding.

"It was so nice to see you all! We'll see you all real soon," Susan assures warmly.

"It sure was good to see you too, Susan, and very nice to meet you as well, June! Chris, always a pleasure," Mr. Jenkins expresses kindly.

Uncle Ed and Aunt Sheila join in the good night wishes at the front door, reaching out with big hugs and handshakes.

"Bye, Roy, see you soon. Don't give Rex too many of those doggy treats he got from Santa," she adds comically.

"OK, Sis!" Roy agrees with a smile. Susan, Chris, and June load themselves up with their beautifully wrapped Christmas gifts, then head out the front door and down the front stairs towards Susan's extremely snow-covered car. Chris places his stack of gifts on top of the dry, fluffy snow, then quickly begins clearing the foot-high snow off the trunk and all the windows. He helps his mother climb into the back seat of the car, along with her newfound Christmas gifts in hand, then helps buckle her up. Susan places all the gifts into the trunk, then gets in and starts the car. Chris does a final sweep over the front windshield, then jumps in the car and buckles up. Roy and his dog stare out the front living room window, watching and waving as their loving sister heads off down the road and disappears into the Christmas wonderland. Warnings of total whiteout conditions are forecasted over the car radio as they head toward their homes. The only guests left celebrating at the Jenkins' Christmas Eve party now are Uncle Ed's family and the old neighbours from across the street.

Susan pulls her car right up in front of June's blue icicle-lit house. "Are you sure you wouldn't like to stay at our house tonight, Mom?" Chris questions thoughtfully with a mint-hidden, six-pack-of-beer slur.

"Yes, you're more than welcome!" Susan kindly supports with a slightly concerned look on her smiling face.

"No, no, no! I'm home now," June conveys with a warm smile. "You know what I mean, that old, home-sweet-home feeling," June softly explains, and they smile with understanding.

"OK, Mom," Chris exits the car and helps his mother out of the back seat.

"Merry Christmas!" Susan and June express with heart-felt emotions.

"It doesn't look like the blizzard will let up anytime soon," Chris mentions as he takes his mother's Christmas gifts and cautiously staggers along the snowy pathway, up the slippery steps, and right into her warm house. "Merry Christmas, Mom!" he says excitedly and gives her a big kiss and hug. He frolics like a kid in the snow all the way back to the bug where Susan waits patiently, listening to a favourite Christmas song, "Silent Night," playing softly over the radio. Chris jumps back in the car and they're on the way home. "That was the best Christmas Eve ever!" he says with a slightly faded six-pack slur attached. "Your Uncle Ed is super hilarious!" he laughs, vaguely recalling one of her Uncle Ed's funnier moments of the evening. The sensational hit song "It's Christmas Time Again" just begins playing over the radio.

Susan's bug has no trouble delivering them home safely. They pull into the snow-drifted garage, then as quickly as they can, they gather up all the Christmas gifts and head up the path and enter their warm and cozy home. They gently place their new gifts around the already highly gifted Christmas tree.

"I'll be right back in a second!" he announces, then flies out the kitchen door and heads right back out to the garage. He just has to have a little Christmas Eve "Night Cap" from the half joint he has stashed in his car ashtray. He lights it up, taking in a big toke, then blows the smoke out through the small crack between the overhead doors, then pops a couple of his special mints in his mouth and heads back up into the house.

Susan already has a small fire going, the tree lit, and some old Christmas music playing softly on the stereo. She whisks down the hall and into the bedroom and quickly changes into her new pajamas and slippers she got from her Uncle Ed's "Santa Claus Christmas bag."

Chris sits staring at the twinkling Christmas tree with its many gifts piled high all around it, reflecting on when he was just outside in the garage, and how immediately after his sneaky puff, he feels the "Got to do right" good guy side shining through a bit more than usual. Chris experiences another bout between good and evil. The good wins this time, with a little help from that good old Christmas Eve spirit. He brushes his teeth and humbly proceeds down the hall and into their bedroom to check out Susan's new Christmas bedtime wear.

"Looking good!" he compliments.

They both head back into the living room and snuggle up in front of the warm, crackling fire for an intimate glass of wine. "Cheers!" they both say at the same time and clink their glasses together.

Dong . . . Dong . . . Dong . . . sounds the old clock on the mantel, right to the twelfth strike.

"It's midnight, Merry Christmas," Susan raises her glass to Chris.

"Merry Christmas," Chris reciprocates, as they clang their glasses together. The bottle of wine is going down smoothly.

"Here's to the best Christmas ever!" Chris elaborates with another cheer, followed by the clanging of their glasses. Before long, the bottle of wine is empty, and their glasses soon follow suit. Susan stuffs the cork back in the top of the empty wine bottle, gathers up the empty glasses, and heads into the kitchen.

Susan re-enters the warm, Christmas-flavoured living room and pulls Chris to his feet. "Time for bed. Santa will be here soon," she reminds with a big smile. The Christmas tree sparkles away as the fire embers fade. They head off down the hallway and straight into their bedroom for a little Christmas Eve loving.

Christmas morning! Susan quietly sneaks out of their bed at 6 a.m. to go fill their large, red, fuzzy stockings that are hung just under the fireplace mantel. "What? They're already half full!" she whispers, a little shocked.

Little did she know, "Santa" had snuck out of bed at 4 a.m. and secretly did the deed of filling the stockings and placing the rest of her gifts from Santa under the tree. All the bad that Chris has done these past few months suddenly and completely dissolves from her heart. After over-filling their stockings and placing a few "To Chris from Santa" presents under the tree, Susan continues into the kitchen to make the morning coffee. The sound and smell of the percolating coffee wakes Chris. He stumbles down the hall and into the living room, where he sinks into the large two-seater chair, waiting to surprise her, but Susan secretly catches his movements out of the corner of her eye and wants to surprise him as well. Chris sits silently, fidgeting, waiting for Susan.

"Merry Christmas!" Chris shouts while jumping to his feet, just as Susan walks into the living room with coffee and Baileys for two. She gently places the coffees down on the table.

"Merry Christmas, to you too, sweetie!" she expresses and gives him a big hug and kiss right on the lips. "Wow, look at all the presents. Holy moley!" she realizes.

"Hey! How did you know I was up, anyway?" he asks, a little puzzled.

"A Christmas elf told me," she confesses and they both laugh as she clicks on the stereo for a little Christmas music. "I love this white Christmas feeling, don't you?" Susan expresses with an added question.

"Love it!" Chris agrees as they continue sipping away on their coffees while watching the falling snow through the front living room window. The Baileys and coffee go down so nicely, they decide to have another while unpacking their stockings and sampling a few of the chocolate goodies inside.

Ring . . . Ring . . . Ring . . . The phone beckons Susan into the kitchen.

"Merry Christmas!" Susan greets upon answering. It's her entire family on speaker phone, simultaneously wishing them both a very Merry Christmas. While Susan chats away on the phone in the kitchen, Chris pokes around at the new development of presents marked, "To Chris, From Santa" lying under the tree he hadn't noticed until just now.

"What a sweetie," he whispers deeply to himself. You can almost see his eyes tear up as he examines the gifts a little more closely. He quickly changes focus and begins digging for the biggest present of all, which he had hidden deep under the tree just a few days ago. He slowly and strategically exposes the large gift while quietly shifting and moving the many gifts that are piled on top of it.

"OK, Mom, Dad, everyone, we'll talk later on today, you're welcome. Love you all, and Merry Christmas!" Susan reaches out, embracing them all with her caring words of sweetness, before hanging up the phone.

Susan is pleasantly surprised as she enters back into the living room where she finds Chris kneeling in front of the Christmas tree, grinning from ear to ear, holding a large colourful, bow ridden Christmas gift out in front of his face.

"Merry Christmas!" He bellows out, then rises to his feet and hands her the extra special gift.

"Oh, thank you!" she shouts with the biggest smile, then quickly sits down cross-legged on the floor in front of the Christmas tree and excitedly begins tearing the present open, just like an excited little kid.

One present after another is being opened. "To Susan, From Chris. To Susan, From Santa." and the list goes on. The occasional present "To Chris" becomes exposed from under the many gifts for Susan. Chris takes a moment and crumples up all the wrapping paper and lights a fire.

"Wow! I think you went a little overboard. Crazy guy," she acknowledges while visually recapping the many gifts that are spread all around the living room. "I love all the presents you and Santa got me!" she conveys sweetly.

"Me too!" Chris expresses right back with a big grin.

"I'll be back in two seconds," she promises and returns swiftly with two fresh cups of coffee and Baileys. "Cheers, Merry Christmas!" she greets and raises her cup.

"Cheers and Merry Christmas to you too, sweetheart!" he expresses back with a big grin, just as their cups clang together. Their warm, spiked coffees go down nicely while sitting quietly on the floor in front of the fireplace, listening to the lovely Christmas music.

"Oh, I better give my mom a call and thank her for the presents!" Chris realizes and vanishes into the kitchen.

Christmas Day has been absolutely perfect. Chris seems on solid ground, laying off the beers and skunk weed on this special day. The only Christmas cheer he has been indulging in is the quite frequent coffee and Baileys that they both seem to be enjoying equally. Chris and Susan stay close together throughout the day and late into the evening, seemingly in a comfortable "Christmas Day" trance, locked-in on one another, creating some much-needed special moments in their relationship. They sit snuggled close together in the big chair in front of the warm, crackling fire, laughing hysterically while watching their favourite Christmas shows. The last show ends and the credits roll. Chris immediately begins tickling Susan to where she just can't take it anymore. She frantically runs down the hall and into the bedroom, trying to escape the "Mad tickler" as she calls him. Chris quickly shuts the house down, all except for the Christmas tree lights, then races down the hallway after her. They kiss passionately, which leads them into a short but sweet lovemaking scene.

"Thank you so much for such a beautiful Christmas," Susan lovingly expresses with a warm smile while looking Chris straight into his unclouded, caring eyes. "Not to mention all the amazing gifts you got me!" she expresses, then sits up a bit.

"Well, Santa got you most of them," Chris admits with a smirk.

"Oh yeah, I forgot!" she remembers jokingly, then gives him a kiss and turns out the light.

Boxing Day 10:30 a.m.

Chris enters the bedroom and startles Susan awake as he dances around the room with his dad's old boxing gloves on. "Come on, get up, get up. It's Boxing Day! Don't cha know!" he proclaims in a fabricated Scottish accent, laughing away as he continues punching in mid-air like an old-style boxer. Susan laughs herself right up out of bed.

They both sit at the kitchen table, sipping away on their extra strong coffee and Baileys that Chris put together before waking her.

Susan jumps into the shower. Chris heads outside and begins building a snowman to surprise Susan. He struggles, huffing and puffing as he pushes and rolls up a huge baseball of snow. "I can't believe I'm all puffed out just from this!" he stresses with a big breath and a backhand wipe across his sweaty forehead. "Speaking of all puffed out," he sinisterly mentions. Chris catches his breath and beelines it straight for the garage. His sentimental craving can't be denied. He grabs one of the few partial joints from his car ashtray, lights it, and sucks in a huge, seemingly long-awaited puff.

Cough, cough, cough.

"Insta-stone." He chokes and takes in another big toke. He pops two special mints into his mouth, grabs the six-step ladder off the wall, and exits the garage, totally recharged for the building of the next few layers of his premeditated "Biggest Snowman ever."

Susan comes outside just in the nick of time to find Chris on top of the sixth step, plugging in the last rock eye of the incredibly massive snowman. "Surprise!" He spazzes out loud, then jumps down from the top of the ladder and lands in a tuck-and-roll.

"I love it!" Susan expresses, then gives the snowman a big hug.

"What about me?" Chris whines sarcastically, standing there with his arms open wide.

"It's nearly ten feet tall!" she estimates with amazement, then hugs and kisses Chris repeatedly. "I was just going to shovel off the front steps and pathway," she explains.

"Oh, right on, I'll help too," he happily volunteers.

"Oh, that's OK, I don't mind at all. I need more than just a little exercise after all the Christmas goodies I've been munching on," she says while smiling and rubbing her hand around in a circle on her exaggerated sticky out belly. They both laugh. "I'll go grab the shovel," she points towards the back of the house. She enters the garage and grabs the snow shovel off the wall. "Sniff! Sniff! Eww, a skunk!" She identifies the smell and quickly exits the garage.

She walks back out to the front of the house where Chris is doing some final touches on his enormous prize snowman. "Hey! I think we've got a skunk in the garage. I smell one anyway," she emphasizes while waving her hand in front of her nose, then carves out a groove down the snowy pathway with her snow shovel.

"Oh, really? Yeah, I thought I saw some tracks in the snow earlier this morning," he lies back to her.

"I better go check it out and make sure there's nothing in there," Chris suggests, then folds up the ladder and heads for the garage. He enters the garage and hangs the ladder back up on the wall. It doesn't take long for his addictive nature to kick in and he indulges himself in one more super quick puff. It's a little close for comfort, but Susan thinks there's a skunk running around somewhere, so it is the perfect decoy. Chris pops a mint in his mouth and heads back out to the front of the house where Susan has just finished clearing the last bit of snow from the stairs and pathways, including the city sidewalk out front. "Nice job," Chris compliments. "Here, give me the shovel. I'll go do the back stairs and pathway, you go inside and get warm. I'll be in soon," he promises.

"Ok, sounds good. See you in a flash," Susan happily agrees, ready for some warmth anyway.

Chris runs up the back stairs and enters the house, visibly exhausted from the snow day outside.

"Well, hello there!" Susan greets as he closes the door. "Surprise!" she announces while holding two large cups of hot chocolate, topped with little marshmallows.

"Right on. Perfect timing!" he says with excitement. "Thank you very much!" He takes a cup from her hand. They wander into the living room and sit side by side in the big chair, staring at the twinkling Christmas tree while symphony Christmas music plays softly in the background. The hot chocolate goes down so well that they slowly drift into a much-needed restful sleep, that is until the old chime clock on the mantel wakes them from their slumberous dreams. They stumble down the hall together and routinely get ready for bed.

"Yay! Back to work tomorrow!" Susan announces sarcastically, and they both laugh. "Yeah, it sure would be nice to have a little more time off, that's for sure," she confesses, accompanied by a mild sigh.

"Yeah, I hear you there!" Chris agrees hesitantly, while uncomfortably remembering his job situation.

"Good night," Susan whispers gently, then clicks out the bedroom light.

"Good night. Sweet dreams," Chris replies in total darkness.

Chapter 14

The alarm rings.

"Ah! Good morning!" They both greet each other with a light kiss, then stretch up into a sitting position on the side of the bed and quickly get ready for the new day.

"I can't believe it! Back to work already. The weekends just aren't long enough!" Susan whines as they head out the kitchen door.

"Well, guess what? New Years is only in another five days!" Chris explains, while displaying five fingers in mid-air, then locks the door.

"Yeah, you're right," she says, clunking down the back stairs and into the garage.

"Oh yeah!" Chris stops for a quick announcement before getting into his car. "We're invited to my friend Dave's house for a New Year's Eve party," he reveals with excitement.

"Did I meet Dave at our housewarming party?" she asks, seemingly a little nervous about a few of Chris's so-called friends.

"No, Dave was in Jamaica with his parents," he recalls, then jumps in his car and quickly rolls down the window.

"OK, sounds good. I better get going. Don't want to be late!" Susan insists with a touch of seriousness and checks her watch. She jumps in her car, presses the fob, then starts the engine and spins herself out of the snow corralled garage.

Chris just barely gets his car out of the garage, slipping and sliding all over the place, until he gets out on the main drag. As he nears his workplace, the reality of him being out of work in only one week's time sets in hard. "Fuck!" he screams out loud in anger, slamming his hands down hard on the steering wheel with a double-palm hit. He quickly glances up to his father's picture on the visor. "Sorry, Dad," he says emotionally, apologizing for hitting the car. He reaches over, grabs a joint from the ashtray, lights it, and burns it right down to complete ashes. He enters the near empty warehouse. "It's like a ghost town around here," he mumbles, then punches his timecard.

The week unfolds like a nightmare as Chris edges closer to his last day of work. He is saddened and frustrated and it shows, but it goes totally unnoticed at home because of all the overtime he still puts in every night. One thing is for sure, he is definitely right back on track with his crazy drinking and smoking habits. "Time for a reload," he says, as if there is no time to waste. The dozen cases of beer he had stashed in the trunk of his car are mere empties now. He pulls into the liquor store and quickly trades off the empties for full ones. "Yeah, woo-hoo! Oh yeah!" he shouts as he pulls out of the liquor store parking lot and bounces through a pothole in the road. Seconds later, he reaches behind his seat and grabs one of the security blanket beers, cracks it open, and guzzles it down faster than ever, immediately reaching around for another. "What else is new?" he chuckles and heads for home.

The last day at his job has come and is going even faster. All the stock in the large warehouse is shipped out by noon. An announcement comes crackling over the intercom. "Attention, everyone. Thank you for all your hard work these past weeks. We emptied the warehouse early, therefore, everyone is free to leave. Your paycheques are waiting in the lunchroom and you have been paid for the full day. And for those who worked overtime all this week, you have also been paid overtime for today as well." A short pause and crackling. "Again, thank you for all your hard work over the years." A short pause, a crackle, then silence.

Everyone looks depressed and angry by their new reality. Chris is definitely angry about it all, but seems to be one of the lucky ones, always immersed in a stoned, drunken state, which eases the pain and the reality of it all.

* * *

New Year's Eve 9 p.m.

"It sure is a crisp, clear, starry night out, eh," Chris points out as they cautiously step down the slippery back stairs and head for the garage. They jump in Susan's weather-capable car and head to Dave's parents' home for the big New Year's party. All the hit songs from the past year are counting down over the car radio.

"Do you think any of your friends are going to show up tonight?" Chris asks while turning down the radio a bit.

"I think so. They said they would anyway!" she confirms, smiling. Just then, Susan glimpses what looks like Brad's truck drive by out of the corner of her eye. Brad sees her for sure and double honks his horn, but they both drive on.

"Who was that?" Chris asks, slightly pre-intoxicated for the party.

"I'm not a hundred percent sure," Susan smoothly confesses as she turns the music back up, and it's left at that.

Chris and Susan enter Dave's parents' home. The party is already rocking with loud music, smoking, drinking, and lots of people scattered everywhere. Amongst it all is that familiar, faint, underlying skunk-like smell wafting in once in a while. Susan is holding a fancy burlap bag containing a bottle of inexpensive champagne and a bottle of white wine, while Chris carries a couple six-packs of beer. Dave is the perfect host and greets them in the doorway.

"Come in, come in. Haven't seen you since you helped me with all the storage stuff." *Wink, Wink, Nudge, Nudge.* Dave

162

secretly communicates with Chris. "This must be your girl-friend Susan. Nice to meet you!" Dave says, then reaches out and shakes her hand.

"Nice to meet you too," Susan says, continuing with a firm handshake.

"Here, let me take this from you!" Dave insists, relieving the bag from Susan's hand. "I'll put the champagne in the fridge for later and grab you a glass for your wine." Dave accommodates and continues to be the perfect host. Chris cork screws the wine open and pours them both a glass of the white wine. "Cheers!" they both say simultaneously, clicking their plastic glasses together. Chris quickly shoots the glass of wine back, then immediately twists open one of his trunk-cooled beers.

"Yee haw! The party's on!" Chris advises with a big grin and a touch of excitement in his voice. Susan's friends, Cathy and her boyfriend Rob, walk in the door. Seconds later Susan's friend Tammy and three of her single girlfriends, Angela, Sherry, and Jennifer, walk in looking like nobody's business. A few of Chris's haywire friends notice the four girls arriving alone and whisper amongst themselves.

"Fresh meat!" one of them disrespectfully blurts out, and they all snicker, then disperse as if they were caught in a spy movie. The girls nonchalantly notice the predatory stares, but fortunately are not totally clear what all the snickering was about, and probably wouldn't even care. Susan walks to the door and greets Angela and her new acquaintances.

"So glad you guys could make it," Susan welcomes with a hug for Cathy and Angela, along with a warm handshake for the others.

Chris walks over slowly. "This is my boyfriend Chris, for those who haven't already met him," Susan politely introduces. Tammy, Cathy, Angela, and Rob definitely remember Chris from the housewarming party they attended on Cook Street, but not in the most favourable light. *Everyone deserves a second chance*, is the vibe lightly discussed between the four of them.

Dave notices the latest arrivals and immediately races over and introduces himself, then politely directs the BYOB holders to place their booze into the already overstuffed fridge, and to throw their coats in the bedroom at the end of the hall. Dave's parents' house is becoming more and more crowded as many party-crazed people continue arriving.

The easy girl from Dave's last get-together arrives, and all the guys notice, single or otherwise. "She's looking a little hotter than usual tonight," is the obvious consensus throughout the party, according to most of the guys.

People have been congregating down the side of the house throughout the night for the seemingly endless chain of available joints being passed around. Chris always manages to not miss out on too much of that action. People are becoming louder and rowdier, but mostly in an overly happy manner, as the clock slowly ticks towards midnight. The overabundance of beer, wine, coolers, and not to mention the THC are taking their toll on most of the guests. The party is rocking. Easy-girl secretly follows Chris around like a lost puppy dog. Cathy and Angela both notice this but decide not to mention it to Susan and her sweet, naïve nature, and continue mingling amongst one another, swaying to the loud groovy music.

"Twenty-nine minutes to midnight," kind-hearted and rambunctious Richie yells out to everyone with double fisted beers in mid-air while moving in more than just a slight drunken right-hand turn. The people who see his performance laugh hysterically, except for Susan, who pretends not to see him staggering around and mumbling like a fool.

Susan instantly gets a series of flashbacks in her mind: Chris's overwhelming behaviours at their housewarming party in combination with prior and more recent strange drunken events that she has unintentionally been taking notes of ever since moving in together. It's like a good movie gone bad and getting worse.

Something else is now going on, even more strange and overwhelming, down around the back of the house near the darkened shed area. Chris and Easy-girl, also known as Sandy, are going at it, grabbing all over one another and kissing hard to where they both fall over into a deep, crispy-coated snow drift along the side of the shed. It seems he's found his perfect match.

Crunch! echoes from the darkness.

"Get up! Quick, get up! I think someone's coming!" Chris whisper-mumbles with intent. He staggers around aimlessly in the darkened backyard and bangs into an old bird bath, tipping it over, then beelines it towards the front of the house. Sandy vanishes around the other side of the house. Chris appears out of the darkness, stops halfway down the side of the house, and easily blends in with a few others for a nice big puff of relief.

Rob, who likes a sneaky puff "once in a blue moon," clearly heard some kind of crunching, thudding noise coming from the back of the house just before Chris arrived. "You were just down there, weren't you Chris? Did you see anything?" Rob asks like a determined detective.

"Aliens! Must be aliens!" Chris blurts out with a chuckle, trying desperately to deflect Rob's bona fide question. The others laugh and begin talking about UFOs. Chris suddenly whisks out of the puffing circle, all the while displaying a touch of guilt on his face that is fuelled by actual guilt and an eight-beer, four-joint, drunken-led stagger. Chris rushes his guilt-ridden self back inside, joining Susan and her friends. Sandy magically appears out of the darkness, joining in with the pot-smoking crew for a few long, drawn-in puffs. Rob and most of the others from down the side of the house follow suit and file back inside to the rocking party.

"It's so close now! Only three minutes until midnight!" Wacky Richie, the human cuckoo clock, cues everyone in his special, very amusing way.

"Ten, nine, eight, seven!" Everyone joins in enthusiastically. "Six, five, four!" Many people scramble to grab refills and search for any type of noise maker, preparing for the eventual New Year's banging, clanging, and toasting. "Three! Two! One! HAPPY NEW YEAR!" Everyone yells out simultaneously while the many bangs and clangs ramp up excessively, especially with the help of that good old hard-hitting, drunken, stoned, vigorous intent. The plastic glasses literally crack together, splashing drinks everywhere, as the party intensifies. People overly announce their drunken emotions, with constant "HAPPY NEW YEAR!" echoing inside and out throughout the night, along with a lot of "Right on, man!" accompanied with the occasional hug.

The music gets louder and louder, along with everything else. Dave brings out a seemingly endless supply of tequila and sambuca shooters, assembled in a long line, for everyone to indulge in, and they do. Susan and all her friends, along with everyone else, join in on a couple shooters. Some go a little overboard with the shooter availability and spiral into a perpetual "HAPPY NEW YEARS" toasting frenzy. Everyone seems to be having a great time, some more than others, with the help of the "DJ guy." Many guests periodically encourage and compliment the "DJ guy" with their "Right on, man" comments and constant "Yee haw!" sparked by the choices of music he's been blasting throughout the night. Certain songs instantly take Susan and her friends grooving onto the dance floor and into a few flashback moments from their high school days.

Meanwhile, down at The Wild Reel, Brad's band is playing to an energetic, crowded New Year's party, easily keeping everyone rocking up on the dance floor. "I want to dedicate this next song, which is also one of the latest songs I've written, to a special friend. The song is called, "We Can Be Together

Now." A few of the local hotties/groupies look around the dance floor, bewildered about who Brad is talking about. Brad doesn't mention the name of the person to whom he is referring, only he and his brother Shawn know the true inspiration behind the new song. "Two, three, four!" People seem love the new song as they dance along emphatically.

Back at Dave's party, the shooters seem to take their toll on many of Chris's friends, but especially on Chris himself, who has been bragging about how many shooters he and "Wacky Richie" have had so far. Susan immediately notices just how far the intensity of his idiotic drunken stupor has gone.

"What have I got myself into?" she whispers, just loud enough for a few of her close friends to become concerned. Susan quivers, feeling more than just a little robbed of her devoted spirit, as her heart quickly sinks, all the while displaying a pale face of sadness and shock. "What the?" Susan whispers, refraining from using any swear words.

"Easy-girl-Sandy," as a few guys now officially refer to her, is now super plastered and is virtually hanging off Chris's arm while mumbling strange, broken sentences.

"Hmm," Susan whispers discouragingly, then looks to her friends, who are gathered close around her.

"They're just drunk!" Rob comforts the situation, but never admits his torn mind about the potential cheating weirdness that he felt might have been going on with Chris and Sandy outside in the backyard just before midnight.

Susan looks to her watch. "It's 2:06 a.m.," she says, then shows Cathy her watch. "I think we better get going, I'm getting a little tired anyway. Not to mention . . ." Susan secretly thumb-points to Chris and everyone gets the message.

"I think we're all going to head out pretty quick as well," Rob confirms with a head nod from Cathy and the other girls. Susan requests help from Rob and Cathy to place Chris in the back seat of her car.

Finally, they're on their way home and leaving the crazy party behind. Susan sees bright lights up ahead that look like they are coming from Brad's old gas station. She pulls into the station to find the entire band unloading their equipment into the garage storage area. Brad immediately notices her and approaches her car, quite excited to see her face, as she quickly unrolls the car window.

"Happy New Year!" Brad greets, while shaking her warm hand.

"Happy New Year to you too!" Susan greets back, accompanied by the biggest smile.

"You're not already bringing beer bottles back, are you?" he questions, overly sarcastic, while grinning from ear to ear.

They both laugh.

"No," she replies softly, almost embarrassed to say any more, but just then, Chris slur mumbles something loud from the darkened back seat of her car.

"Oh, there he is. I was wondering where he might be, especially with it being New Years!" Brad confesses, now realizing her predicament.

"I better get him home," Susan says while thumb-pointing to the back seat and displaying a slightly crinkled face. "Happy New Year!" she wishes once again with a slightly forced smile because of the revealing and embarrassing Chris situation.

"Drive safely!" Brad encourages thoughtfully as she rolls up the car window and slowly drives away.

"Finally home," Susan says sadly. Tears well up in her eyes as she views Chris passed out in the rear-view mirror as they pull into the garage. Susan gets out of the car and pulls the seat forward. "Wake up, Chris!" she says sharply while reaching in and moderately shaking him.

"What? What? Where are we?" Chris asks with a drool-dripping slur.

"Home. We're home. Now, come on, please get out of the car. We're home," she encourages as nicely as she can under the circumstances. "Chris! Come On. Let's go," she pleads with an unusual touch of aggression in her voice. She continues to encourage him out of the car, waving her arm, now leaning towards a little taste of "vamoose jerk," then reaches in and firmly tugs on his arm. Chris seems to be having a really a hard time vamoosing from the car. He finally crawls out of the back seat and onto the garage floor like a dog on all fours.

Susan huffs and puffs while helping him to his feet, or at least into a half-standing position. It's a good hard go navigating him down the path, up the stairs, into the house, and right into bed. She makes a quick, easy decision to sleep in her own bed as she closes the door on Chris, who is now laying on the bed with his clothes on, totally passed out.

"It's like an instant replay of the housewarming party, but without the smelly mess. Thank God!"

She consoles herself before drifting off into a deep, dreamy sleep of slow-motion replays, seeing herself from above, walking into the bar the night of their housewarming party. Brad is singing up on the stage. She dreams on, throughout the night, right to the end when she had butterflies in her gut. She watches these feel-good moments, with the occasional flash back shot from all the gas station moments they shared.

Chapter 15

Monday, January 2.

Back to work—or so *she* thinks. "It would be better to not mention anything to Susan about my stupid job-loss situation until I at least find another job!" He reconfirms, whisper-mumbling to himself as he shaves in front of the steamy, towel-wiped bathroom mirror. It seems he is experiencing one of his few, good-guy, guilty, conscientious, sobering moments.

Chris follows the regular motions and emotions of heading off to work to a tee, just like he normally would. He drives off down his normal route then smoothly ditches out of sight for a while, then heads back towards the house and secretly parks his car away in the garage. He is trying his hardest to lay off the beers and pot while pondering just what to do about his job-loss situation. He flips through the newspaper searching for a new job but can only seem to find a lot of really low-paying jobs available, as per his skill level. Only a couple days into this harsh reality is seemingly too much for his "be a good guy" conscious to handle, so as soon as Susan drives off to work in the morning, he slips right back into his usual groove of heavy drinking and pot smoking, and actually kicks it up a notch.

Days, weeks, a month passes by. Chris's credit card bills keep rolling in relentlessly, but he's good for about another eight grand, according to the three combined credit card statements.

He seems to look a little rough around the edges these days, and Susan notices. Every day Susan enters the kitchen door from work, she finds Chris sitting at the kitchen table drinking a beer. He always appears tired, half cut and stoned, continually claiming how hard of a day he had at work.

"Something's just not quite right," Susan says. Her intuition keeps trying to tell her something is more than a little off as she heads to work every morning and returns home in the evening. She tries reaching deep inside herself for that special feeling she experienced with Chris at Christmas time, but sadly, there is just no luck there.

The heavy rains have not let up for two weeks now, and all the while, Susan is being constantly haunted by the daily calculating events of her relationship with Chris. All the snow has almost disappeared, except for some mountainous piles that the snowplows created along the sides of streets and in shopping mall parking lots.

Friday, late afternoon. Chris has been fidgeting around the house for most of the day, waiting for that special phone call from Dave to confirm when he can come over and pick up another arranged, put aside, big bag of skunk weed.

Ring . . . Ring . . .

"Finally!" Chris shouts, jumping to his feet.

"Hey, man! I'm home! Come on over!" Dave demands enthusiastically.

Chris is about halfway to Dave's house and has already guzzled down a couple beers from the old secret stash behind his seat. "Oh, oh, I better stop off at the liquor store on the way back from Dave's," he mumbles to himself while reaching around for another, and simultaneously takes inventory of the minuscule beer situation. He cracks open the beer and quickly sucks in a long guzzle. "Only thing left in the trunk are empties," he confirms mumbling, as if proud of his accomplishments, then takes another swig of beer.

Suddenly, red flashing lights appear in his rear-view mirror from a motorcycle about fifty yards behind him. "The cops. Oh no!" Chris scrambles to put his seatbelt on, then quickly reaches for the "super mints" stashed in the console. He grabs a couple half-burnt roaches from the ashtray, quickly eats them, then washes them down with a dribble of beer. He slams at least six of the "super mints" into his mouth just for insurance and immediately begins frantically crunching them up, which causes his eyes to water up profusely. "Ah, it burns!" he screeches while displaying a scrunched-up face as he secretly slips the empty bottle behind his seat.

Seconds later, the cop knocks on Chris's car window, signalling for him to roll the window down.

"Good evening. Licence and registration please."

"What did I do?" Chris asks nervously as he hands his driver's licence to the cop.

"Taillight's out," the cop confirms, pointing as he leans in a little closer for a suspicious sniff. He immediately spots the two unopened beers and the freshly consumed empties on the floor. "I'll have to ask you to step out of the car, sir!" The officer instructs professionally.

Chris slowly unbuckles and steps out of his car and into the pouring rain. The cop gives him the breathalyzer twice, but no accurate reading is present because of the "super mints" he just consumed. The cop is quite aware of these types of mints and gives Chris "the look." The cop gives Chris a sobriety test at the side of the road. Chris fails big time—his sway was a dead giveaway. The tow-truck driver hooks up Chris's car and takes it straight to the impound lot. A police car arrives on the scene. Chris is cuffed and thrown into the backseat of the police cruiser to be taken downtown to the police station for booking and further questioning. The arresting cop speeds off with lights flashing in pursuit of his next victim.

Chris will not be getting his car back anytime soon. He has officially been ordered to appear in court in ninety days for a verdict on his drinking and driving charges, and has bail set at $1000, which must be paid before he can leave the police station. Chris calls Dave and briefly explains the situation. Dave hesitates, but shows up an hour later with a thousand dollars all in small bills.

"Thank God you came. Thanks, man. I'll give you back the grand later, for sure!" Chris pleads. "I've only got the $300 for the pot right now." He exposes the money from his pant pocket.

"No worries," Dave assures, then fires the double-bagged skunk weed right into Chris's lap. Dave sparks up a freshly rolled sample joint and is savouring every bit of its taste.

"Nice!" Chris craves his turn for a wrenching toke.

"Hey, you mind stopping off at the beer store before dropping me off?" Chris asks, from happy land.

"No worries, mate!" Dave obliges without hesitation.

Chris enters the front door of the house, still soaking wet, with a fresh twelve-pack of beer in his hand and the double-bagged stinky pot stashed up the sleeve of his jacket. He doesn't waste any time getting right down to business and rolls up a big fat skunk joint and guzzles down a couple beers.

One hour later, Susan is just turning onto Cook Street. "Oh man, Chris!" she says, seemingly a little annoyed he hadn't picked up the mail once again, showing that he has most likely been drinking. She pulls the car over right in front of the mailbox that still displays the red flag up. She quickly runs to the mailbox, grabs the stack of damp mail, pulls the flag down, and runs back to her car, all the while getting pelted by heavy rain. She drives around the back, clicks open the garage door, and drives her car into the empty garage.

"Hmm, Chris must not be home from work yet," she says, now feeling a little guilty about the mailbox accusations. She enters through the kitchen door, clicks on the light, and is startled to find Chris in his usual drinking position at the kitchen table.

"Happy hour!" he immediately declares, but that doesn't seem to work anymore, and Susan's heart slowly sinks along with her facial expression.

"Why are you sitting in the dark? And where's your car?" she double questions, a little puzzled, seemingly a bit angry, as she plops the stack of damp mail down onto the kitchen table, then slips out of her wet coat and shoes and whisks them off to the front hall closet.

Chris avoids the car question, giving him a little more time to make something up. "Hey, so how did it go at work today?" he asks, over vivaciously, in hopes of instantly swaying her views on his power drinking and their rocky, unknowing, deceptive relationship, all of which have been created by his own demons. Susan can't hear him over the closet door noise, and Chris thinks she's ignoring him. "Oh, crap," he mumbles to himself, feeling kind of busted. Susan enters back into the kitchen where Chris immediately hands her an opened beer.

"Oh, what the heck," she obliges with a can't-beat-them-join-them attitude.

"Cheers!" Chris reaches out and clanks his beer bottle with hers.

"So, how was your day at work?" he asks again.

"Well, it's been super busy with this new system and all, but all right I guess. I think I'm getting the hang of it, slowly but surely," Susan says with confidence. "So, where the heck is your car, anyway?" she asks once again, accompanied with a puzzled look.

"Oh, Dave drove me home. I . . . I've got to get some work done on my engine . . . And Dave told me about this fantastic mechanic guy he knows . . . So, I dropped the car off at his place after work. I've already arranged for this guy from work to pick me up Monday morning," he rambles deeper into the lie.

"Oh yeah, that's good," she happily conveys without hesitation. Halfway through her beer, Susan stands up, places the beer bottle down on the kitchen table, then picks up the wet stack of sticky mail. "What do we have here?" she says out loud, as she sorts through the sticky wet mail.

"Bills, bills, junk mail . . ." she rambles while sorting the various envelopes into different piles. "Hmm," she emphasizes her curiosity while holding up a bulky, brightly coloured piece of mail addressed to both of them close to her face.

"What's that one?" Chris asks, then perks up a bit in his seat, worried it might be something that will reveal one of his various past or present disastrous realities.

"Not sure," she says, appearing a little baffled, and begins tearing the letter open with her sharp fingernail. She slips the four-page letter from the envelope and unfolds it.

"Holy shit!" she screams loudly.

"What does it say?" Chris asks, with a big, worrisome gulp as he rises to his feet.

"We won! We won! I can't believe it! We actually won!" she continues shaking the letter around and jumping up and down.

"What do you mean? What the heck did we win?" Chris asks, wide-eyed, leaning in for a closer look at the vibrating letter in Susan's excited hands. She holds the letter right in front of his face and points frantically.

Congratulations! You are the lucky Grand Prize Winners of our promotional two-week All-Inclusive Vacation to one of three Five-Star Resorts in Mexico.

Each destination has its own colourful promotional page, with many photos of the hotels they are to stay at, and in-depth information about each holiday resort.

"Unreal!" Chris says loudly, appearing a little shocked.

"And look!" Susan points. "$1000 spending money too! And—Oh my God! Shorts, T-shirts, snorkels, masks and hats. Oh, and even a little video camera! Wow!" she expresses with amazement while reading further into the Grand Prize Winners list.

"Holy crap!" Chris shouts out while displaying a huge grin. "Right on!" He blurts and quickly snatches the letter from her hands.

"And you said we would never win anything!" she boasts.

"Well, I take it all back," he sincerely apologizes while reviewing all the facts right there in the letter. He gives her a big hug filled with gratitude. All the excitement of winning the trip seems to have a positive candy coating and could be the one thing to break Chris's spell of disaster, or so Susan hopes. "Only one thing," Chris playfully mentions while looking over the colourful destinations. "Where would you like to go, out of these three places, Susan? Riviera Nayarit, Cabo San Lucas, or Cancun?" he inquires with a big kid grin, gently flashing each exciting place right in her face.

"Hmm, not quite sure," she admits, displaying a crinkled face while holding one hand on her chin. "Hmm, maybe Cancun," she imagines. A short pause. "Yeah. That's it, Cancun! That's where I'd like to go," she confirms with confidence, poking the letter with her finger, right on the Cancun brochure. "What about you? Where would you like to go?" she asks excitedly, then unexpectedly opens the cupboard and grabs a bottle of red wine and two glasses to celebrate their winning moment.

"Well, I was hoping you wanted to check this area out," he politely urges while displaying his choice. "Riviera Nayarit. It's about thirty minutes from the Puerto Vallarta airport, according to this right here." He points right on the brightly coloured mini map and photos on the Puerto Vallarta page. "That's right around where that alien movie was filmed with what's his name, you know who I mean." He adds in the perk for a vote of confidence.

"Oh really? I didn't know that." A silent, pondering pause. "I still think I would like to go to Cancun though," she reconfirms.

Chris appears to be sulking from her choice. A short pause. "Tell you what. My dad and I would always draw straws," she explains as she opens the drawer and grabs a couple skew sticks and breaks them into various lengths to prepare for the so-called "Final Draw."

Susan stands holding the various undeterminable lengths of broken skew sticks in her left hand right out in front of Chris. "Go ahead, pick one," she encourages.

"Hmm," Chris contemplates as he bites down on his bottom lip in hesitation. He slowly reaches out with a calculating look on his face, takes a moment, and then suddenly makes his choice. "Your turn!" he says excitedly, not revealing his true skew stick length, squeezing it tight in his hand, with only an inch of it sticking out. Susan slowly reaches out to her own clenched fist that contains the remaining skew sticks, then just goes for it.

They stand silent, face to face, ready to reveal who the winner is. "Wait!" Susan says and pours them both a glass of wine. "Cheers," she says with excitement.

"Cheers," Chris concurs as they reach out and simultaneously clink their glasses together.

"OK, good luck!" Susan expresses with a touch of suspense in her voice. "On three," she continues, "One . . . two . . . three!" They count down together.

Chris stands before her with the longest skew stick in his sweaty hand.

"Ah!" Susan screams out, seemingly very disappointed. "Oh well, I would go anywhere just to get out of this rain anyway," she admits with a big smile and positive sportsmanship. "But it would have been nice to be heading off to Cancun. Oh yeah, Cathy and Rob went there and they said it was amazing. But . . . Oh well," she rambles, adding a long sigh.

"You make me feel bad now!" Chris says. "You're the one who came up with the great drawing straws idea," he confirms, grinning from ear to ear while holding his winning skew stick right up in front of her face.

"Yeah, I know I did," she admits smiling. "I remember playing the draw straws game with my father when I was just a kid. I always seemed to win back then," she recalls humorously, and sips her wine. "Let's pick a date and book first thing in the morning," Susan encourages.

"Sounds good to me," Chris agrees.

"My boss will give me the time off, for sure," she explains with positivity.

"Mine too!" Chris lies.

Chapter 16

Next thing you know, the plane is coming in for a smooth landing at the Puerto Vallarta airport, gently touching down onto the scorching, radiant tarmac. Mexican music and sunshine accommodate the great mood they are both feeling. They get directed onto one of the resort shuttles and are handed a Corona beer with lime. Before long, they arrive at the resort.

"Wow, look at this hotel!" Susan elaborates while looking out the window of the shuttle bus.

"Nice," Chris agrees with a final swig of his beer as he scans the grand structure. An announcement comes loud and clear over the bus intercom.

"Welcome to your Grand Prize Five-Star Resort," the bus driver politely informs as he opens the automatic bus door, then jumps out to grab their luggage.

"That's us!" Susan quickly confirms, while looking over their "Grand Prize Winners" itinerary papers.

"Right on," Chris blurts out as he exits the shuttle. He takes her hand like a gentleman and helps her out from the shuttle.

As they approach the front desk to check in, they are graciously greeted by two travel agency representatives responsible for the contest. "Welcome, and congratulations you two!" The representatives immediately place nice straw hats on their heads and hand them both a tropical drink, along with one-thousand dollars in cash and a large bag with many more of their prizes inside. The representatives proceed to strap multicoloured bands onto their wrists, identifying them as the "Grand Prize Winners." The colourful wrist bands entitle them to anything and everything that the Five-Star Grand Resort offers, including various water sports and excursions.

They enter the largest, most beautiful ocean-view suite. There's a king-size bed, big screen TV, luxurious furnishings, and a huge balcony with a table and chairs for two, topping it off with their very own jacuzzi.

"Very nice," Chris relays respectfully as he hands the bell boy an American five-dollar bill.

"Thank you very much, señor," the bell boy blesses with hand gestures, conveying genuine gratitude.

"Well, let's get down to the beach!" Susan directs excitedly, seconds after the bell boy closes the door.

"What did you call me? A son of a beach," Chris says, then bursts out laughing, and Susan laughs right along with his cliché humour. Chris quickly fires on his new holiday shorts while Susan privately slips out of her clothes and into her sexy bathing suit.

"Let's head to the beach!" she encourages.

"Wow! Look at this place! Hey, let's go have a couple straw-berry margaritas over at the pool bar there and get this vacation started," Chris says while pointing across the huge, gorgeous pool towards the swanky little Mexican hut bar.

"Good idea. It's super hot out here!" she says, easily accom-modating his idea. The Mexican Five-Star Resort and hot sun are just what the doctor ordered to smooth over their relation-ship troubles at home. Just the fact that they are on a vacation away from the heavy rains back home is like a dream come true. They're sipping away on their refreshing tropical drinks while sitting on the underwater seats in front of the fun, crowded, energetic, poolside bar while Mexican dance music plays loud and crisp.

"Ok, let's head on down to the beach," Susan encourages with her incredible smile as she finishes her lovely strawberry margarita. They both slip on their sunglasses and their newly acquired straw hats, then continue down the path towards the sandy beach where they are both handed a thick, luxuri-ous beach towel. "Nice, beach chairs!" Susan says as they claim the two most perfect spots about twenty feet from the crash-ing waves. They plop their towels down onto the beach chairs, along with their new holiday bag filled with sunscreen, some T-shirts, a video camera, flippers, masks, and snorkels.

"Right on! Love this place," Chris can't help expressing.

"I know exactly what you mean!" Susan strongly agrees as they gaze out to sea and melt into their beach chairs for some much-needed relaxation time.

Moments later, one of the many resort waiters approaches them smiling, carrying a large tray with ice waters and menus. "Good afternoon, señorita, señor," the waiter greets as he places the tray down on their side table. "Would either of you like anything from the bar or restaurants?" he encourages with his solid-gold-tooth smile that sparkles in the sunlight while gracefully bowing towards them.

"Sure," Chris replies. "How about you, Susan? Would you like something as well?" Chris asks politely, all excited to order something.

"Sure, how about some nachos?" she quickly decides, pointing at the picture on the beachside menu.

"Oh, and a couple Coronas and two piña coladas!" Chris quickly adds in. Susan does a double take at his order, but just smiles. Three Mexican singers and guitar players show up wearing large sombreros and begin singing and playing "Guantanamera." Everyone in the vicinity applauds when the song ends. The three amigos immediately break into the song, "La Bamba."

"Love it!" Susan expresses with her beautiful smile.

"Living the dream!" Chris adds in while nodding his head along to the beat of the song. Out of nowhere, the waiter's serving tray comes in for a landing, filled with their drinks and nachos. "Thank you!" Chris appreciates while handing the waiter a tip.

"Gracias, señor," the waiter says with sincerity.

The song ends with much deserved applause from everyone. Susan and a few other guests toss money into the entertainers' sombreros before they move on down the beach in search of their next audience.

Chris guzzles down his first beer in about five seconds. "Ah, excellent!" he expresses, then wipes his lips with the back of his hand.

"Hey, you don't have to rush, you know. We've got two weeks here, silly. Or is it because everything's free? Crazy guy." She smiles jokingly, yet seemingly a bit nervous about his radical beer guzzling actions, while praying to God in her mind that Chris's home drinking situation hasn't followed them all the way to Mexico. Her worrisome feelings quickly blow away like the warm breeze that blows through her hair. She lays back in her beach chair, enjoying that special first time, sunshiny, Mexican holiday experience. The waiter zeros in and picks up the tray of dishes and empties.

"Would you like something else? Señorita, señor?" the waiter asks.

"Sure, two more piña coladas!" Chris speaks up with two fingers in mid-air. "Thanks, man," Chris adds before the waiter whisks away with their chattering tray.

Chris routes through the straw bag and assembles his flippers, mask, and snorkel at the foot of his lawn chair to prepare for an ocean adventure. "Hey, let's go check out the water," he encourages, jumping to his feet and pointing to the sea.

"You just ordered two piña coladas," Susan reminds, chuckling.

"Oh yeah! OK, after that," he remembers, and chuckles right along with her.

"Sure," she happily agrees. "I used to love swimming in my Uncle Ed's indoor swimming pool with my flippers, mask, and snorkel on," she reminisces. "So, this is going to be absolutely amazing, I'm sure, especially snorkelling around that reef there." She points excitedly, then reaches in the straw bag, pulls out the video camera, and clicks it into record mode. She catches the waiter approaching with their fresh drinks high on the tray, then slowly pans over to Chris, who resembles a frustrated child sitting in the sand, fiddling with the mask's adjustable strap.

"Cheers!" Chris greets as he takes one of the piña coladas from the waiter's tray, then slips him a tip.

"Gracias, señor," the waiter reacts to their generosity. The drinks go down like a tasty treat, cooling the heat.

They walk towards the ocean, past the waterline, into three feet of water. They both put on their flippers, mask, and snorkel, and are ready to dive under. Suddenly, without notice, Susan dives under and completely disappears for at least thirty seconds.

"Holy crap! I thought we lost you!" Chris yells out as she reappears from under the water, at least forty feet away.

"Come check this out," she shouts at Chris, then disappears under water.

Chris swims to where he last saw her go under and looks around. "Holy shit!" he shouts as Susan pops to the surface, right beside him, totally freaking him out.

"Follow me," Susan directs and dives under. Chris follows close behind, into what looks like a massive aquarium. There are clusters of multicoloured fish all around a very camouflaged reef. Twenty seconds later, Chris comes to the surface gasping for air while Susan rises gently from below.

"Wow, that was incredible," Chris expresses with amazement.

"Hey! Look, windsurfers. We have to go give that a try on one of our days here too," Susan expresses with enthusiasm as she lifts the mask from her face to the top of her head. They both tread water for a few minutes, observing the windsurfers off in the distance who are constantly being driven by changing winds into action-packed sequences. "Yeah, and I think it's included in the 'All Inclusive,'" she displays with comical air-quotes with her fingers. They both laugh. "If I remember correctly, that is," she adds with a smile. "Well, one thing's for sure, I don't remember seeing any photos of this amazing reef in the brochure," she admits, then pulls the mask back down over her face and disappears under the water. Chris quickly dives under and races after her. They play a little game of underwater tag amongst the beauties of the hidden reef until it's time to relax once again.

They lay back comfortably in their beach chairs, basking in the hot sun throughout the afternoon. Chris has a few more drinks, and Susan happily drinks right along with him. The incredible scenery and warm breeze comforts them into a deep relaxation, and before they know it, the day is trickling towards night. They shuffle to the edge of their seats. Romance is in the air as the sun softly sets. In a flash, the sun completely disappears below the far away waterline.

"Wow! Amazing sunset," Susan expresses perfectly.

"Yes, very nice one. That's for sure," Chris whisper-slurs back. They rise to their feet and immediately begin packing up their stuff.

"Wow, the hotel looks really nice at night too," Susan can't help mentioning. They enter their suite, and quickly get ready for dinner and a night on the town.

They step off the elevator, looking like a million bucks. "Mexican tonight, right?" Susan strongly suggests.

"Keeping it real, I see," Chris says jokingly. They both laugh, then take each other by the hand. They are enjoying the perfect candlelit Mexican-style dinner while romance still lingers in the air since the beautiful sunset on the beach.

"Holy! Look who's here! The singers from the beach," Susan says while lightly pointing. The three musketeers begin with a soft, appealing song. Everyone applauds when the song ends.

"Excuse me! Sir," Susan directs to the singer she recognizes from the beach earlier today. "Can you play Guantanamera?" she asks excitedly. "I just love that song!" she expresses with her hands clasped together.

"Yes, of course, señorita," the singer says, gentlemanly like. They break into song, and sound even more fantastic than they did at the beach.

"You really love this song, don't you!" Chris says, with a high-in-the-air cheers as his glass clangs against hers.

"Living the dream!" Susan quickly adds in while moving to the groove of her favourite Mexican song.

"Copy that!" Chris agrees with his crooked grin, then drinks to her, 'living the dream' toast.

After dinner, they hop onboard the resort shuttle and head towards town, all pumped up with excitement and a bit tipsy from the wine. They discuss happily where they might want to go while sifting through a few of the many travel magazines that are tucked into the slats at the backs of the shuttle bus seats.

"How about Max Margaritas," Susan suggests excitedly while pointing directly to the flashy coloured picture in the magazine.

"Sounds good to me!" Chris agrees. "I overheard someone mention that place while we were sitting at the pool bar earlier today. They said it was a really happening place to go. If I heard correctly, that is," Chris explains while looking at the picture.

"Hey! Excuse me, can you let us out here!" Susan prompts the shuttle driver excitedly while viewing the dolphin statues along the side of the cobblestone roadway.

"Cool! Right on!" Chris couldn't agree more. They exit the shuttle about ten blocks from Max Margaritas.

"Wow! It's packed down here!" she mentions with a smile as they pass by many authentic Mexican stores and restaurants that seem to attract many cheerful tourists. They get lured into a few of the colourful stores along the way and politely take a moment to browse around in each one of them. Every merchant says that they have the best price while relentlessly coaxing them into purchasing something. "We will come back later, or tomorrow," Susan explains politely as they exit each store.

"Nine and a half blocks pass without a single purchase! But we'll definitely come back down here another day though, and maybe get some of those colourful Mexico T-shirts and hats back there for you and me and our families. And even for a few friends, maybe, OK," Susan generously contemplates.

"Of course. We got that thousand dollars spending money!" Chris slurs into her ear while simultaneously wrapping his arm around her waist. They approach the massive front entrance of the very busy Max Margaritas bar.

Mexican dance music plays loudly over the incredible sound system, and people are dancing and drinking holiday spirited margaritas everywhere. Chris and Susan get lucky. A table right near the main bar comes available just as they're walking beside it.

"Oh, excellent. Thanks," Chris acknowledges his gratitude toward the couple who are just leaving the table. Right away, chips and salsa arrive at their table. A Mexican waiter stands before them, displaying a silver-toothed smile.

"What would you like to drink tonight, señorita, señor?" The waiter asks, ready to take their order with his pen already touching the pad.

Susan and Chris look at each other, a bit wide-eyed.

"I'd like a strawberry margarita!" Susan quickly announces.

"Me too!" Chris copycats as he dips a chip in the salsa.

"Beautiful," the waiter compliments their choice. "But you must have a look in the Max Margaritas book there." The waiter points. "We have every flavour under the sun, in regular size and mini sample size, señorita, señor," the waiter explains before whisking away.

Midnight rolls around quickly, and by now, both have devoured more than just a few tasty margaritas. Susan innocently overindulges on many of the mini-size margarita flavours listed in the Max Margaritas book, and has become quite drunk along the way, yet continues to make her way down the list of many flavours.

"Ah, brain freeze!" She laughs loudly while holding her head with both hands until the pain passes.

Chris laughs, never once hesitating to keep up with her crazed mission to sample every one of the multicoloured margarita flavours, and even slips in a few Corona beers along the way. The party's on.

They're enjoying a fantastic first-time Mexican vacation, dancing, laughing hysterically, and occasionally mingling with other holiday couples from all around the now louder and seemingly more drunken Max Margaritas bar. Susan isn't really the type to let loose like this, but tonight she seems to enjoy making this the perfect moment for an exception to her rule.

"Two more margaritas please, guava flavour!" she orders directly from the bartender while pointing to a picture in the Max Margaritas book.

Chris is in heaven as Susan easily keeps up with his notorious drinking ways.

"Cheers!" she overly expresses with a heavy clink against his glass.

The popular holiday song "Pour Me Another Margarita" begins playing loudly. The bartender immediately jumps up on to the bar and dances along. Next thing you know, there are two more people up there going nuts as well.

Susan takes a big gulp of her margarita and places it down on their table. Suddenly, she climbs onto the bar and joins in on the dancing fun.

"What the!" Chris shouts, not believing his eyes.

"Come on, Chris. Come up!" She coaxes loudly while swaying around in a small circle and reaching out her hand. More and more people join in on the bar-top dance craze until there is not even an inch to spare. People are now even dancing on the tabletops, and everyone is singing along loudly to the suggestive song, "Pour Me Another Margarita."

Six Mexican waiters shuffle around from person to person, pouring on-the-house tequila from large, squeezable funnels into the mouths of many brave, already half cut holiday patrons. Susan and Chris can't help joining in on some of that holiday action and both take a good long shot.

"Play it again!" some hot chick standing on the bar screams out a second after the song ends. The song instantly loops around and continues the hyped atmosphere of the holiday-crazed Max Margaritas bar.

"Holy, I can't believe it's already 2:30 in the morning," Susan realizes while glancing at a waiter's digital watch as he pours tequila down some poor bastard's throat right next to them.

"Yeah, let's head back to the hotel," Chris slurs up a storm. Both of them are more than just a little plastered by now, staggering out the front door of the Max Margaritas bar and into the warm cobblestone streets while clinging on to one another for stability.

"Wow! I'm loaded!" Chris admits for the first time.

"Me too!" Susan says, laughing hysterically at anything and everything as they zigzag amongst many other plastered party animals lingering and swaying in the streets. They veer off the street and continue staggering arm in arm down the cobblestone sidewalk, then must stop for an adjustment in Susan's shoe.

"Listen to the waves out there!" She suddenly perks up while fixing her shoe. They become fixated on listening to the powerful waves crashing loudly in the darkness along the not-so-far-away shoreline. Just then, a Mexican cab driver appears alongside of them, recognizing their resort bracelets.

"Good evening, señorita, señor. You need a ride to your hotel?" the cab driver asks while smoking his flimsy "roll your own" cigarette with his arm dangling from the car window.

"Sure!" Susan blurts out, giggling for no apparent reason. Before long, the cab is pulling right up to the front of the resort entrance.

Chris pulls out a crumpled twenty-dollar bill from his jeans pocket. "Keep the change," he mumbles.

"Thank you very much, señor, señorita," the humble cabby expresses with gratitude. Susan giggles into laughter and begins singing "Guantanamera" as they exit the cab. She sings all the way across the resort lobby, giggling frantically as they barely make their way up in the elevator, down the hall, and into their gorgeous room. Fortunately for them, moments later they're in bed fast asleep.

Chapter 17

S usan is woken by the scorching sun beating down on her face through the undraped balcony windows.

"Oh my God! The pain!" she accentuates while holding her swollen head with both hands. "Close the drapes! Please!" She continues whining, now shading the sun from her eyes with her forearm.

Chris easily accommodates and instantly springs out of bed, seemingly unscathed from their night of unconscionable proportions they equally consumed at Max Margaritas the night before.

"I can't even remember coming home!" she confesses. "Unbelievable! 1:13 in the afternoon already?" she whisper-shrieks, totally in pain, holding her head with one hand while looking directly at the side table digital clock.

"Well, don't forget the time difference, its actually only 11:13 back home," Chris saves the moment.

"Oh. Yeah, right! Two hours difference," Susan remembers. "I've got the worst pounding headache ever!" she unwillingly admits as she moves to sit up on the side of the bed. "I think I've actually got a hangover," she confesses in a low, whining tone while continuing to hold her head, and yet she's still able to crack a cute, beautiful smile.

"Well, I know exactly what the cure is for that!" he boasts.

"What? Coffee?" Susan answers back.

"Ah!" Chris blasts her with an irritating buzzer sound. "Nope, hair of the dog," he says, grinning away.

"Hair of the who?" Susan pretends she didn't hear that right.

"You know. You have another like the one that bit you. If I remember correctly, something like that anyway!" he elaborates. "In other words, let's go down to the poolside bar for a Margarita," he suggests persuasively.

"Oh, yeah, I get it now. No way!" she strongly disagrees. Even though she's heard the popular quote "hair of the dog" somewhere before, she is obviously not too excited about giving it a whirl.

"OK, it's your head," he reminds her in a long, drawn-out, sarcastic tone.

"OK, well, can you please make some coffee first!" she innocently demands. "And I'll go have a quick shower," she says, then drags herself into the bathroom and straight into the massive marble and glass shower stall.

Chris opens the minibar, slides out one of the six Corona beers, and walks out onto the balcony. "What a view," he says to himself before guzzling down the first beer of the day. He quickly walks back inside and heads straight for the minibar for an instant replay, then back out on the balcony for some more tantalizing holiday views. There's just no nursing that beer either. He shuffles back inside, remembering to make coffee before heading for the shower. He sneaks in the shower, startling Susan when he touches her in a certain way.

"Not now. Later," she suggests as Chris tries to get a little more than fresh as she exits the shower. "Mmm, the coffee smells so good. Thanks, Chris!" Susan warmly appreciates while exiting the bathroom wearing one of the hotel's complimentary, white, luxurious robes. She pours herself a coffee then steps out onto the balcony, taking in the beautiful tropical views while Chris lathers up in the shower.

The elevator door opens revealing Chris and Susan, all ready for another day at the beach. They slowly flip-flop their way through the lobby towards the front desk, then out through the massive sliding doors and straight to the poolside bar, for a little "hair of the dog" action.

"Good afternoon, señorita, señor," the bartender greets.

"Good afternoon," they greet back simultaneously.

"Two strawberry margaritas, please!" Chris quickly orders without an ounce of hesitation as they plant themselves down on the warm underwater bar stools.

"I really hope this works. My God, what a pounder!" she expresses in a wishful tone while holding one hand to her forehead.

"It will. I promise," he conveys with undeniable confidence. It's another beautiful hot, sunny vacation day: there's a warm breeze fluttering the edges of the thatched roof, and Mexican music sounds just right for this tranquil moment in time as they sip away on their margaritas.

"I feel my headache already going away!" Susan says with amazement, having never had to test this hair-of-the-dog theory.

"I told you!" Chris boasts, grinning from ear to ear. "Do you want another?" he asks as she noisily hits bottom of the Margarita glass while slurping it up through the straw.

"Hmm. Not yet. Let's get down to the beach and check out that windsurfing," she encourages happily, seemingly totally cured from the night before, energized and ready to get on with their holiday.

"Are you sure?" Chris asks with a touch of disbelief. "It sure didn't take you very long to recuperate," he adds, expressing his sincere feelings of happiness for her fast recovery.

They stroll down the pathway towards the beach in a peaceful manner. "Hey, Susan, look! A peacock!" Chris points out, absorbing the beauty of their much-needed, very fortunate, romantic holiday experiences.

They check out two beach towels, then continue to claim two nicely situated beach chairs right near the water line, in perfect view of the many windsurfers flying around way the heck out there.

"Living the dream," Chris can't resist claiming as he spreads both towels over their beach chairs.

"Thank you," Susan says before sitting down, slipping on her sunglasses, and slowly laying back. Seconds later, the same waiter from yesterday shows up out of nowhere.

"Good afternoon! Señorita, señor, how are you both today? Beautiful day!" He politely greets while placing ice waters and menus on the side table.

"Good afternoon, we are fantastic! Good to see you!" Chris says with an added compliment, then grabs the menus and passes one to Susan. The waiter stands patiently, smiling, ready to take their order.

"So, what can I get you two today?" he enquires, as his gold tooth sparkles with every word.

"Hmm, I think I'll have the fruit plate," Susan orders calmly, then places her menu back on the side table.

"And you, señor?" he asks, focused on Chris's response.

"I'll get three chicken skewers and a small order of nachos. Ah, what the heck, make it the large order," he decides, pointing at the menu. "And a shrimp cocktail as well. Oh, and a couple Coronas too," he quickly adds in.

"Holy moley." Susan laughs out in disbelief while smiling.

"How about you, señorita. Would you like a drink?" The waiter asks once again, not wanting to miss anything.

"She'll have a piña colada. Or maybe another strawberry margarita?" Chris attempts to answer for her as he looks straight at her sweet innocent face.

"Oh, OK. I guess I'll have a piña colada," she decides.

"Thank you, señorita, señor. I'll be right back with your orders!" he speaks up, smiling big, then gathers up the tray and heads back towards the hotel.

"Wow, you must be starved!" Susan states the obvious with a beautiful smile, then applies sunscreen all over her body.

"Yeah, pretty hungry!" he admits. "Besides, it's All Inclusive, remember?" he adds, portraying the double-handed air quotes. They both laugh.

"Yeah. You're right. Were so lucky to have won this trip. It couldn't have come at a better time. That rain was really getting on my nerves," she continues happily.

"Yeah, I know exactly what you mean," Chris agrees as he slips on his sunglasses, then leans back in his lawn chair, relaxing with his eyes closed, totally forgetting about his secret realities back home.

The shiny, gold-toothed waiter, along with another backup waiter, approach carrying two fully loaded trays of food and drinks. The backup waiter grabs another side table along the way. They place the food and drinks down on the matching side tables.

"Oh, thank you!" Susan says sweetly as Chris hands them both a five-dollar tip.

"Thank you, señor, señorita!" Both waiters show gratitude for the tip.

"Hey, how much money do we have left out of that thousand? After last night's adventure?" Susan inquires curiously.

"Oh, about $822.15," he estimates, chuckling.

"Nice! Right to the cent," she chuckles along. "I can't believe I can't even remember what went on last night at the bar—since about the halfway point," she laughs nervously. "Not to mention getting back to the hotel and into bed," she chuckles in disbelief.

"Well, that's OK. We're on holiday, you know, so there's nothing wrong with a little extra fun," he consoles her worries. "And don't forget, it's an "All-Inclusive" one too, I might add!" Chris says, pointing out the obvious with a touch of sarcasm in his voice while displaying the classic air quotes. They both laugh.

"Right, and quit stealing all my lines!" she warns, sending a little sarcasm back his way. "Oh, cool. Here come those Mexican singers again!" she points out discretely.

Their lunch is going down so well with the ocean views and the Mexican songs echoing along the beach.

"Excellent lunch. Wow!" Chris points out while dabbing the sides of his mouth with his napkin.

"Yes! Delicious!" Susan can't help agreeing. They lie back relaxing, sun tanning the day away, occasionally drifting in and out of sleep. Susan suddenly sits up and looks at her watch.

"Holy. 4:13. I wanted to go check out the windsurfing before the sun goes down. You're coming too, right?" she asks, totally refreshed from their after-lunch naptime. "Well, what do you think?" she urges while rising from her lawn chair, then discretely adjusts her sexy bathing suit.

"Nah, you go ahead. I think I ate too much." Chris demonstrates by rubbing his stomach in a circular motion. "I'll just stay here and watch you, OK?" he whines with exaggerated moans in his defence.

"Oh, all right!" Susan says with understanding. "See you in a few," she promises as she walks towards the windsurfing shack.

Susan seems a little nervous while holding onto the windsurf sail bar, but her stress is short-lived with the guidance and patience from the windsurfing instructor. She sails through the rigid waters, just barely staying erect for more than a few seconds at a time, while fighting back and forth with the unpredictable, strong wind.

A few girls about the same age as Susan come flying along like pros on their wind boards.

"Hey, how's it going?" one of the girls asks as she flies on by.

"Well," Susan says with a big grin as she is tossed around like a rag doll and repeatedly thrown into the water. The girls instinctively help her out with a few of their own simple staying-up strategies. They easily become friends along the way, always laughing and continuously rooting her on. Before you know it, Susan has got the hang of this windsurfing thing, and nothing seems to be stopping her now. She zips around with the girls for a while and her skills improve by the minute. She can just make out Chris sitting back on shore, drinking one of his two freshly arrived Corona beers and smoking a Mexican cigarette.

Susan slowly and stiffly walks towards Chris, who has been kicking back the free beers and smoking Mexican cigarettes the entire time she was out there mastering her windsurfing techniques.

"Hey, how was it? You looked pretty good out there!" he says undeniably with a mild slur.

"It was excellent!" she confirms, then plops down onto her warm, towelled beach chair. "Yes, it was definitely fun. I met some really nice girls out there too. And they gave me some tips," she explains excitedly.

"Oh good. I'm glad you had fun! I wouldn't mind giving you a few tips later on tonight," he jokes, then finishes the last of the many beers he's consumed since she was out there.

"Nice one! Ha Ha," she responds to his dirty humour. "Wow! 6:10 p.m. already!" she informs as she looks at her waterproof watch. "I'm suddenly super hungry!" she hints.

Chapter 18

As if in response to Susan's hunger, an army of Mexican waiters and hotel staff arrive on the beach carrying tables, chairs, tablecloths, dishes, flowers, and there's even a seven-piece band following right behind them with all their instruments.

"Hmm, what's going on, I wonder?" Susan asks while scanning the activity.

"Not sure!" Chris mumbles back. Their friendly gold-toothed waiter notices them looking around and approaches them, smiling away.

"Good evening, señorita, señor!" he greets.

"Good evening!" they both reply.

"So, what's going to be going on down here tonight?" she asks while displaying her puzzled-eyebrow look.

"There is a dinner and dance on the beach here tonight. Did you not receive the notice in your hotel room, señorita?" The waiter seems a little puzzled and concerned.

"Well, maybe we did, but we just quickly ran out the door this morning to get in some sun and do some windsurfing," she explains, pointing towards the many windsurfers still flying around way out there, never revealing the true unconscionable state they were both in the night before.

"I see, señorita." He totally understands and displays his golden smile. "Well, we hope to see you down here tonight for the festivities!" he graciously re-invites.

"Sounds good to me!" Susan says excitedly.

"Yeah, me too!" Chris blurts out and sits up.

"What time does it start?" Susan asks as she rises to her feet.

"In one hour, señorita," he responds while looking at his watch.

"Thank you!" Susan replies, then begins loading their stuff into the straw bag.

"Oh, you're very welcome, señorita, señor!" the waiter responds graciously, then races back to help the other hotel staff finish setting everything up for the "Five-Star Dinner and Dance on the Beach."

"Ok. Got everything. Let's head back up to the room. I need a good shower!" Susan insists excitedly. "I'm starving too. And I can't wait to see what they're going to be serving for dinner tonight!" she adds as they walk up the path towards the hotel.

"Yeah, I'm pretty hungry now too" Chris insists with a touch of sway in his walk and a slight slur in his voice.

They enter the beautiful resort lobby, where Chris quickly notices who he thinks is a tasty chick, standing there reading a brochure behind a marbled counter booth, which contains a multitude of various holiday, touristy brochures situated right behind her in a nice wooden slotted wrack against the wall. "Wow, she's hot!" he speaks in his mind while slipping into beer motion.

"Hey, check it out!" He points towards the "Fiesta Holidays" booth about forty feet across the way. Chris beelines it right towards the girl. He approaches the counter. "Oh, hi," he says in a flirtatious way, revealing a slight quiver in his voice before he suddenly and completely loses his nerve to say another word, especially now that Susan is standing right beside him. He quickly zeros in on the bright-red brochure "Rent a Jeep! Only fifty USD a day!" he says, creating a little underlying distraction as to why he actually walked over to the booth in the first place.

"Um, I noticed that, 'Rent a Jeep' one. Right there!" He points with an ever-so-slight sway while still displaying a touch of nervousness in his voice from the girl's incredible sexiness. The girl immediately picks up on his promiscuous ways, but just does her job while smiling anyway. She turns and pulls out one of the many shiny, bright red "Rent a Jeep" brochures from its wooden slot and politely hands it to Chris.

"Can I see that one right there? Swimming with the dolphins!" Susan points, totally unaware of Chris's lustful attraction towards the hot Mexican señorita.

"Of course!" The booth girl happily hands her one of the "Swimming with the Dolphins" brochures. "I see that you guys are the Grand Prize Winners. You can book any of these adventures for free," the girl ensures with a smile.

"Thank you!" Susan appreciates politely.

"Right on!" Chris accentuates while secretly giving the girl one last sneak-peak as they turn and make their way through the lobby towards the opened elevator doors.

"Hey, let's rent a jeep tomorrow!" he exuberantly suggests while holding the bright red "Rent a Jeep" brochure right up in her face as the elevator door closes.

"Yeah, Ok. Good idea," she agrees without hesitation. "And maybe we can go do the swim with the dolphins thing later on too, or the next day. Or even the day after that," she continues excitedly. "It doesn't really matter what exact day we go because we've still got twelve days left on our holiday anyway!" she calculates excitedly with her cute, slightly sunburnt face, smiling away, then flashes the four-page fold-out "Swimming with the Dolphins" picturesque brochure.

They continue down the hall and into their beautiful suite. Susan immediately jumps into the shower while Chris beelines it straight for the minibar and quickly guzzles down one of the freshly restocked Corona beers, then enters the shower.

"Wow! Look at all the sand that came off you!" he says jokingly, swaying and pointing to the floor of the shower. "You must have collected about ten pounds of sand during your windsurfing adventure today," he jokes again and they break into laughter.

"The windsurfing was amazing, but it definitely took its toll on my body, that's for sure!" she admits, then leans back under the showerhead. "My entire body is tight. Especially my arms." She massages them up and down.

"Tight is good!" Chris jokes and moves in for a kiss.

"Not now!" she pleads softly. "Later, after dinner. Later on tonight!" she promises. "I'm starving. Let's get down to the beach!" she encourages him further as they step out of the shower.

"Oh, OK!" Chris regretfully accepts, then secretly checks to see if his beer breath had something to do with the refusal.

They stroll down the twinkling tiki-torch-lit pathway towards the beach. The Mexican band sets the perfect holiday mood. There are already about a hundred people sitting at the many spread out, festively decorated tables, and at least a hundred more tiki torches burning all around the area, adding to the special flavourful atmosphere of the evening.

"Nice!" Susan emphasizes as they are directed by the host to a candlelit table of their own. A totally decked out waiter in a sombrero approaches the table. "Good evening, señor, señorita. Can I get you something from the bar?" he asks with a strong accent as he places two ice waters down on the table.

"I'll have a glass of white wine," Susan requests politely.

"I guess I'll have a Corona, if you don't mind." Chris orders his, as per usual, still a bit tipsy from the ten previous beers he's consumed throughout the day. "But who's counting?"

"Yes. Please help yourself. The dinner is over this way," the waiter kindly directs. The music and Susan's hunger quickly whisk them over to the tiki-torch-lit buffet. They return to their table with plates piled high.

"So, what time should we get up in the morning to rent the jeep?" Susan asks while savouring her dinner.

"Um, I don't know. How about eight, to get there by nine?" he suggests without hesitation.

"Sounds good. I'll make sure we get a wake-up call from the front desk," she volunteers. The atmosphere is a constant holiday flavour as they devour their delicious dinners, all the while grooving to the continuous music from the seven-piece Mexican band.

"Hey, I wonder which way Cancun is from here?" Susan asks curiously while glancing all around.

"Hmm, I'm not quite sure," Chris says in slow motion as he joins Susan in her side-to-side search.

Suddenly, from out of nowhere, the gold-toothed waiter appears with the answer. "That way, señorita, señor." He points his hand precisely in the direction of the quarter moon.

"Oh, thank you. Cool!" Susan graciously appreciates.

"Would you like another drink, señorita, señor?"

"Sure!" Chris answers immediately. "She'll have a strawberry margarita, and I'll have another Corona, please."

"Make mine a lime this time," she decides, changing it up a bit.

They dance along to more than just a few Mexican beats. The band just finishes a song, and Susan rushes up to the stage.

"Can you play Guantanamera?" she requests nervously, with her hands clasped together.

"Yes, señorita!" The Mexican front man agrees to do so and breaks into song.

Susan sways to the beat and is quite mesmerized by the song. "Did I ever tell you why I like this song so much?" she angelically asks Chris.

"No, you didn't, actually!" he confirms curiously. "Why do you?" he asks.

"It's like this special memory I have of when I was a kid. Almost like a dream," she reminisces. "My dad would sing this song every time it came over the car radio. That was a long time ago, I know, but it just does something to me," she confesses all, with the help of a few margaritas under her belt. "I'm super stiff! And I'm suddenly really sleepy too!" she explains while displaying the obvious signs. A pause.

Chris takes a step back to look at her to see if she's just joking around but quickly finds it's not the case. "Ok, let's head back to the hotel room, wink, wink, nudge, nudge!" he sarcastically throws in, hoping for a little support on his lovemaking idea.

"I'm just so tired! Wow, those margaritas are super strong!" Susan stresses with a slight slump in her posture. They enter the resort lobby and approach the front desk.

"Hi. Could we get an 8 a.m. wake-up call for room 422?" Susan politely requests of one of the three girls working at the front desk.

"Yes, señorita," the girl accommodates and immediately programs the info into her computer.

"Thank you!" Susan appreciates in her kind, usual way and goes totally unnoticed as tipsy.

"Finally in bed!" Susan whispers softly. "Good night, Chris!" she expresses lovingly, just before drifting off into a deep sleep.

"Good night!" he replies, dimming the lights, then kissing her on the forehead. He immediately grabs a bottle of Corona from the minibar and steps out onto the balcony. He quickly devours it, then heads back inside, slips into bed, and falls fast asleep.

Chapter 19

Ring... Ring... Ring... Ring...

Susan reaches out and answers the phone. "Hello?" she greets with a sleepy whisper.

"Good morning. Front desk calling for your 8 a.m. wake up call."

"Oh, right. Thank you! Could we also get a shuttle to the jeep rental place. About 9 a.m. this morning?" Susan asks respectively with a stretched-out yawn."

"Yes, señorita," the front desk answers.

Chris lays there motionless. "Time to get up!" she coaxes while lightly shaking him. "Jeep day!" she announces happily, now suddenly seeming very refreshed and full of energy, anticipating an exciting day ahead. She gives him another shake, then quickly pops out of bed and heads for the shower.

Chris roles over, groaning, then sits up on the edge of the bed, rubbing his thick head with both hands. He stumbles his way into the bathroom and slips into the shower with Susan. She instantly notices his strong, stale beer breath and quickly shies away.

"Yuk!" she emphasizes while waving her hand in front of her face. Seconds later, she steps out of the shower and grabs the toothpaste and his toothbrush from the bathroom counter. "Sorry, but, that breath has just got to go!" she insists with a sarcastic tone and a big grin as she hands them off to Chris. He fixes himself up as quickly as possible, hoping for a little action when he gets out of the shower. He exits the bathroom and finds that Susan is already dressed and ready for the day. "Room service should be here with our breakfast in about ten minutes," she surprises excitedly.

"Cool," Chris says, not having a choice, and must settle for food over sex. The front desk informs them that there is a private shuttle waiting to take them to the jeep rental place. They devour their breakfasts and head down to the lobby.

They step onto the shuttle, sit down, and immediately pick up a few of the flashy holiday magazines that are lying around on the seats. "Oh, I know, I'll pick us up some stuff for a picnic lunch today, OK?" Susan volunteers enthusiastically.

"Sure, sounds good to me!" Chris agrees while secretly flipping through the sexy, colourful pages in the travel magazine.

Upon signing the jeep rental agreement, the attendant politely informs them of the areas in which they can and cannot go with the jeep. "Just stay on the green lines. Stay off the black lines," he drills in strongly while pointing to the small, etched-out plastic road map firmly attached to the glove compartment door.

"Thank you!" Chris and Susan respond simultaneously.

"Have a good time, señor, señorita. See you at 6 p.m.," the attendant confirms.

They drive around town with the tunes cranked and eventually stumble upon a very busy Mexican produce and textiles market. Susan shops from place to place, half filling her straw bag with various items for their picnic lunch. Chris quickly sniffs out a good place to buy cold Corona beer. He buys three six-packs and secretly stashes them behind the driver's seat, strategically covering them with his large beach towel. He definitely doesn't want her to know about the overabundance of beer he has made available for their lovely jeep day trip. "Out of sight, out of mind," he whispers to himself as he spots Susan approaching with her weighed down straw bag. "Hey! What the heck do you have in there?" he asks, trying to direct any focus away from his lumpy beach towel.

"You'll see!" she promises sweetly.

"We're off, down the tropical highway!" Chris announces with a big, devious grin as he slips on his sunglasses. Upbeat Mexican music plays loudly over the jeep's kick-ass stereo system as they happily make their way along the everlasting, sunshiny, palm-treed, oceanside highway.

"I wonder where this highway will take us?" Chris asks, as if in suspense, just as he turns down the stereo.

"Well," Susan reminds as she puts her finger right on the etched-out map. "We're approximately right here, and if we just stay on this oceanside road, the green line, like that guy said, it looks . . ." A pause. "Hmm, well, it looks like this map ends at about 220 miles away, but I'm sure . . . wait!" she says, suddenly remembering seeing something in the glove compartment when the attendant placed the agreement in there this morning. "Yeah, another map!" She unfolds it.

"Cool! What does it say?" Chris asks.

"Wow! We could drive all the way to Ixtapa or Acapulco or Managua or even Costa Rica by the looks of it. And maybe even Cancun. Holy moley," she continues ecstatically, following her finger across the map. "But they all look like they are a million miles from here!" she adds with a smile, then places the map back in the glove compartment.

"Oh well. We'll just keep driving and see where we end up!" Chris says with a confident, beer-craving attitude as he turns the stereo up a little louder.

"Yeah, it's still early!" Susan shouts happily while looking at her watch, then out to the sparkling ocean. "I'm sure we'll find an excellent spot somewhere along this beach for our picnic lunch!"

Chris reaches behind his seat and grabs his first beer of the day.

"Hey! What the? Drinking and driving? I don't know about that!" Susan smiles nervously but just leaves it alone, mesmerized by the addicting holiday mood. She leans back in her seat, bopping along with the holiday-flavoured music cranked over the stereo as the beautiful views just keep coming.

After another seventy miles down the highway and a few more nonchalant beers for Chris, Susan perks up. "There's a good spot!" Susan suddenly notices and points towards a beautiful, picturesque seascape off in the distance. They approach the spot, then Chris immediately swerves the jeep off the road and drives on a bumpy angle, straight for a big, thick foliage-and-palm-tree patch about forty feet in from the road.

"The jeep is completely camouflaged now!" he states the obvious with a sudden hidden agenda master plan attached.

"Wow!" Susan shouts. "Who do you think you are? Indiana Jones?" They both have a good laugh. Chris slips four beers into the heavy straw picnic bag while Susan grabs their flippers, masks, and snorkels along with her beach towel. They slowly emerge from the foliage onto the most beautifully secluded and completely deserted beach. "It's like a dream here. Wow, I love this view," she conveys joyfully while spinning around a couple of times. An angelic trance washes over her smiling face. The white-capped waves constantly rush in and crash loudly down onto the shoreline. The sun is hot, the sand is fresh, and the palm tree leaves are ruffling in the warm breeze.

"It almost feels like were stranded on a desert island," Chris sarcastically adds in his vision of the whole thing. They both laugh.

"Crazy guy. But I know what you mean," she explains with a chuckle, then begins strategically placing all the surprises she picked out for their picnic lunch onto a large, brand-new, funky, colourful, Mexican blanket that she bought this morning while at the market.

"Wow! You could be in charge of the 'All Inclusive' at our hotel," Chris jokes, yet complimenting Susan on her picnic efforts, all the while displaying the famous two-handed air quotes. They both laugh. "This looks fantastic!" He slightly slurs while reaching out for more than just a little of each of the many food selections Susan just finished placing out on her proud, new, colourful, Mexican blanket. "You are the best picnic maker ever, sweetheart!" Chris praises, then devours it down as if he hasn't eaten in a week.

"You *are* hungry!" Susan states the obvious.

"Do you want a beer?" he asks as he instantly cracks one open.

"Sure," she gladly accepts and takes it from him. "Oh, I got some mango juice too!" She pulls a couple small bottles from the bottom of her straw bag.

"Oh, good! Thanks!" Chris pretends to be thrilled about it, and cracks open another beer for himself. The mood is quite tantalizing, especially with the incredible scenic location and the beautiful colourful picnic lunch spread out along the waterline. Susan seems to be so enthralled with the relaxing holiday spirit of things that she doesn't even notice, or possibly doesn't care, that Chris's notorious drinking habits may have followed them all the way down to Mexico.

"High noon. Wow, its super hot. Good thing I brought our new hats along." Susan packs the leftovers back into her straw bag. She straightens and realigns her beach towel, then strips down to her sexy bathing suit and slowly lies back onto the beach towel. "Hey, where's your towel?" she asks as she looks from side to side while squinting from the bright sun in her eyes.

"Oh. It's still in the jeep," he realizes. "I'll go get it!" He takes off running.

When he gets to the jeep, he is totally out of breath from the quick jaunt. The run seems to have instantly re-stimulated the many beers he previously consumed since the beginning of their road trip. He pulls his beach towel off the nine remaining beers. "Right on!" he says as he cracks one open and quickly guzzles it down to the bottom. "Ah… Refreshing!" He gasps for a little air. He gathers up the empties, then recklessly fires them into the thick foliage. "Out of sight, out of mind!" he says and laughs. He grabs his towel and two more beers and heads back to the beach. "I brought you a beer. And they're still cool too!" he says with a slight slur, then cracks it open and hands it off to her. He wastes no time cracking the other open for himself.

"Cheers!" Susan says while holding her bottle up towards Chris. "Here's to our amazing holiday!" she adds sweetly. *Clink! Clink!* The bottles double hit together.

Susan is just finishing her beer when Chris suddenly attacks, frantically tickling and kissing her. "Ah!" she screams out, then jumps up from her towel and begins running down the smooth, sandy water line. Chris chases after her but is having a hard time catching up. Susan suddenly dives into the water. Chris finally catches up to her and immediately pulls her in close to his sweaty body and begins kissing her hot juicy lips. She playfully breaks away from him and begins running through the knee-deep water. Chris slowly gains on her, reaches out and accidentally pulls her bathing suit top right off.

Her perky breasts are only revealed for a split second before she realizes exactly what's happened and quickly covers herself with her arms. "Chris!" she screams loudly. "Give it back!" she pleads while giggling and stomping her foot in the water.

"Oh? You mean this!" he taunts while twirling her top around in mid-air.

"Yes, that!" she confirms with a big grin.

"You know, I read somewhere that it's illegal to go topless on these beaches," he teases as he stops twirling her top for a second.

"So then give it here!" she continues pleading with a little more serious intent attached, yet still revealing a slight playful smirk on her face.

"You'll have to come and get it!" he coaxes, then resumes twirling her top around his finger. She slowly and cautiously moves towards Chris in desperate hopes of getting her top back on. Just as she is close enough to grab it, Chris pulls her in tight to his body and kisses her again. Her bathing suit top remains clutched tight in his hand all the while. They continue kissing romantically as the waves crash gently against their slightly sunburnt bodies.

Then suddenly, like a lightning bolt, Susan snags her bikini top from his clutched hand, turns away, and discreetly slips it back on. They hold hands and slowly walk back to their picnic spot. Chris spreads his towel out alongside Susan's. They lay baking in the hot sun for about a half hour. A flock of Mexican seagulls squawk on by and startle Susan up to leaning on her elbows. A bead of sweat trickles down her face from the heat. Chris struggles to sit up.

"We must have dozed off." She looks at her watch. "12:36," she says.

Just then, Chris notices a family walking along the water line towards them. "Hey, look over there!" he whisper-shouts while pointing towards the family. "You're lucky they didn't see your boobs, eh?" he pokes at her sarcastically.

"Yeah, more like *you're* lucky," she pokes back.

"Hey, let's get back in the jeep and drive a bit further down the highway or road or whatever they call it out here," he coaxes with a crinkled burnt face and a slight slur attached.

Susan looks towards the family still approaching. "Yeah, OK. Good idea. I had the perfect private picnic today!" With the biggest smile, she rises from her damp towel.

"Me too, and guess what? We can always come here another day too!" Chris realizes.

"Yeah, you're right!" Susan agrees wholeheartedly.

They quickly pack everything up and head back to the jeep. Chris immediately throws his beach towel over the remaining six-pack of beer behind the driver's seat, hoping to maintain his famous out-of-sight-out-of-mind mode. Susan slips on a colourful breezy blouse and buckles up.

"We're on the road again," he announces and starts the jeep, backs it up, then swings it around and heads for the highway.

"We better keep these straw hats on! Or else our faces are going to get super burnt," she advises for obvious reasons as the sun beats down intensely.

"Yeah, and good thing we parked the jeep in that shaded area back there too! Or these seats would have melted. Not to mention our asses would have been burnt off too!" He sarcastically exaggerates while secretly reaching back to check the temperature of his beer, then turns up the stereo.

"Too funny!" she stresses while laughing along with his humour. "Yeah, well, if it gets too hot, we have our damp beach towels to sit on anyway!" She enthusiastically giggles.

Ten minutes later. "Hey, hmm, the stereo, I mean the radio, is getting a little crackly." Chris points out while trying to pinpoint a clear station.

"Yeah, I guess we're slowly getting a little out of range." Susan guesses right. "Hey, I brought a few good CDs along with us. Do you want me to slip one in?" she asks innocently.

"Slip one in, hmm?" Chris slowly repeats with a devilish smirk on his face while looking directly at her, hoping for some kind of positive reaction.

"Yeah, right, good one!" She finally gets it and slaps him hard on the arm. "Tonight!" she promises, gently patting him on the shoulder. Susan pulls a few CDs out of the straw bag and places them between their seats.

"Well, if the radio gets too crackly, just, you know!" he couldn't resist mentioning. They both laugh. A few miles pass by. "Excellent CDs you brought, cool," Chris approves while checking out the selection, then slips one in and cranks it up. Susan sits back in her seat, relaxing until she finally closes her eyes and dozes off into a deep relaxing slumber. Chris looks right at her. "She's totally out to lunch," he says, then quickly reaches behind the seat for a beer, and then another, and another.

Chapter 20

The music takes them sailing another sixty-six miles down the tropical highway until they come to a fork in the road. "Stay right, go left" echoes throughout Chris's intoxicated mind. He abruptly makes a hard left that eventually has them traveling down a gravelly dirt road to who knows where. Two and a half more miles of dusty gravel road pass by. Chris suddenly veers left onto a faint trail-like road that leads them up a steep mountainside. The road slowly becomes nonexistent and totally covered with thick foliage. Chris fires another couple empty beer bottles overboard, then reaches behind his seat and grabs the final beer from the now empty six-pack case. He cracks it open and guzzles it halfway down. The steepening trail has now become a self-made road and is becoming bumpier and bumpier the deeper they go. The jeep suddenly hits a good-sized bump and comes crashing down, instantly startling Susan awake.

"Hey! Where are we?" she shouts, extremely concerned, while frantically wiping the sleep from her eyes. "I don't think we're supposed to be in this area!" She panics while looking in every direction. "We're way off the main road!" she continues shouting, very terrified.

"Ah, don't worry about it. We're having fun!" he boasts, slurring heavily, then leans way back and takes in a smooth "Mr. Cool" swig of beer.

"No! Look, Chris!" she persists frantically, trying to get his attention while pointing right at the etched-out map on the glove compartment. She rises from her seat and quickly turns around, suddenly realizing that the ocean is now far, far below. "Seriously!" she pleads. "I'm not joking!" she continues and slaps both hands down hard on her lap. "Turn around, Chris. Please!" Susan continues pleading, but there just seems to be no stopping him now.

"But we're almost at the top!" he slurs with excitement as the jeep peeks over the crest of the mountain. Suddenly the jeep's brakes squeal loudly as they must come to a complete and abrupt stop. They stare straight forward, frozen with fear.

Nicker, whicker, sounds a horse.

Right in front of them are fifty of the meanest looking bandits you have ever seen. Chris gulps, then stagger-steps out of the jeep. He solutes the bandits with the small trickle of beer he has left at the bottom of the bottle.

Bang! echoes the heart-stopping bullet fired from the bandit leader's old-fashioned, six-shooter pistol. The bullet rips right through Chris's chest, sending him flying backwards through mid-air in slow motion. His lifeless body slams down hard onto the ground, creating a thick puff of dust all around him.

Chris lay dead, right in front of Susan, who is now going into a white-faced shock. She has a sudden flash moment of hope that this is only a crazy dream, but reality quickly stares her right in the face as the dust settles around Chris's lifeless, bloody body. She maintains her silent screams while displaying an extremely terrified look across her entire face. Her breathing becomes frantic as her body shakes uncontrollably. She is becoming more and more petrified by the second until she cannot make a sound or even look up at the bandits, who have been constantly peering into her soul. Cool tears flow from her frightened eyes, down her extremely saddened face, and drip over her sweet puffy lips.

"Bring her to me!" the four-hundred-pound bandit leader growls to one of his men, revealing his deep, scary, thick, rumbling Spanish accent. The chosen bandit gets off his horse and approaches the jeep. Susan realizes what is about to happen and begins screaming for her life. She frantically unbuckles her seatbelt and tries desperately to escape the ugly bandit, who is now racing toward her with a creepy grin on his face. The bandit swiftly grabs a hold of Susan's arm before she even has the slightest chance of slipping away, then aggressively yanks her out of the jeep and unknowingly rips her precious diver's watch off her wrist, sending it flying into some foliage. She screams frantically for her life while kicking and punching the ugly bandit who eventually slams her down sideways on the back of the bandit leader's horse and ties her down. The main bandit reaches back and slaps her on the ass, as if to announce to the others that she is his prize possession. Another bandit jumps off his horse and searches over Chris's dead body, quickly revealing a stack of American twenty-dollar bills inside a small waist-pack, then fires it directly into the hands of the bandit leader. The cash-finding bandit then proudly slips off Chris's slightly bent straw hat from his lifeless, bobbling head, claiming it as his own.

"You won't be needing this anymore, gringo," he sarcastically announces while looking down at Chris's lifeless body. All the bandits have a good laugh as the cash-finding, seemingly sadistic bandit tugs and pulls down hard on his new hat, barely able to stretch it over his big, fat, greasy head, before remounting his horse.

"Please. Let me go!" Susan demands while sobbing uncontrollably. "Please!" she continues sporadically. The bandits laugh and joke amongst themselves, totally ignoring her pleas. The bandits slowly disappear into a thick, green, mountainous jungle terrain while buzzards hover high above the jeep.

* * *

Later that evening, the jeep rental manager is corresponding over the telephone with the resort manager. The conversation quickly escalates into a closed-door discussion about the jeep that these guests had rented earlier that day, that is now several hours over the return time specified in the agreement. The resort manager quickly makes photocopies of their passports, and has his staff thoroughly search the entire resort, but they are nowhere to be found. The resort manager immediately calls the police and explains the situation.

The next day, in the late afternoon, a chopper searches far and wide, eventually locating and reporting the jeep's whereabouts to the chief of police. Soon after, a half dozen khaki-clothed, five-foot nothing, old-school Mexican police scout out the jeep's reported location. The six police officers eventually find the jeep along with Chris's buzzard-tattered remains lying right beside it.

"Stupid gringo!" one police officer rambles to himself as he zips up the body bag, then nervously looks towards the jungle as if he had the feeling of being watched. He wasn't wrong. Chris's body is quickly loaded into the back of a police jeep. Another two jump into the second jeep, while the remaining two climb aboard the rental jeep. All three jeeps slowly convoy their way down the mountainous terrain. Once on the road, they speed all the way into town.

Chapter 21

Three days later, back home, the paper boy approaches the old gas station riding his bicycle. He tosses one of his old-school, pre-folded newspapers hard towards the old gas station door, and quickly rides on by. Seconds later, Brad pulls into the gas station driving his old '47 pickup. He exits the truck, walks to the door, slips in the key, and pushes it open. The newspaper instantly flops open, revealing Chris and Susan's faces plastered across the front page. He quickly snatches the newspaper up from the floor and reads on. "Local Girl Missing, Boyfriend Found Dead On Mexican Fiesta Vacation."

"What the! Holy shit!" Brad shouts loudly, shocked and in disbelief at what he is seeing and reading on the front page of today's newspaper. He holds the newspaper clinched tightly in his hands, staring at her picture for another "Twilight Zone" moment, then re-reads the headlines just to be sure. "Holy shit!" he shouts, confirming the terrible and unbelievable situation that Susan has gotten herself into, then slams the newspaper down hard on the countertop and quickly proceeds to dial the old gas station wall phone.

"Shawn, hey. Sorry for waking you but you've got to cover me for a while! It's an emergency. It's that girl, Susan, the one I introduced you to . . . Yeah, I think she's in deadly trouble . . . I've got to go out of town . . . Well, just grab today's newspaper on the way in. I'm taking this one with me. The front page will explain everything! OK, I've got to go, I'll see you soon. I'll call you. Oh, and call Grampa to cover for me too. OK, bye!"

Click.

Brad quickly snatches the newspaper from the countertop, locks the door, then sprints out to his truck and jumps in. He drives faster than usual all the way back to his place and comes to a screeching stop into the driveway. He flies out of the truck and sprints into the house. He heads straight to his secret hiding spot above his closet and pulls down a shoe box, opens it up, and pulls out a thick stack of cash. He folds it in half then stuffs it deep into his pocket. He runs downstairs into the basement and locates an old knapsack carry-on bag, then frantically gathers up a few small items that he may need for the trip.

Brad arrives at the airport and quickly slips into the lineup to buy a ticket bound for Puerto Vallarta, just as indicated on the large digital screen under the heading, "Mexican Destinations."

"Last call for passengers heading for Puerto Vallarta, Flight number 1892," echoes throughout the airport.

Brad waits patiently in line while desperate thoughts of where to look for Susan play out in many scenarios in his mind as he stares down at the front page of this morning's shocking newspaper. "Oh, good! I'm up next," he says to himself, then carefully rolls the newspaper up, passionately clutching it with both hands. "How much to Puerto Vallarta?" he asks firmly without his usual smile as he steps up to the ticket and baggage counter. He swiftly cups the newspaper under his arm, then reaches deep into his pocket for the stack of cash and passport.

"Just in the nick of time," the cute ticket agent confirms while looking toward the time of departure listed on the digital board. "You still have ten minutes, you'll make it," she promises, recognizing a slight urgency in Brad's demeanour.

The plane is just leaving the runway. Brad leans back in his seat, unrolls the newspaper, and reviews the front page once again. While reading a bit further, he is directed to "story continued page 13." Page 13 gives a more descriptive account of the situation in these parts of Mexico politically, indicating that troubles with kidnapping for ransom has been more frequent.

"That's a terrible story, poor things," the elderly woman beside him snoops out loud.

"Yes," is all Brad can say in a soft, concerned tone as the seatbelt sign rings off. He slips on his headphones, cranks up his band's music, reclines his seat, then closes his eyes and mentally prepares himself for the unknown adventure ahead. He drifts off to sleep for the rest of the flight.

"Attention! Please fasten your seat belts in preparation for landing," blares loudly over the intercom, startling Brad from his deep sleep.

Screech! The plane touches down on the heat radiating tarmac.

Brad is wide awake now, and seemingly quite eager to depart the plane. He quickly exits the plane, runs through the terminal, then jumps into the back seat of the first cab that becomes available.

"Puerto Vallarta police station please," Brad demands politely, but with a quite obvious intent to get there as fast as humanly possible.

"OK, señor," the Mexican cabbie says, then switches on the metre that doesn't seem to be fully functional, as its lights flicker off and on. Brad takes in the scenery along the way as Mexican music plays over the cab radio. He occasionally glances down at the front page of the newspaper where Susan's passport picture stares right back at him.

The cab comes to a complete and abrupt stop, breaking Brad out of his daydream state.

"Police station, señor," the cabbie shouts.

"How much do I owe you?" Brad enquires while reaching in his pocket.

"One hundred fifty pesos, please, señor," the cabbie adds with his hand out.

"How much is that in American money?" he asks, ready to peel off some cash from his wad.

"About ten dollars," the cabbie quickly calculates in his favour. Brad pays without hesitation, then exits the cab, and beelines it straight inside the police station.

"Excuse me, officer!" Brad politely requests the attention of one of the few police officers.

"Yes, señor," the police officer says as he approaches the counter.

"I'm here about this girl." Brad points at Susan's face on the now slightly wrinkled newspaper. "Have you seen her? Or know where she might be right now? Or where she was last seen?" Brad asks intensely, seemingly a bit scattered, while displaying major concern on his face. All the other police officers hear Brad's request and have now perked up. The police officer slowly turns to look at his superior officer, who is now approaching the counter.

"Can I help you, señor?" the chief officer asks in broken yet understandable English, knowing all too well what Brad had just been pointing out.

"Have you seen this girl?" Brad gladly repeats. The chief abruptly grabs the newspaper from Brad's hand, as if to inspect, then slowly peers around the station, then back to Brad.

"Sorry, señor, we do not know where this girl is, but we are doing all what we can to locate her," the chief explains as if he is hiding some details about the truth, which Brad easily picks up on. Brad smoothly slips the newspaper from the chief's hands and looks at Susan's picture.

"You're sure?" Brad checks once again.

"Sorry, señor," the chief says with both hands up in mid-air. "We are doing all we can to locate her, señor." The police chief then walks back to his office.

All the while, there has been a little Mexican kid constantly poking his head around the corner, as if playing some kind of spy game with the police officers, sneak-peeking into the police station and absorbing more than anyone knows.

Brad is angered by the Mexican police, with their tight-lipped attitude, but maintains his cool. "Thank you," he sarcastically compliments their nonexistent efforts to find Susan, then turns, and slowly walks out the front door of the police station and onto the busy main strip.

"Señor! Señor! Señor!" shouts the same Mexican kid who was peeking his head around the corner at the police station. "Señor! Señor!" the kid continues.

Brad is finally stopped by the kid, who is now tugging on the side of his shirt. Brad appears puzzled, while looking down at the little, spunky, enthusiastic, wide-eyed Mexican kid.

"Yes? Is everything all right?" Brad asks, quite concerned.

"I tell you everything!" the boy assures with determination.

"What do you mean? A tour?" Brad guesses. "No, sorry, kid. No time for any tours today," Brad confesses and waves his hand down and continues walking.

"No! No! Señor, señor. I tell you everything you want to know about the bandits that took the girl in your newspaper. For twenty American dollars!" the boy promises, with pure conviction, while pointing to Brad's newspaper.

"What?" Brad asks, wide-eyed with amazement, compiled with disbelief. "How do you know this?" Brad asks, then crouches down to eye level with the boy.

"My uncle, he is a journalist here in Puerto Vallarta," the boy informs. "I practice reading with all the stories he writes every time I visit, but they don't always print what he writes. My uncle always gets, very, very mad at them and says to me, 'At least someone is reading the truth,' so now I tell you the truth, señor, for only twenty American dollars. OK, señor?"

"What's your name, kid?" Brad asks, impressed by the boy's demeanour.

"Pedro!" the boy replies.

"Wow, chances are," Brad says to himself and is very intrigued by Pedro's stories. He reaches into his pocket and pulls out the wad of cash, then secretly peels off a twenty-dollar bill and hands it off to his newfound friend. "OK, Pedro, let's hear all the stuff you know about this girl, and where she might be!" Brad demands while holding up the newspaper, displaying Chris and Susan's pictures.

"Not here on the street," Pedro secretly communicates. "We will go to my friend's home and I will tell you everything. He is a good friend. He will help too. He has maps and everything,"

Pedro promises with a continuous breath of excitement as he guides Brad down many cobblestone streets.

"Here it is!" Pedro points, then does what seems like a secret knock on the old metal door with a hammer. The door clicks, then slowly slides open, revealing a room that is filled with what appears to be one of everything you could ever imagine, neatly stacked or hung, from floor to ceiling. Pedro enters. "Come in, señor," Pedro says while waving his hand inward. Brad enters, then Pedro quickly hammers out the secret knock, magically resetting the spring-loaded, self-locking door that is rigged with ropes, wires, springs, pulleys, and leavers.

Brad follows Pedro down a narrow path through a few more stockpiled rooms, then eventually into an office, deep in the back of the building. Pedro's good friend sits behind a grand antique desk with his back to them, hidden behind his high-back, black leather chair, looking over some trinkets. Suddenly, the chair spins around, revealing Pedro's extremely tough, weathered-looking friend.

"Who do we have here?" Pedro's scary friend asks in a deep, gravelly voice, then slowly leans back in his noisy, spring-loaded chair.

"Oh, hi, I'm Brad. Pedro came out of nowhere saying he could help me find this girl," Brad emphasizes with confidence as he hands the newspaper over to the seemingly crazed local.

He looks over the front-page photo for a short moment. "I see! Yes, I know this situation all too well, it isn't the first time someone has gone missing or been found dead. The bandits that took this girl are the most ruthless of all the gangs, so they say," he regretfully confesses.

"So, you think you might know where this girl is?" Brad asks with driven hope in his voice.

"What did you say your name was, kid?" The crazed local asks, while leaning forward in his chair.

"Brad, Brad Conners," he quickly repeats.

"Sit down, Brad. Pedro! Cerveza," the tough guy barks out his requests.

"OK, señor CC!" Pedro instantly responds as Brad takes a seat.

"Well, I'm Charlie," he introduces. "People call me Crazy Charlie. But I'm not really crazy; it's a good nickname though. Keeps people off my back," he admits with a chuckle, then opens the desk drawer and pulls out a cigar-sized joint.

"Mmm." Charlie gestures as his lungs fill with Columbian gold, then hands the joint out towards Brad.

"Oh, no thanks, man!" Brad politely refuses while putting his hands up.

Pedro smoothly intercepts the joint. "You're relentless!" Crazy Charlie growls directly at Pedro, then breaks into laughter. "You better eat an orange before you go home tonight. Your mother is worse than any of those bandits out there if she catches you smelling like, you know, the good stuff," CC explains.

"OK, señor CC," Pedro says with a grin. Pedro pretends to take a puff as Brad does a double take, and quickly understands that Pedro is not really smoking the marijuana, but still must genuinely cough from the intense smoke that streams from the cigar-sized joint. Pedro's face scrunches up as he waves one hand to clear the smoke while simultaneously handing the joint back over to CC. Crazy Charlie takes in a huge puff, then slowly exhales, filling the room with smoke. A silent pause.

"So, Pedro, you said you were going to tell me everything about the girl I'm looking for," Brad nervously speaks up, hoping to bring them back to the urgency of finding Susan alive. CC now sees more of Brad's respectful determination to find Susan and can tell that he is stressed throughout his entire mind and body.

"OK, OK, yes, señor," Pedro speaks up.

Red-eyed Charlie grabs hold of the newspaper and slowly sits back in his squeaky chair. He looks at it for a moment, then throws it back on top of the desk. "Well," Charlie emphasizes in a deep, drawn-out voice as he rises to his feet. "Do you know what you're getting yourself into here, kiddo?" he asks with a slightly aggressive tone while staring Brad right in the eyes.

"What do you mean?" Brad asks in a worrisome tone while appearing slightly puzzled.

"Well, the bandits that supposedly took your girlfriend there," Charlie drills in hard while pointing at the newspaper, "they are a pack of scary dudes, no one would ever mess with them, not even the police," Charlie admits, then walks over to the large wall map. Brad and Pedro listen carefully as CC rambles. "They are well armed and invisible while in the jungle. They hang out up in this area." Charlie touches the map with his finger. "You'd have to travel about a hundred and fifty miles up along the ocean road here, then hike quite a few miles up into this thick, jungle, mountainous terrain."

Brad moves in for a closer look at the map. "Not to mention the snakes and spiders and many other nightmare animals. It's become a pretty hush-hush situation here in Mexico within the government and tourism as to what's really going on," Charlie elaborates. "They don't want to be scaring off all the tourists with any publicity about kidnappings and murders, that's for sure. They'll go broke!" he shouts. "And the bandits know it too, so . . ." CC concludes, with a silent pause. "The bandits used to get what they wanted. But now . . ." CC hesitates to say anything.

"What do you mean, *used to get?*" Brad probes while appearing puzzled.

"Well, things have just recently changed. The government had to put a strong hold on the bandits and not pay them any more ransom money. They say it's gotten way out of hand over the years, now every wannabe bandit is trying to get in on the action, and there just isn't enough money to keep paying them off. That's what they say in the newspapers, anyway. You know how sometimes a story leaks out," CC confesses while grinning as he and Pedro have a moment with their secret wink.

"I see," Brad drawls with a touch of shock, remembering a bit about page 13 of the newspaper and a sudden sense of hopelessness is revealed in his voice. A silent pause. Brad walks around the room with both hands rubbing hard over his face.

"So now everyone just gets killed?" Brad abruptly asks, now sounding more panic stricken.

"Well, yes. Not long after they're kidnapped, they've been killing them," Charlie brutally confesses. "Usually within a week or two," he hesitantly concludes.

"Holy shit! How much time do I have? When did they go missing?" Brad double questions, obviously quite frustrated, while pointing at the newspaper.

"About four or five days ago," Charlie calculates. "But you can't just go waltzing into the jungle to look for that girl," Charlie tries to explain while pointing to Susan's face.

"Can you, or can you not, take me into those mountains?" Brad asks with a shivering calmness in his voice while pointing at the map and looking CC right in the eyes.

"You're joking, right?" Charlie expresses with a jovial chuckle, then re-lights the joint.

"You can take him, can't you, señior CC?" Pedro speaks up enthusiastically while secretly rubbing his fingers together, showing the signal of cash for what he thinks only Crazy Charlie can see. "Can't you?" Pedro pleads for his usual percentage.

"Well," Charlie says in a long, drawn-out way, then sits back down in his chair and takes another big toke.

"I'll pay you," Brad says as he reaches deep into his pocket and pulls out the wad of cash. Pedro's eyes instantly light up as he calculates the wad of cash before him. Pedro silently encourages CC to take Brad into the jungle. He is very convincing with his wide-eyed stare and rapid up and down head movement while looking CC right in the eyes, then back to the cash. Dead silence, all except for a huge exhalation sound of marijuana smoke that fumigates the room.

Smash!

"Shit!" CC shouts, as he slaps his hand down hard onto the newspaper, then quickly rises to his feet. "You do know what you're getting yourself into here, right?" CC dramatically emphasizes. "And you know what you're getting us into as well," he grumbles while leaning forward, wide-eyed, pointing to Pedro and then himself. Intense silence floods the smoky room. "Well, you're going to need a few things if you're planning a trip into the jungle, my friend," CC states with his crazy child-like grin.

Brad's face lights up with excitement.

"How much money you got in that wad there, anyway?" CC asks while pointing outward.

"About three thousand," Brad approximates.

"I'll take half. We better get started, we haven't much time," CC speaks with conviction as he firmly closes the deal and walks past Brad and Pedro, then out into another room.

CC turns the lights on, revealing his somewhat organized hoarder's delight. "You're going to need a few more things to take along with you on your little adventure besides that big, old, empty knapsack!" CC says with a gravelly persuasion in his voice as he lifts the lid off an ancient, large, squeaky, dusty trunk. He reaches deep inside and pulls out his very own invention of an automatic mini three-shooter crossbow. "She's a beauty!" CC says as he hands it off to Brad. "Go ahead. Oh, take the safety off first!" CC explains as he reaches over and simply releases the safety with his thumb. "Fire it at that box of wood there," CC says while pointing.

Brad slowly lifts the mini crossbow and without hesitation, fires an arrow right into the box. "Wow, this thing has kick!" Brad says as he moves in for a closer look at the arrow's penetration.

"Here's more ammo. Reload it now," Crazy Charlie says as he hands Brad another arrow. "Oh, yeah. Put the safety back on, or else!" CC reminds with a raised eyebrow and a smirk. "You'll need some water and some of these," CC says while handing Brad six bottles of water and a twenty-four pack of potentially stolen power bars. "That should just about do it!" CC calculates.

"Unreal, man! You've got one of everything in this place," Brad compliments as he finishes loading his slightly overstuffed knapsack while peering around the room. Brad quickly rises to his feet and flips his knapsack over one shoulder, then reaches deep into his pocket, pulls out his cash, and begins peeling off twenty-dollar bills. Crazy Charlie and Pedro stand silent, staring as the money rolls off the wad. "Here you go," Brad says with appreciation as he hands CC half his cash.

Chapter 22

Pedro is now the richest kid in town, or at least he feels that way as he stands tall, looking up with both hands reaching out in anticipation, trying to imagine what his cut might be. All the while, Pedro displays the biggest grin a kid could ever have, plastered right across his entire face, accompanied by an occasional twitch and a squirm, almost as if he had to go to the washroom. CC quickly peels off fifteen twenty-dollar bills, right into Pedro's open hands, which is double his usual percentage.

"Wow! Three hundred, plus twenty!" Pedro shouts out while shuffling the bills like a deck of cards, then walks off in a mist of glory.

"OK, we better get the hell out of here. You got everything?" CC directs his question to Brad with authority.

"Ready to go!" Brad says immediately while slapping the knapsack with his hand.

"Pedro!" CC shouts. "Go warm up the boat," he orders and fires the keys over to Pedro.

"Come, señor!" Pedro shouts, motioning for Brad to follow him.

"The boat?" Brad says under his breath with a slightly concerned look on his face.

"I'll be right there!" CC shouts loudly from his office while gathering a few things into a large leather bag.

Pedro and Brad approach Crazy Charlie's long, yellow, overloaded, nineteen-foot-long, shockless, peel 'n stick woodgrain LTD 1972 Country Squire Station Wagon. Pedro unlocks the door, jumps in, and starts the car. The interior of the car takes on the geographical environment well, with the ceiling covered in multicoloured dingle-balls, along with seat-covers that could easily remind you of an old spaghetti western. CC approaches the car as the power windows are going down.

"You're the boss while I'm gone," he firmly directs as Pedro leaps out of the driver's seat, and onto his feet.

"Yes, sir, Señor CC," Pedro shouts excitedly, then looks up and proudly salutes him, conveying total respect, as if being entrusted with this responsibility for the first time.

"Jump in!" Crazy Charlie says. Brad instantly obliges and slides into the front seat of the old, motorized, Mexican-flavoured stagecoach. CC immediately clicks on the CD player then gently shifts the boat into drive.

Ka-Bang!

The sound from the tailpipe shoots as he puts on the gas. "Been a while, since I had this old boat out," CC remembers, then gives the dashboard a few good, firm taps of appreciation. He pushes in the ashtray lighter, then reaches into his bag, pulls out another marijuana cigar, and lights it when the lighter pops. He reaches back into his bag and grabs a crinkly old map, then fires it at Brad. "Study this!" CC says as a thick stream of smoke billows from his mouth and out the window. "We're right here." CC points to a red scribbled circle on the map. "And we've got to get right about here," he figures while pointing on the spot marked in pencil.

"OK. Now I know where I'm going anyway," Brad finally realizes. CC takes a big puff, then cranks up the music. Brad looks over the ruffled map for a moment longer, then folds it into a perfect square and hands it out toward CC. "No, you keep it," CC says with a distorted voice as the cigar joint dangles from his lips. "Here, try it, it will calm your nerves," CC shouts over the music, persuading Brad with the cigar joint remedy up close in his face.

"Oh, no. Thanks, man. I'm good. Thanks anyway," Brad says politely, then gives Crazy Charlie a quick double look at his super red eyes. Brad leans back, taking in the lush greenery and oceanside views as they speed along the road towards their destination. An old-school rock song just ends.

"Brad!" CC shouts out and snaps Brad from his daydream. "Open the glove box!" CC orders. "Take that too. Just in case," he demands while pointing to the huge bone handled bowie knife.

"Wow! Thanks CC," Brad obliges with more of a personal note. Brad pulls the knife from the sheath and examines it for a moment before strategically placing it into his knapsack alongside his other arsenal. CC takes a big puff, then slips in another rocking CD. Many more miles and many more songs pass by.

Brad opens the map and runs his finger along the coastline, then looks out the window. "We are about three-quarters of the way!" CC suddenly shouts out in a deep, gravelly voice.

"Oh, thanks!" Brad says as he props himself up in the seat and looks from side to side. "Yeah, I was wondering how much further it was," he explains with gratitude. CC takes a puff and cranks up the music. "Don't Let the Devil Bring You Down" rocks them much closer to their destination than they realize. CC rocks out to the beat with one-handed drumming on the dashboard.

"Oh, holy shit. We're here already!" Crazy Charlie announces while looking down at the malfunctioning odometer. He cranks the boat over to the side of the road and comes in for a smooth, dusty landing. "This is as far as I can take you, I can't go down that road!" Charlie explains while pointing, seemingly with regret. The music suddenly stops as CC turns off the engine. A dead silence enters the midday heat as they both exit the car simultaneously.

"It's going to be a warm one," CC expresses as he pulls both hands over his sweaty face. "Let me see that map," CC demands, unintentionally snatching it from Brad's hands. CC quickly unfolds it out over the hood of the car. "Here's the fork in the road. Right here!" CC points out while they both hover over the map. "And here's approximately where the cops found the jeep," CC explains with the movement of his finger.

Brad studies the map for a moment, then quickly folds it up and stuffs it into his shirt pocket.

"Good luck, kid!" CC growls sincerely as he reaches out and shakes Brad's hand.

"Thank you, Charlie. You're not so crazy!" Brand conveys kindly while firmly shaking CC's hand.

"Well, don't tell anybody, kid," CC jokes back while squinting from the beating sun. "Oh, wait. One other thing!" CC mentions as he walks around and opens the back of the station wagon. "Here, take this too!" he says while revealing a cool hat.

"I've got a baseball cap in my bag," Brad explains while slightly holding up the knapsack.

"This is better than any old baseball cap when you're in this kind of heat, kid," CC rumbles out as he frisbee throws the hat to Brad.

"OK, thank you, Charlie!" Brad accepts sincerely and places the hat on his head. "Do I owe you anything for it? Oh, and what about the knife?" Brad asks as he reaches into his pocket.

"They're on the house, kid," CC confirms with ease.

"Thank you, CC. You're a real life saver," Brad conveys emotionally.

"Well, kid, I hope you're right," CC says with all honesty. Brad walks with his sights set on the last location of the jeep.

CC jumps in the car, starts it up, then cranks the wheel over hard to the left. He stomps the peddle to the metal, inducing a rock-spitting, dust-spewing U-turn before quickly barreling back down the oceanside highway towards town with the music cranked past ten. Crazy Charlie's car slowly fades into silence.

Chapter 23

Brad walks a few miles down the so-called forbidden road, stops, and slips off the knapsack. He reaches deep inside, pulls out a bottle of water, opens it, and takes a conservative sip. He unbuttons his shirt pocket and rechecks his approximate location on the map. "Must be around here somewhere," he assures while looking closely down along the left side of the road. He slips the map back in his pocket, buttons it up. then continues down the rough gravel road for a couple more miles.

The blistering heat of the sun forces him to stop once again. He slips off his hat, wipes the sweat from his forehead, drops the knapsack on the ground, pulls out a bottle, takes a sip, then puts the bottle back into the knapsack and continues onward for a few hundred yards.

"Hmm, what's this? Interesting. Yes, this must be the way!" he says, hopeful, then moves in for a closer look. He focuses in on what appears to be a faint, slightly overgrown, ancient-looking roadway. With further observation, he notices some freshly broken foliage, most likely caused by vehicles. "This has got to be the right way!" he confirms with a double-check of the map.

He immediately begins trekking along the vine covered roadway, up the mountainside, and deeper into the jungle. He stops for a quick rest about a mile up. He finishes the first bottle of water, then stuffs the noisy empty back into the knapsack. He continues onward and upward for another couple sweaty miles as the path becomes steeper by the minute. Brad can see a clearing up ahead in the distance and begins moving a little quicker. The hill crests into a wide-open space, exposing a vast array of mountainous, thick-foliaged jungle that seems to go on forever.

"Tire tracks, horse tracks, footprints, OK!" Brad strongly emphasizes out loud. He inspects the area and discovers what appears to be a large patch of dried blood soaked deep into the ground. This instantly alerts his adrenaline. He peers towards the edge of the thickening jungle, then places his knapsack onto the ground and pulls out the large bowie knife that CC gave him and quickly loops his belt through the sheath.

"What the! What is that over there?" he questions out loud. He walks over to the small flicker of light coming from an object partially hidden amongst some sparse foliage, then reaches in and plucks it out. "Holy shit! I think this is Susan's watch! Holy shit, I think it is!" he repeats, then turns around and takes one last look down the long, steep path from which he climbed, staring to the ocean far off in the distance as if he were in some kind of trance.

He places the watch in a small pocket inside the knapsack then grabs a bottle of water, cracks it open, and takes a small, seemingly more rationed drink. He holds the bottle up in front of his face, then looks down. "Five left, including this one. Hmm," he says, then tosses it back in the knapsack. He fires the knapsack over his shoulder then turns and looks down at the blood-stained ground. "Bastards!" he whispers to himself with absolute anger, then pulls the knife from its sheath and begins hiking his way down the steep mountainous terrain into the seemingly infinite jungle. He must slash his own pathway through the thick foliage, occasionally cutting location identifi-cation notches in the palm trees as he consciously searches on.

With every passing moment, the jungle becomes more and more alive with its many animal sounds and has become much thicker with its various trees and lush foliage. Brad finally arrives at the bottom of the first mountainside and stops for a still moment. He stands gazing upward to where he must even-tually travel, and all the while listens intensely for any unusual sounds. He looks down to his watch and realizes that several hours have passed by very quickly. Without hesitation, he snaps into gear and firmly attacks the next mountainous incline. He hikes on hard for five more hours and is now approaching the peak of the second mountain just as the deep, orange-coloured sun slowly descends behind him.

"Definitely time for a break, anyway!" Brad admits as he stops and wipes his forehead with his forearm. He immediately engages in cutting and gathering large bits of foliage, and quickly constructs a thick-walled, almost invisible home away from home to spend the night in. Complete darkness is just arriving, and with it comes a chill in the air as he slowly climbs inside his new home, then quickly covers the entrance with some super large, pre-cut leaves. He slips off the knapsack then reaches in and pulls out his truck keys, revealing a small LED light attached to the keyring. "Wow, this thing is pretty bright!" Brad realizes as he clicks it on. He reaches in the knapsack and pulls out some water and a power bar, then snatches the map from his top pocket for a quick review. While reviewing the map, he unknowingly drifts off into a deep sleep with the light still on.

The crack of dawn begins with a loud squeaking and squawking from a group of blue parrots perched high in the trees. They seem to be chatting it up with a tiny yet vociferous monkey that is only about fifteen feet above Brad's temporary domain. Brad twitches awake from all the chatter with his keys still clutched in his hand and immediately realizes that there are only very faint spots left in his LED flashlight.

"Son of a—I left it on. I can't believe it!" He whisper-shouts, startling the now intrigued monkey into silence. Brad devours the bar and water from the night before, then poofs the doorway open with a kick and crawls out of his green cave. The curious monkey stares in disbelief from above while remaining totally unnoticed.

Sounds from all creatures manifest, echoing throughout the jungle as the sun slowly rises. Brad stretches his arms high above his head, yawns, looks around, then carefully continues down the next mountainside in his desperate search for Susan. Brad has unknowingly gained a curious new friend, who is now gripping a big yellow banana in one hand and seems to be quite adamant about keeping up with him. Hours pass by, then suddenly, a banana magically drops from the sky, landing only a few inches from Brad's feet.

"What the!" Brad says as he bends down and picks up the banana. He looks high into the trees for any signs of a banana tree. "Interesting. No banana trees anywhere around here," he says mysteriously, then quickly peels the banana and devours it. All the while, his only friend remains invisible, swinging high in the trees.

Brad continues his downward trek, heading deeper and deeper into the jungle, and before he knows it, a few hours have passed by like the blink of an eye as he slowly scrambles towards the bottom of the second mountain.

"Finally!" he gasps, then plops his knapsack down onto the jungle floor. He rifles through his knapsack for a much-needed drink of water and a power bar. "Holy shit!" he can't help cursing while observing the next task before him.

Brad instantly realizes that the mountain is much too steep for him to climb in this particular area, and must trek on, to his right, in search of an easier way to continue his upward journey. Another couple of hours fly by. He stumbles onto what appears to be a horse trail, which is easily confirmed when he kneels down to examine the many hoof impressions embedded into the pathway. Brad's adrenaline immediately spikes, jolting him into a sprint up the narrow, uneven pathway. He runs until he can't run anymore and must stop for a moment to catch his breath. He leans over with both hands on his knees, totally exhausted, then looks up to realize that this is a much steeper mountainside than the previous ones he had conquered. He sits down for a moment and takes a rationed sip of water before moving onward and upward. After several more hours of gruelling climbing, another day is about to end. He finally reaches the top of the third mountain, where there is more level ground that spreads far off in the distance. The sun begins its quick departure.

"Shit, right! No more flashlight!" Brad suddenly remembers and instantly prepares his sleeping quarters for another night in the jungle. Totally exhausted from the day, he quickly climbs into his leafed tent, then slowly lays down onto the thick bed of foliage. The rising moon and stars above instantly reveal a missed open slit between two of the large roof leaves. "Where are you, Susan?" he whispers to himself, then slowly rolls over into a fetal position, and closes his eyes.

Brad slowly enters a vivid dream about being back home at the bar the night Susan walked in. Suddenly, he is startled from his dream by a cackling laughter echoing throughout his head, or so he thinks. He immediately crawls out from the tent and jumps to his feet, puzzled and not able to confirm if he was just dreaming or not. He stands motionless and listens intensely for a long moment for the ghostly laughter to begin again. "Must have been dreaming," he says, then crawls back into the tent, and lies back down.

A few moments of dead silence pass, then suddenly, echoing from far off in the distance, comes more of the same cackling laughter he thought he might have heard in his dream.

"Holy shit!" he whispers, then sits up. "Now, that's no dream!" he says, conclusively, now being fuelled by a steady stream of adrenaline pumping through his veins. He instantly jumps to his feet, bashing right through the top of the large, leafed roof, then quickly straps the knapsack over his back.

He rips through the tent wall like it wasn't even there and begins moving swiftly through the thick, slightly moonlit, face-slapping foliage. Adrenaline and sweat pour, accompanied by his audible pounding heart, as he comes closer and closer to the source of the cackling laughter that hauntingly echoes through-out the jungle now more than ever.

"A fire!" Brad whispers as he spots a small dancing flicker of light several hundred yards away. Wide-eyed with sweat pouring down his face, he slowly and cautiously approaches the exact location of the fire in almost complete silence, except for the sound of his pounding heart and his deep breaths of air, which are both accompanied by sheer adrenaline. He crouches down low and slowly approaches the very loud, smoky, fiery, camp. "Are these the guys that took Susan?" he asks with his inner voice. "There must be fifty of them!" he realizes. One of the many heavily armed bandits suddenly throws a huge pile of wood and foliage onto the small fire, creating a massive flame, exposing the murdering, kidnapping bandits' hideout.

"Susan!" Brad whispers, as he invisibly rises for a closer look. Susan sits motionless, leaning forward with her hands tied behind her at the bottom of a palm tree as the intense fire dances upon her.

What appears to be the second-in-command bandit drunkenly approaches Susan. He leans over, grabs her hair, and pulls her head back, revealing her sweet, fire lit, puffy lips, then moves in for an aggressive kiss, accompanied by the fondling of her breasts. Brad must bear this sight from a distance, for he knows he would surely be killed if he acted out right at this very moment. Susan struggles herself away from any lip contact. The huge, scary bandit leader suddenly appears out of nowhere.

Smack! echoes loudly throughout the camp as a powerful backhand from the bandit leader strikes the overindulging second-in-command bandit directly across the side of his head, sending him flying ten feet away from Susan and right onto his back. Blood trickles down the face of the second-in-command bandit.

"Touch her again and I kill you!" the bandit leader promises while pointing directly at him as he lays on the jungle floor holding his ugly, sweaty, injured, mean, vengeful, twitching face. Drunken laughter, along with indecipherable whispers from all the other bandits, echoes across the camp. Totally humiliated, the second-in-command bandit rises to his feet and staggers out of sight.

Brad watches on as the bandits drink themselves into a macho, ranting, who's tougher, who's faster, sporadic shooting contest that continues long into the night. Then, sure enough, one by one, the bandits drop like flies as the crackling fire slowly transforms itself into only slightly glowing embers before disappearing into almost complete darkness.

"It's time!" Brad faintly whispers to himself, then slowly removes his knife from its sheath. He cautiously inches to his feet, then silently and intensely begins to tiptoe into the camp with the knife in one hand and the knapsack strapped on his back. He must move super slow as he makes his way in, around, and over the maze of many scattered, loudly snoring bandits. "Almost there," is written all over Brad's face as he gently approaches Susan, who appears to be sleeping, and is slumped over and still tied tightly to the bottom of the huge palm tree, wearing her straw hat cinched up tight under her chin.

He kneels down alongside Susan and carefully begins cutting the thick rope. She immediately becomes startled from her sleep as Brad is cutting through the last strand. Susan instantly becomes very frightened and attempts to let out a full-blown scream, but ninety-nine percent of her scream is foiled by Brad's quick hand over her mouth.

"I'm here to help, don't say a word," he whispers from the unrevealing darkness, straight into her ear. He slowly removes his hand from Susan's trembling lips, then firmly takes her hand and helps her up as they simultaneously rise to their feet.

Without a word, they cautiously sneak out of the bandits' camp. A few of the bandits' horses become spooked as Brad and Susan slip their way through the intricate maze of bodies. The noise from the horses instantly wakes one bandit who is only a few bodies over from where they are standing. The bandit struggles a bit, but eventually sits up and looks around. Brad and Susan instantly freeze in their tracks and remain invisible enough in the darkness not to be seen. The bandit mumbles something in Spanish, then plops back down, quickly falling back into a loud snoring sleep. All the while, Brad keeps a firm grip on Susan's hand, as if it extended his own arm.

The escape exit proves much more difficult than the entry now that the two of them are clenched together in total darkness, stepping over and bending around the many sprawled-out, snoring bandits. They are almost in the clear when Susan accidentally steps on a bandit's arm and immediately alerts him to his knees. The bandit shouts loudly, firing his gun into the air, and wakes the entire intoxicated camp.

"Run!" Brad couldn't shout any louder. Susan immediately lets out a piercing screech as she is tugged swiftly by Brad's adrenaline-motivated desire for them to escape this very real nightmare.

Bang! Bang! Bang!

The bullets fly from all directions towards the outskirts of the camp. The bandits drunkenly mount their horses and continue firing multiple bullets into the dark of night.

"Faster!" Brad shouts with undeniable conviction. Susan is having a hard time keeping up. The bandits are closing in fast. Bullets whizz by their heads while the rumbling hooves of the bandits' horses become ever so increasingly present. Susan cannot keep up with Brad's sprinting pace. She is now being dragged along the jungle floor at full speed by Brad's determined-to-live strength.

Bang! Bang! Bang!

Bullets riddle the foliage as the horses close in on Susan's heels.

The cloud covered moon ensures the state of almost total darkness, which seems to be the only thing saving them from the many random bullets and sure death. Susan's adrenaline suddenly kicks in as she twists her dragged body around and gets back to her sprinting feet. They run faster and harder, smashing through the dense foliage, miraculously avoiding the seemingly endless gunfire. The bandits and their horses are unknowingly right on their heels and are about to trample both of them down. Brad blindly changes their sprinting direction and avoids being trampled under the horses' hooves.

Suddenly, the jungle floor completely disappears from under his feet and Brad is going over a small cliff with Susan still attached.

Thud! Crack! Thud! sounds as they hit the jungle floor, then uncontrollably roll right into a small, spring-loaded, foliage-covered cave.

The blood thirsty bandits are totally unaware of Brad and Susan's sudden invisible drop off and continue on while drunken voices scream out and bullets continue to fly in all directions throughout the darkness. A few straggling, torch-carrying bandits catch up and illuminate the surrounding area. The bandit leader gruffly orders the torch carriers to spread out and search in different directions. Brad and Susan lay side by side in total darkness, petrified as the crazed horse-riding bandits slowly dissipate off into the thick, dark jungle, until there is finally a peaceful silence in the air.

A warm gust of wind stirs up and slowly disperses the thick layer of cloud that once surrounded the moon. Susan lays closest to the opening of the foliage-scattered cave and witnesses the beautiful luminous transformation.

"Cancun moon," she whispers, embracing the moment as moonbeams softly trickle through the cracks in the foliage.

"What's that?" Brad whispers faintly.

"Oh, nothing!" Susan answers back with a sadness in her voice, then slowly turns her head around, only to find her symbolic Cancun moon illuminating Brad's unforgotten face.

"Brad!" Susan whisper-shouts, wide-eyed in disbelief, then immediately wraps her arms around him and begins crying. "I can't believe you found me! I didn't know it was you! I thought you were the police!" she cries on.

"Shh. They might hear us," he whispers compassionately. "I'm here now, we're going to be OK, I promise," he pleads softly while gently holding her cute, dusty face in his hands and looking right into her beautiful, teary eyes.

"Thank you!" is all Susan can say before clinging tighter to Brad's body.

"Anytime," Brad whispers back. The wind swishes by and covers the moon once again. They lay peacefully, in total darkness, then drift off into a deep sleep.

Squawk, squawk, sounds an overhead parrot.

Brad opens his eyes and ears to the already hot, sunny, loud, misty jungle morning. A moment later, Susan wakes startled. "Ah," she shrieks, then sits up a bit.

"Good morning," Brad whispers.

"Thank God!" she says. "I wasn't dreaming. I forgot where I was for a second!" She then gives Brad a strong, gripping hug. "Thank you again!" she pleads before letting up on her grip.

Brad rifles around in his surprisingly soaked knapsack. "Oh, no, I wondered what that crack was when we fell down here!"

"What happened?" Susan asks, seemingly more alert.

"Looks like two of our water bottle lids popped off and one of the arrows is snapped right in half." He regretfully removes the broken arrow from the crossbow.

"Arrows? What is that thing?" Susan asks with a puzzled look while reaching out to touch it.

"Just a little insurance a new friend of mine gave us! It's a mini crossbow," Brad says, obviously quite disappointed with its condition, along with the diminished water supply. "Well, at least we still have two shots left, and two waters," he concludes while inspecting the wet-bottomed knapsack. He holds up the two dripping water bottles in mid-air and quickly realizes that there is still an ample trickle of water left in each to start their day. "Thank God!" he says and hands one of the bottles to Susan. He reaches into the knapsack, pulls out a couple of power bars, and passes her one.

"Thank you, I'm literally starving!" she expresses while holding her empty stomach.

"Oh, I have something else for you too," Brad says mysteriously while reaching into the small pocket inside the knapsack.

"What?" Susan asks, quite intrigued.

Brad casually pulls her diver's watch from the knapsack pocket and proceeds to strap it onto her wrist.

"Perfect fit!" he confirms by the outline on her white skin where the watch used to be before it was lost on that horrible day.

Susan sits there, wide-eyed in disbelief, with her mouth hanging wide open.

"Oh my God! I can't believe it!" she cries. "Thank you so much! This watch means the world to me!" she admits, along with a touch of sadness in her voice.

"Anytime!" Brad says promisingly. "Come on, let's eat! We've got to get moving right away," Brad stresses and takes a bite from his bar, followed by a cool sip of water. Susan inhales her bar and finishes the rest of her water.

"That should get us back on our feet," Brad insists, then begins quietly gathering everything up and stuffs it back in the knapsack. He effortlessly snaps the foliage back with his foot, making it easy for them to crawl out from their secret, and very fortunate, hideout. As they rise to their feet, they instantly feel and see the aftermath from last night's near-death escape, all over their tattered bodies.

"Ow," Susan whimpers as the morning sun reveals her cut, swollen elbow, along with many scrapes and bruises that she has up and down both legs. Brad slowly looks her over while underplaying the many cuts and scrapes that are slightly hidden from the sweaty dust, covering her entire body.

"It doesn't look too bad," Brad examines. Susan suddenly notices his banged-up condition as well. "What about you? Are you OK?" she asks while examining him from head to toe.

"I'm good, I think," Brad underplays, while dusting himself off. "We've got to get moving before those crazy bandits head back this way." Brad quickly straps the knapsack over his shoulder and pulls the knife from its sheath. "We also have to remember to be super, super quiet," he cautions with a subtle hand gesture, all the while scanning the area for the real possibility of any stray bandits that may have overheard their immediate conversation and may be upon them right at this very moment. Susan nods in silence.

"OK, let's go this way," Brad directs confidently while pointing towards an off-beaten track. As the sun rises, the thick, hot jungle becomes more alive by the minute with all its various tropical animal sounds. Brad and Susan quickly and silently create their own unidentifiable pathway along the top ridge, then slowly and cautiously make their way down the steep mountainside.

Hours of hiking finally take them near the bottom of the first mountain. "Let's hold up for a minute and take a break," Brad says as he crouches and sits down. Susan immediately sits across from him.

"Perfect timing," she admits.

"I cut markers on some trees to help find our way back but I'm pretty sure we're way off the pathway I came in on," Brad quietly clarifies as he wipes the sweat from his forehead and looks around. He reaches in his knapsack, pulls out one of the two slight rations of water they have left, and hands it to Susan. "Just a sip. There's not much left," he suggests politely.

"OK," she says softly and takes a conservative sip. Suddenly, a banana falls from the sky and lands right between them. "What the!" Susan says, quickly looking up.

"Funny, I had the exact same reaction when it happened to me," Brad admits with his addictive smile, then looks to the thick greenery above for any sign of a banana tree. "Let's just say they're bananas from heaven," he calculates with a snicker, then immediately peels the banana down and hands half off to Susan.

"Wow! You're not kidding!" she agrees with her dusty-faced smile, then devourers the heavenly banana.

"Shh, listen," Brad insists while displaying one finger on his mouth. "I think I can hear them over that way!" He points towards the many bandits scouring the area. Susan instantly switches from a smiling face to a terrified face as they crouch down a bit further onto the jungle floor. They huddle in silence while both their hearts beat loudly, but thankfully not loud enough for anyone else to hear. The second-in-command bandit and a few of his crazed companions are moving around extremely close to where Brad and Susan are situated.

Brad moves quickly in silence with an instant adrenalin rush, pulling Susan down into thicker foliage with him. The second-in-command bandit and his horse suddenly stop with a jerk of the reins. The bandit looks around in suspense, but only for a moment, then pulls out an old-school, self-rolled cigar from his vest pocket, strikes a wooden match on the saddle, then calmly cups his hands and lights it. A silent pause as smoke billows from his first exhalation.

Suddenly, out of nowhere comes a loud, angry stream of Spanish words. "I know you are out here somewhere, gringo," echoes quaveringly throughout the jungle from the mouth of the scariest, most mean-faced bandit of them all: The bandit leader. "I get you, gringo!" he continues to threaten.

That instantly prompts the second-in-command and his posse to spur their horses forward and onward. "I get you! I promise, gringo!" concludes the last of the faint threatening echoes, as the scary, horse-riding, foliage-slashing bandits finally disappear into the hot, hazy jungle.

"That was way too close for comfort," Brad quietly confesses as he rises to his feet, pulling Susan up with him. "Come on!" he says enthusiastically as he takes her by the hand and begins carefully weaving through the large, leafed foliage towards a hopefully safe destination.

"It must be noon already," Brad says as he stops and looks down at his watch. "Yes, pretty close," he confirms while looking up through a small opening in the tops of the thick jungle.

Just like magic, the blazing rays of the noon sun sift down through the opening and shine directly upon them.

"Wow! It's like someone is watching over us," Susan says, amazed by the sight.

"Yeah, you could be right about that," Brad says with hope and sincerity. "How are you doing? Are you hanging in there?" Brad asks as he reaches into his knapsack and pulls out some water and hands it off to Susan. "We only have one bottle left after this one," Brad confirms while looking into his knapsack.

"I'm good for now," Susan conservatively holds back from drinking any water and hands the bottle back to Brad.

"You're sure?" he asks as he holds the bottle up in front of her.

"Oh, yes, I'm sure," Susan says softly. The magic moment slowly fades from above as the sun repositions itself and urges them to do the same. Several hours of intense hiking passes by.

"We better stop right here," Brad decides while looking around, then immediately begins his race with darkness. He pulls out his knife and begins cutting and gathering large leaves from around the area, then strategically places them down on the jungle floor to prepare a bed. He pulls out the partially filled bottle of water from the knapsack and passes it off to Susan. She takes a small sip and hands it back to Brad. He obliges with a small sip, then passes it back to her. "Here, take another," Brad insists with a short gasp. Susan easily takes another swig, then quickly hands it back to Brad, who does the same. Moments later, they lay close together on their fresh, spongy-leafed bed, clearly exhausted from the day's excursions, and without even a whisper, they abruptly fall into a deep sleep. Morning comes quickly with its loud, awakening jungle sounds, and they slowly rise to their feet.

"Good morning," Susan greets while stretching her arms high above her head.

"Good morning to you too," Brad says kindly. "We were out like a light last night." He reaches into his knapsack and pulls out the one and only full bottle of water that is left, along with a couple power bars.

"We're a bit off course now, I'd say!" He sips the water and glances far off in the direction they really need to be travelling. "It was the only way we were ever going to lose those maniacs!

But we've got to go that way." He points, quietly reconfirming definitively, seriousness etched across his brow.

"Well, thanks to you we've made it this far," Susan says softly with a humbling smile, breaking the air with a positive note.

"Well, Susan, I wouldn't have it any other way," Brad says back as he hands her the water and a power bar.

Suddenly, the shocking snort of a horse echoes from nearby.

"Shit! The bandits must have coincidentally set up camp only about fifty feet from us," Brad says. "Shh!" he demands with one finger to his lips as he crouches and pulls Susan down with him. "How the heck, did they find us? They must have doubled back!" Brad quickly realizes, restraining from the use of any harsh vocabulary. "Let's get out of here! Now!" he says with immediate intent. "Stay as low as possible," he gently pleads while glancing back and forth to her, then back to the bandits' suspected location.

This latest dart to escape absolute death takes them through several hours of fresh, self-made, somewhat undetectable pathways into a thicker, tunnel-like jungle. All the while, not a word is spoken to avoid the possibility of being overheard by one or more the wild dog-style bandits.

"Let's rest up here a bit," Brad finally breaks the silence.

"Phew." Susan gestures with a gasp of breath. "It's so hot! Already!" she stresses as she leans into a palm tree and wipes the sweat from her eyebrow with the back of her hand.

"Yeah, a little muggy too, I'd say. That's for sure," Brad agrees, sounding a little dry as he flips the knapsack from his sweat-drenched shoulder onto the ground, then reaches in and pulls out the remaining bottle of water that is less than half full. He holds it up in front of them.

"Is this where you say I've got some good news and some bad news?" Susan jokes with a nervous smirk on her face.

"Well," is all Brad can say as he hands her the bottle. "Drink half, we're going to need it today," he estimates.

"You sure I should?" she asks, double checking.

"Yes, drink, oh and here," Brad reconfirms as he hands her a power bar as well. "We still have at least a dozen of those," Brad assures as Susan gently leans her head back, sipping the water.

"Oh, look, a coconut!" she says, while pointing to the top of a palm tree, then immediately begins choking from the water that apparently went down the wrong way, which was totally induced from the sheer sudden excitement of seeing the real-life coconut.

"I see that. Good eye!" Brad admires. "You OK?" He pats his hand on her back.

"Oh, yeah, I'm fine now," she admits, seemingly a little embarrassed. Brad quickly scurries up to the top of the palm tree.

"Incoming!" he whisper-shouts a second before he safely drops the freshly picked coconut.

He slowly slides back down the rigid palm tree and instantly goes to work on the coconut with his knife.

"Wow!" Susan whisper-shouts as this new experience unfolds before her. Brad exposes the little brown hairy coconut, then strategically pokes holes in the top and immediately taste tests the milk inside.

"Mmm, very good!" He hands it to Susan.

"Mmm. Yes, it is good!" she agrees then hands it back to Brad. "So, how did you learn how to do this?" she asks, impressed.

"Saw it in a movie once," Brad sarcastically states with a grin.

"Oh, what movie?" Susan asks innocently, not realizing his intent to humour her.

"Just kidding," Brad quickly admits. "I saw it done a few years ago while I was in Maui." They both laugh while looking closely at one another. Brad takes another sip, then hands it back to Susan. "Finish her off!" he insists.

Susan wastes no time polishing off the remaining coconut milk. "It's empty now." She reveals softly, along with a slight gasp of breath before passing it back to Brad. He instantly flips his knife around in mid-air, then strikes the hairy coconut with the butt of his knife, breaking the nut into a few large, sharp-edged pieces. He quickly flips the knife back around and peels out a small slab of fresh coconut meat, then hands it to Susan.

"Amazing," she says after her first bite.

Brad peels out a small piece for himself and slips it in his mouth. "Nice flavour, I'm so glad you saw this old coconut up in that tree, it will come in handy." He packs the rest into the knapsack.

Squawk, squawk, squawk! Suddenly alarms one of the many parrots scattered throughout the jungle.

"OH, OH, let's go!" Brad says while peering all around, fearing the parrot squawks are a warning that someone may be approaching. "They might have heard me breaking the coconut," he suddenly realizes, then takes Susan's hand and begins quietly scurrying through the jungle, away from any imminent danger.

Hours of hiking in the intense heat, along with the steep upward slope of the mountainside, take a gruelling toll on both of them. They finally collapse dead in their tracks for a well-deserved rest.

"If you see any more coconuts, let me know, will you," Brad says, with a touch of reality and sarcasm mixed tightly together. "We could definitely use a little drink right about now!" He is a little dry-mouthed and slightly heat stressed.

Susan immediately looks up to the treetops for any signs of another refreshing coconut. "Don't see any yet," she says, disappointed. "I am so thirsty right now!" she whines unintentionally, then takes a seat on some foliage.

"Here, let's eat some more of this coconut, it may help quench our thirst," Brad says as he lowers to his knees and pulls a piece of the broken shell from the knapsack and quickly chips out a couple small pieces of the coconut meat. He places some coconut right into Susan's mouth, then into his own. They look closely at one another in a long moment of silence while savouring the coconut.

The water shortage has definitely put a scare into them both. "Let's look around for any palm trees, there's bound to be a coconut on one of them," Brad encourages with positivity. They rise to their feet, full of hope, and exhaustedly engage themselves in a serious search for any palm trees in the immediate area. They slowly become separated from each other in their desperate search for another delicious, watery coconut, but remain in perfect view of one another.

"Ah," Susan grunts loudly, then disappears right before Brad's extremely shocked eyes. He rushes as fast as he can towards the area where Susan was just standing, and instantly realizes that she has stepped over the edge of a somewhat invisible and very steep, foliage-covered cliff that veers down into an abyss to who knows where.

Chapter 24

B rad immediately begins strategically sliding his way down the steep mountainside in a frantic search for Susan. All the while, Susan is twisting and turning and tumbling down faster and faster through the thick mountainside. Suddenly, she becomes completely airborne and screams out before plunging deep into the unsuspected, cool, crystal blue water below. Brad faintly hears her scream and a wide-eyed look of fear comes over his face as he frantically continues down the steep incline. Susan quickly shoots to the surface of the water, gasping in a much-needed breath of air, then becomes instantly mesmerized, while gazing up at the incredible white waterfall crashing down about a hundred feet from where she treads water. She grabs her hat and quickly swims for shore, then takes a seat on the edge. She looks way up the mountainside where she had just fallen from and sobs. The coolness of the water soothes the minor scrapes and scratches she has all over her entire body from the fall.

"Susan!" Brad calls out repeatedly, but she cannot hear him over the white noise of the totally dreamlike waterfall. The mountainside has become too steep and the foliage too weak to support Brad's weight, but he must continue on.

Snap!

The foliage Brad is grasping breaks, sending him free-falling one hundred feet down towards the unsuspected safety net of water below. "Ah," he wails as he is falling.

Splash!

Susan instantly dives back into the water and swims toward the bubbling splash area. Brad suddenly shoots up past the surface of the water, gasping in some air, seemingly unscathed from his fall.

"You're OK!" he confirms with great happiness in his voice while still grasping the piece of foliage that freed him to fall in one hand and his soaked straw hat in the other.

"You are too!" Susan expresses along with some happy tears. They hug each other in the water for a moment, then slowly make their way to shore.

"Wow! Look at this place!" Brad says with amazement while looking up and down at the waterfall. "Holy shit! This is fresh water!" he confirms with a double-take taste test. He quickly unstraps the totally soaked knapsack from his back and begins rinsing and refilling the crumpled, empty water bottles. He immediately hands Susan one of the newly filled water bottles and without hesitation, she quickly guzzles it down.

"Ah," she emphasizes with instant relief.

Brad easily drinks two bottles down, then refills them again. "Unreal, this place is right out of a movie. What are the chances?"

"Of what?" Susan asks.

"A few moments ago, we needed water so bad, we were nearing the desperate mark, and now, look!" he concludes, amazed by their new, incredible, everlasting water supply. Brad suddenly realizes Susan has way more scrapes and scratches scattered from head to toe. "Are you hurt bad anywhere?" He gently spins her body around.

"A little stiff on my left shoulder, but that's about it!" She emphasizes with a turn of her head and body movement. "Are you OK?" she probes sweetly.

"Well, we must have hit the same tree on the way down because I've got the same sore left shoulder!" Brad confirms jokingly while stretching it out. He suddenly displays a serious look on his face and Susan notices instantly.

"What happened?" She asks, holding her hands to her chest.

"Nothing. Yet. But I can't help wonder if anyone heard our little adventure falls and screams echoing throughout the jungle." Chris fearfully peers all around the top edges of their new nestled sanctuary. "Quick, let's get out of sight, we'll go over there. By the waterfall!" He indicates the spot. "It's going to be dark very soon anyway. So we better set up camp for the night."

He guides them through thick foliage, towards the waterfall. "Out of sight, out of mind," Brad jokes, but with serious intent, as he slips off his knapsack, places it down on the jungle floor, and marks their spot for the night.

The adrenaline still flows from their fall. They work fast, setting up camp about thirty feet from the waterfall, inside the most secluded, dense foliage area, ensuring their invisibility. The orange sky dissolves into darkness much quicker than normal down in their little paradise.

"It's a little chillier out tonight," Susan notices with a slight shiver.

"Yeah, you're right, it is much cooler down here," Brad agrees. "Probably because our clothes are damp and we're so close to the water. Not that we're complaining about the water being there or anything," he adds in sarcastically.

Susan smiles along, agreeing with his humour.

"I'll light us a little fire, but I sure hope those bandits won't be able to see it way down here." He hesitantly fears that truth, but they must get warmed up. "We've got about forty-five minutes before we're in total darkness," he calculates. "Come on, let's collect some dry foliage so we can get that fire going, ASAP and try to dry out a bit before it gets any chillier."

It isn't long before they have a small, warm, crackling fire. They sit close together around the fire and share a piece of coconut, a piece of bar, and a couple bottles of water.

"I still can't believe all this is happening. It's like I'm in a dream, or a movie, or something!" she admits in a tone of disbelief, along with an added touch of sadness in her voice as she gets a flashback of Chris getting shot. Susan's eyes fill with tears but go unnoticed.

"I know. It's definitely something," Brad conveys compassionately. "Don't worry, Susan, I'll get us both out of this nightmare if it's the last thing I do," He strongly reassures, then tightly wraps his arm around her. White noise from the waterfall, along with the warming fire, radiates a soothing, comforting atmosphere, causing them to become very sleepy. They sit holding one another as the fire dries their tattered clothes. They lay down on their soft leafy bed, holding each other close, and quickly slip into a deep sleep as the fire dwindles into total darkness.

Crackle, crackle, echoes above the sound of the waterfall just before the break of dawn.

The sound instantly wakes Brad. He sits up and peers all around into the quickly dissolving darkness.

"What is it?" Susan whispers and sits up alongside him.

"Not sure," Brad whispers back, with a slight tremble in his voice. He slowly slips his knife from its sheath, then reaches over and gently pulls the crossbow out of the knapsack. "Stay down!" he whispers while gesturing with the wave of his knife. He slowly and silently rises to his feet to further investigate.

Crackle! Frightfully sounds again.

Brad instantly ducks down behind some large foliage, then gently moves a leaf with the tip of his knife. He tries to peek between the foliage in the direction the sound just came from, but see's nothing out of the ordinary.

Crackle, sounds again. Suddenly, a white-tailed deer springs six feet into mid-air.

"Ah," Brad shouts out, instantly positioning himself into a fierce fighting stance. The deer takes off running and disappears into the dense foliage. Brad eases up on his fighting stance, then slips the knife back into its sheath. All the excitement seems to have triggered the jungle's awakening. Susan lies petrified, unsure about the earie crackling sounds.

"It's all good, it was only a deer," Brad assures as he approaches Susan, then quickly stuffs the crossbow back into the knapsack. She jumps up and squeezes Brad tightly. The squawking jungle intensifies as the sunlight rapidly appears.

"Look!" Brad points to the water's edge. "All those different animals are drinking the fresh water. It must be the only fresh water for miles," he calculates with dead accuracy.

"Wow!" Susan emphasizes with disbelief as they both watch.

"Time for a long-awaited morning shower under that waterfall," Brad coaxingly invites, while moving towards the water's edge. He steps behind some foliage and privately slips off all of his freshly washed and dried clothes, then enters the cool morning water with a splash and quickly swims toward the waterfall.

Susan unintentionally zooms in on his tight butt while he stands naked under the soul-cleansing waterfall. "Come on!"

Brad gestures with the waving of his hand while his nakedness is shrouded by the white water splashing over his body.

Susan appears hesitant as her genuine shyness kicks in while nearing the water's edge. "Turn around!" she shouts out, motioning with a hand gesture and smiling nervously.

Brad cannot hear her over the waterfall but is prompted by her hand signals and respectfully turns around. She quickly strips off her clothes and cautiously makes her way over to the waterfall.

"Holy, this is amazing," she can't deny. "Oh, don't turn around!" she stresses strongly out of complete and utter shyness while attempting to cover up. Brad obliges without a flinch as she moves in close behind him and slowly immerses herself into the shower of fresh water. "This is more than just a shower, it's a massage!" She shouts while leaning forward, letting the water pound down onto her naked body.

"Love it!" Brad agrees while doing the same. They stand back-to-back as the glistening, sunlit water pours down upon them, rejuvenating their tattered bodies. "Now, this is definitely out of a movie," Brad suggests with enthusiasm.

"Amazing feeling," Susan says, forgetting that she is completely naked. They simultaneously turn to one another. Brad quickly and romantically pulls her in tightly against his ripped body. They gaze into each other's eyes, but only for a moment, then suddenly begin a long-awaited, reciprocated first kiss. The magical, glistening, cool water pours over them in slow motion, but fails to soothe their simmering, naked bodies.

Suddenly, a *Roar!* echoes from across the other side of the water.

Holy shit. Look!" Brad shouts, while pointing to a huge black jaguar pacing off in the distance. "Quick, go back behind the waterfall!" Brad naturally directs them to safety. They become invisible as they step in behind the wall of water.

"Hey, Brad. Look!" Susan shouts while pointing to a small opening in the rock face.

"What the? Wow! Good eye!" Brad compliments while examining what appears to be a cave opening leading into a tunnel and maybe even a way up and out.

"It's cold under here," Susan says while mostly covering herself. Brad does a quick double-take at Susan's nakedness.

"Yeah, it's definitely cooler under here, that's for sure," he admits without going into much detail. "We've got to get our stuff and get the heck out of here before we become the pussy cat's breakfast," Brad says with a little realistic humour thrown in. He pokes his head out through the waterfall and notices the jaguar is already preoccupied with a white-tailed deer breakfast.

"OK, let's go get our stuff," Brad boldly suggests. "We're safe until lunch, by the looks of it," he reveals calmly while pointing out the situation to Susan.

"Yuck!" is all she can say as they nervously swim back to shore. They gather all their belongings, cramming mostly everything into Brad's knapsack. He holds the knapsack and their hats above the water as they make their way back towards the waterfall. They slip through to the other side of the waterfall.

Brad maintains the knapsack's dryness, as is revealed when he hands Susan all of her clothing and her hat.

"Still dry. Good," she remarks shyly while standing naked in the shadows. They quickly dress then take a moment to top up all the water bottles. Brad takes Susan by the hand as they shuffle their way through the opening of the tunnel. The damp, darkened tunnel eventually turns into a swift moving stream, starting out in ankle deep water, then swelling up to just above their knees as they slowly incline through a maze of swishing tunnels.

"So much for our dry clothes," Susan chuckles sarcastically.

"It's all good. I'm sure we'll dry out as soon as were out of this dark, damp maze," Brad predicts with confidence while holding Susan's balance from the slippery rocks under foot. Twenty minutes of sloshing up through the various water-filled tunnels pass by.

"Look! Up that way!" Susan points up one of the few choices to travel. "It seems to be a lot brighter up that way!"

"Yeah, you're right. Let's go!" Brad happily agrees with her findings.

The light at the end of the tunnel gets brighter by the second as the incline gets steeper, and quite slippery, with every step, making it extremely difficult to maintain their stability.

"Hold on to my belt!" Brad shouts as they fight against the ever-increasing downward flow of water gushing against their bodies. They struggle relentlessly up through the slippery, rugged, narrowing incline.

"Keep your head down!" Brad shouts meaningfully as the water pours heavily upon them. "Another twenty feet!" he calculates excitedly. It takes all of Brad's strength to pull them up and out the last bit of tunnel.

"Wow, we made it. Phew! We're out of there!" Susan acknowledges, quite relieved. "Oh, look, your hands, they're bleeding!" She notices, seemingly quite concerned as blood drips onto the ground. She gently takes his hands and reveals the many rips and tears across his palms and fingers.

"Yeah, those rocks are pretty sharp. But I wasn't about to let us fall back down through that tunnel over a little trickle of blood, that's for sure!" he explains while tearing a couple strips off his wet t-shirt and wrapping them around the wounds.

"OK. Where the heck are we? Hmm," he directs his question to the jungle while spinning right around. "The sun is there. So, the ocean has to be back that way," he easily calculates while holding his chin and pointing way off in the distance, towards the rugged mountainous terrain. "So glad we came out on this side. Holy, shit!" Brad suddenly realizes the many pockets of false floor foliage all around the vast ravine. "We wouldn't want to have to go around that way and possibly end up down at the bottom of that waterfall again, just in time for Big Spook's lunch," Brad happily realizes while adding in a little humour.

"I'm glad too!" Susan expresses humbly while squinting from the morning sun, then blossoming a beautiful, freshly washed smile. "Someone's been watching over us. That's for sure!" she says, with the grace of God. A moment of silence as the sun reveals a bit more of itself.

"OK, let's go up this way," Brad directs eagerly without hesitation. He takes Susan's hand and pulls her right up in front of him. Brad immediately becomes embarrassed, catching himself staring at Susan's exquisite, tight, little, wet butt as she walks slightly ahead of him. The jungle quickly thickens and Brad must gracefully take back the lead to ensure they are travelling in the correct direction. They beat onward, gently creating their own invisible pathways through the thick jungle that constantly screams sounds straight out of a Tarzan movie.

Seven hours of intense travel has brought them down into a valley, which is unknowingly at the very bottom of the last large span of mountainous terrain, or about five or six miles as the crow flies before hitting oceanfront. "We're way off track from where I came in, probably about five miles. But I know for a fact we're heading right towards the ocean," Brad reassures with confidence while squinting at the sun's position. "I totally lost track of which mountain is which, but we must be really close by now," he predicts with a touch of hope. "Definitely time for a break though," Brad stresses with a deep breath and a sigh.

He slips off the knapsack then kneels down and opens it up. A silent pause as he sorts through the knapsack.

"I'm still alive, thanks to you. You know that, right?" Susan expresses deeply as she moves up close and places both hands on his warm, sweat-drenched head.

"Like I said, I wouldn't have it any other way," he lovingly expresses while looking straight up at her. He pulls out their usual rations and they waste no time digging right in. "Man, these power bars are definitely a lifesaver!" Brad realizes while taking the last bite.

"Yes, they sure are!" Susan can't agree more.

Seconds later, *Thud!* A banana lands right between them, startling Brad to his feet.

"Bananas from heaven again, unreal!" Susan comforts as they both look up, searching for the welcomed culprit. "There! Look, it's a tiny little monkey," she says while pointing directly at its current position high above in a tree.

"So, that's our little buddy, eh," Brad concludes with a smile. "I wonder where he learned to do that with the bananas?" Puzzled, they watch their little friend swing from tree to tree, then disappear into the jungle. "Cool, we'll save this one for later," he suggests, then picks up the banana and slips it into the knapsack.

"Now, where were we? Oh yeah, a little break!" he remembers jokingly. They finally sit down across from one another, sipping away on their own fresh bottle of water, enjoying the peacefulness of the squawking jungle.

"Don't move," Brad mysteriously pleads in a tone of complete seriousness. He slowly pulls the knife from its sheath, then shuffles to his feet. Susan's eyes become as big as saucers. "Get ready to duck, when I say," Brad directs, then raises the knife above his head. "Are you ready?" Brad asks firmly.

"Yes, but what is it?" she whimpers while slowly nodding her head up and down.

"OK, get ready. On three! One, two, duck!" he shouts, then fires the knife right at the huge, long, yellow-headed snake as it slowly slithers down the tree right behind Susan's head. The heavy butt end of the knife miraculously strikes hard, directly onto the snake's wide, yellow head with a tremendous *Crack!*

"Ah!" Susan shrieks, lunging forward onto the ground and quickly scurrying to Brad's feet. The large snake drops to the jungle floor and quickly disappears into the infinite carpet of foliage.

"I absolutely hate snakes. Good thing you didn't tell me what it was!" Susan quaveringly emphasizes with great relief and rises to her feet while pressing tight against his body.

"I'm not a big fan of snakes myself!" Brad admits, then kisses her on the forehead. He gently eases from her clutches and quickly pinpoints his shiny knife amongst the thick foliage and slips it back into the sheath. "You ready?" Brad asks, then flips the knapsack on his back.

"I've got to talk to the union about these five-minute breaks," Susan jokes while brushing herself off. They both laugh.

"Well, what I'm a little worried about right now is the fact that those bandits might have overheard us for sure this time. We were pretty loud." A silent pause. "But let's hope not! Anyway, we better get moving," Brad encourages. "Or we can just hang around here until the snake comes back, or the bandits show up again. Whichever come's first!" Brad unintentionally jokes harshly while seriously peering all around for any threatening signs of sound or movement.

"Oh, yeah. Ah. No, thank you!" Susan says. "I never want to see another snake, or any of those bandits, ever again. Trust me on that one!" She immediately begins hiking up the steep mountainside.

"Copy that. I couldn't agree with you more," Brad says with a big smile, then catches up behind her. He gently takes her hand and guides them up the steep mountainside.

Chapter 25

Meanwhile, far off in the distance, a few of the bandits think they have just faintly overheard Susan's scream echoing throughout the jungle. The bandits immediately shout out their findings across the camp to catch the attention of the bandit leader, all the while pointing in the direction they think the scream might have come from. The bandit leader immediately rises to his feet and orders everyone to mount their horses and follow him in pursuit of the scream.

Brad and Susan are totally unaware that the bandits are now in hot pursuit of them as they peacefully trek up the steep mountainside.

After several minutes of intense riding and slashing out their own trails through the thick foliage, the bandit leader suddenly raises his arm. "Stop!" he grumbles loudly with force. The gang of bandits simultaneously pull back hard on their horses' reins as they all stutter to a complete stop at the edge of a mountainous ridge.

The bandit leader slowly and intensely looks from side to side, then suddenly spurs his horse back into action in search of the quickest route down the treacherous mountainside, and the others quickly follow in a cluster. The bandits ride hard along the top of the vast ridge, becoming frustrated while searching for a pathway the horses can safely negotiate down the steep, crumbling rock face.

Brad and Susan are more than halfway up the side of the mountain where the foliage is becoming quite sparse.

"OK, time for that banana and a drink," he stresses and plops the knapsack down. He pulls out the banana and some water. They quickly devour the banana and indulge themselves in a long, healthy swig. Brad's sharp eye suddenly catches some movement far and high across the valley.

"Holy shit!" he shouts and instantly rises to his feet.

"What?" Susan shouts back in terror.

"Look! Over that way!" Brad points to the many horse-riding bandits way off in the distance.

"Can they see us from there?" Susan asks frantically.

"Well, if we can see them, there's a good chance they might have seen us too. We better get going, right now!" Brad firmly grabs a hold of Susan's hand and begins racing up the mountain.

"Ay caramba!" one bandit suddenly shouts out while pointing towards the ant-sized movement of Brad and Susan as they scurry up the sparse, rock-faced mountainside. The main bandit instantly raises his arm and they all reef on their horses' reins, stopping dead in their tracks. The main bandit squints from the blazing, blinding sun while glaring straight across the valley in search of the reported movement.

"There! There!" one keen-eyed bandit alerts while pointing and shouting. The bandit leader finally zeros in on their movement, then abruptly and violently spurs his horse to continue down the immediate steep incline. The horses tiptoe their way down the sharp crumbling ridge while the bandits lean way back in their saddles to keep from tumbling headfirst off their horses.

Brad and Susan must stop to catch their breath about three-quarters of the way up the mountainside. They both look back across the valley. Susan unwillingly witnesses the bandits travelling down the adjacent mountain far off in the distance and right in their direction.

"Oh no, I think they see us!" she regretfully informs with a touch of fear in her voice while pointing directly at the bandits' current location. Brad quickly zeros in on the horse-riding bandits.

"You're right! Let's move. Come on!" Brad can't stress enough as he suddenly jerks Susan's entire body upward.

"Ah!" Susan shrieks piercingly as they must climb much harder and faster than ever before.

"It's like we're in a fishbowl way up here," Brad realizes as they fight their way uphill over the sparse rockface. The bandits have now become completely invisible and have quickly slashed their way down through the thickly foliaged mountainside, just past the halfway mark.

Vigorous, intense, nonstop climbing has finally brought Brad and Susan about a hundred yards from the top of the mountain. Winded and dry-mouthed, they both must stop to catch their breath. Brad quickly pulls out a bottle of water and hands it off to Susan. She immediately indulges in a gasping, much-needed drink before handing it back to Brad.

"Holy shit!" Brad curses just as he lowers his head from a bottle-emptying drink.

"What!" Susan shrieks in an anxious tone.

"Don't look now. Holy shit!" he continues in a sharp, derogatory manner while pointing right down to the bottom of the very mountain they are standing on. Susan follows his intense finger that instantly reveals the many bandits appearing from the thick foliage right at the base of the mountain. "Well, they definitely see us now!" Brad uncomfortably informs, as he crushes and drops the empty bottle into the knapsack. He frantically flips the knapsack over his back then firmly takes Susan's hand.

They run for their lives and are now right at the crest of the mountain. They look back down the steep mountainside when they hear some faint yet very aggressive shouting coming from the many horse-riding bandits, who are now more than a third of the way up the mountain and are gaining on them quickly.

"Run, Susan, run!" Brad pleads as he pulls her along at top speed. Several hundred yards of sprinting across the rugged mountaintop takes them right to the edge of an incredibly steep cliff. "There it is! The ocean!" Brad screams out.

"Holy, how do we get down this crazy mountain?" Susan shouts in desperation.

"I know, I was just thinking the same thing," Brad admits with a serious look on his face. "Come on, this way!" he demands with an unintentional forceful tug on her hand as they quickly travel toward a more secluded, foliaged area.

"Can't see them yet," Brad confirms while peering far across the top of the flat, sparsely covered, foliaged ridge.

"Thank God!" she says, fearing the worst as she tries her hardest to keep up with Brad's powerful sprint while the horse-mounted bandits slowly inch their way to the top of the mountain.

Brad and Susan sprint a hundred yards down the ridge into a more densely foliaged area.

"Ahh!" Susan suddenly screams out loud as she twists her ankle and now must come to a complete stop.

"Here, put your arm around me," Brad quickly remedies, and they continue to travel a little further.

"Oh, no, there they are!" Susan literally cries out as the bandits appear over the top of the ridge, several hundred yards away.

"Look, what's that up there?" Brad questions, totally baffled by what he sees tangled up in the foliage. He gently lowers

Susan's arm from around his shoulder and races in for a closer look. "It's a hang glider!" He draws the knife from its sheath.

"What? A hang glider?" Susan repeats with concern.

Brad literally springs up the sturdy foliage and wastes no time cutting the intricately intertwined rope-like branches away from the seemingly Godsent two-seater hang glider. He drops the glider safely to the ground then immediately jumps down after it. He races towards Susan, carrying the glider above his head, then crashes it down right beside her.

"What? I can't!" she cries out.

"You must! We have no other choice! You mentioned, God help us! Well, this is God helping us! Trust me," he pleads calmly as the bandits rapidly close in. Brad immediately fastens Susan into the glider, then straps himself alongside of her while many bullets ricochet intensely all around them.

"Lift your feet!" he screams, and Susan instantly raises her legs. Brad begins running at top speed towards the edge of the cliff. The quickness of Brad's feet and the warm breeze makes the weight of the glider almost effortless as they race away from the rampaging bandits, and their rapid gun fire.

Ting, Ting, sounds out like a chime as bullets hit the glider's tarnished aluminum frame, slightly damaging it.

The bandits are now only sixty feet away, still firing their guns and screaming like maniacs.

"Ahh," Brad moans as he is grazed in the lower leg by a bullet. He reaches behind his head, pulls out the mini crossbow, releases the safety, and aimlessly fires into the cluster of crazed bandits.

The arrow cuts through the hot jungle air like a lightning bolt and miraculously strikes the bandit leader right in the middle of his throat, sending him plummeting to the ground in slow motion, creating a big puff of dust around his fat, dead body. Brad locks the safety on the crossbow and quickly passes it off to Susan.

"Ah," Susan screams at the top of her lungs as they leave the edge of the cliff. The glider surges down fast, miraculously regaining altitude under the power of the glider's wings and Brad's relentless determination to keep them afloat. Brad grabs the crossbow from Susan and stuffs it back in the knapsack. The bandits are seemingly stunned as they slowly gather their horses around the bandit leader's dead body. They stare down at their scary boss, who now lays in a pool of blood with an arrow sticking out of his throat upon the dusty ground right before them. All the while, the second-in-command, who is now the leader, smiles deviously in the background.

"Come on!" he abruptly demands with his newly warranted authority.

"No! No! No civilization!" A few bandits grumble while shaking their heads and pointing towards the ocean below. Not one bandit budges to his order, as if challenging their new leader's authority.

"I am in command now!" he screams at the top of his lungs while rapidly punching his chest and forcing his horse to scamper from side to side. "After them! Now! Come on!" he orders relentlessly, but is not taken seriously by any of the other bandits, who are now whispering and arguing amongst themselves about who they think should be the next in command.

Bang! Bang! suddenly echoes deafeningly across the mountaintop as the self-promoted bandit fires his guns high above his head, instantly startling the bandits and their horses. "Good riddance!" he shouts out aggressively as he spurs his horse towards the edge of the cliff. He rides intensely all along the jagged edge, searching for the quickest way down the treacherous mountainside, all the while keeping a keen eye on the everescaping hang glider that carries his prized possession on it.

Brad smoothly navigates the glider, sweeping from left to right, high above the vast mountainous terrain, while the selfproclaimed new leader has just stumbled upon a very dicey, yet potential access point down the mountainside. His horse is reluctant to continue down the steep, crumbling cliff, but is brutally influenced by the sharp, heavy blows from the bandit's spurs. The bandit leans all the way back as the horse strategically places one slipping hoof in front of the other as they inch their way down the steep, rocky mountainside. The bandit regains his posture as the incline lessens. He whips his horse into a gallop with a constant cracking of the reins, all the while keeping a sharp eagle eye fixed on the hang glider, flying high above, far off in the distance.

"We're almost there, Susan! We're almost there," Brad repeats ecstatically.

"I can really smell the ocean air from up here." Susan takes in a deep breath through her nose, then gently exhales out through her mouth. A warm gust of wind suddenly picks up and flutters Susan's silky hair right across Brad's slightly stubbly face, tickling his lips and nose as they magically make their way towards the picturesque ocean below.

All the while, the possessed bandit has been in constant pursuit, raging on invisibly through the vast foliage below, and has unknowingly been slowly gaining on them.

Bang! Bang! Whizz. Whizz. The bullets fly by from out of nowhere, just missing them.

"What the!" Brad nervously shouts while frantically looking to the vast jungle below.

Bang! Bang! Whizz, Ting.

"Ah!" Susan shrieks as one of the bullets ricochets off the glider's frame.

"Let's get out of here!" Brad shouts intensely as he shifts his weight, sending them veering off in a totally different direction. The bandit loses sight of them but still rides on hard while slowly reloading his pistol with the few bullets that are left strapped across his chest.

"I think we're safe now," Brad confirms while looking back. He slowly redirects the glider more towards the beach, which now appears to be just over a half mile away. Suddenly, a huge gust of cool wind stirs up and begins fluttering them around like a rag doll.

"Hold on!" Brad shouts while struggling to maintain their inflight stability.

"Ah!" Susan screams out and closes her eyes.

The glider continues fluttering but Brad eventually pulls them out of danger and right back towards that beautiful ocean off in the distance.

"Nice recovery!" Susan says with gratitude and a heavy sigh.

"Thank you for that. It was a little shaky there for a second," Brad admits humbly. They continue gliding smoothly towards the beach as the wind peacefully sounds all around them. "Well, I don't see that wacko bandit down there anymore. Sure hope we lost that crazy bastard," Brad stresses.

"Yeah, I sure hope so too," Susan says trembling.

"I just hope he doesn't follow us all the way down to the beach," Brad prays while glancing below.

"I'm sure they are all wanted men so I can't see any of them coming down this far." Susan re-enforces hope and lightens the terrible thought.

"Sure hope so," Brad says under his breath.

Normally, that was the case, but this crazed, egotistical, bastard bandit wanted another taste of Susan so bad that pure evil took over his being, driving him on in a focused pursuit of the hang glider, no matter what the consequences.

Brad cautiously glides towards the crashing waves below, then shifts his weight, redirecting them right along the sandy shoreline, and prepares for a landing.

"Look Mommy!" a little girl suddenly shouts, startling the rest of her family to move in around her. "Look, Mommy!" she repeats excitedly while pointing and filming the gliders descent, as viewed on the camera's little LED flip-out screen.

The crazed horse-riding bandit suddenly appears, riding wildly along the shoreline.

"Oh, look, honey. A Horse!" The mother points out while the little girl continues filming.

Bang! suddenly echoes from the bandit's freshly loaded pistol.

"Holy shit!" Brad shouts out as he turns around to see the possessed bandit racing along the shoreline towards them.

Bang! Bang! He fires again.

The family quickly flees from the dangerous situation.

"Lift your feet and hold on!" Brad screams seconds before they are about to land.

Thud, thud! sounds as Brad's feet slam down hard onto the wet sand. The glider instantly pivots into a nosedive and flips upside down. Brad immediately releases himself then quickly helps Susan.

The crazed, screaming bandit closes in fast.

Bang! Bang! Bang! Click, click. He fires relentlessly then tosses the empty pistol into the ocean.

Brad quickly side steps away from the glider. He reaches behind his head and grabs hold of the mini crossbow.

"Shit!" he curses, realizing that it is caught on a strap and it just cannot be pulled out. He quickly flips the knapsack off his back and frantically tries untangling it. The horse's hooves are literally upon them. "Son of a bitch!" Brad curses loudly.

"Ah! I kill you, gringo!" the bandit screams savagely. The bandit dives off his horse, right on top of Brad, knocking him to the ground, sending the knapsack flying several feet away.

The fight is on. Brad and the bandit cling to each other, rolling back and forth across the sand, desperately keeping control of each other's arms from striking a blow. Brad pulls his knife from its sheath but is quickly controlled by the strong arms of the bandit. The knife flails in all directions as they struggle intensely for the dominance of the blade.

"I kill you, gringo!" the bandit screams out while twisting the knife around and inching it towards Brad's face.

"Ah, someone please help!" Susan cries out. Brad's adrenaline immediately kicks into the next level when he hears Susan's pleas, bursting them across the sand and closer to the crashing waves. Brad grips both hands tightly around the bandit's knife-wielding hand while frantically refraining from being stabbed.

Swish! A large wave comes crashing down upon them, triggering Brad to smash the bandit's hand hard against some rigid coral. The knife finally drops free from the bandit's bloody hand and roles away with the force of an outgoing wave.

The bandit manages to release himself from Brad's clutches and quickly crawls into the water in search of the knife. Brad jumps to his feet and thrust kicks the bandit right on the butt, sending him splashing face-first into the water. The bandit quickly emerges from the water empty handed, then fiercely resumes his attack on Brad with a flurry of connecting punches to the stomach and head. Brad fights back hard, striking the bandit with several blows to the face and body.

The family man cautiously rushes in to help Brad fight the bandit.

Crack! echoes loudly as the family man is punched on the nose by the swift hands of the bandit, sending him flying back, bloody-faced, onto the shoreline.

"Honey!" the wife cries out then quickly rushes in and leads him, stumbling, away from the fight. Brad's and the bandit's faces are becoming bloodier by the second as they slowly stumble into deeper and deeper water with every striking blow. They wrestle in the waist-deep water as the waves constantly slam against them.

A very large wave creeps in, suddenly swishing them both off balance. The bandit lunges at Brad, wrapping both hands firmly around his neck. Brad struggles to release the bandit's solid grip from around his throat but is unable. The bandit is getting the best of the situation as Brad's air supply is being cut off by the bandit's relentless choking hands. Slowly but surely, the bandit is winning the battle and now has Brad's head submerged under the water and is holding it there.

"I kill you, you bastard!" the bandit curses with his back towards the shore.

"Brad!" Susan cries out. "Let him go, please!" she pleads on, totally panic stricken as tears stream down her face.

"Please, someone help. Please!" she begs while peering all around in search of the now much farther away family, who are trying desperately to get cell reception in order to call the police.

"Brad!" Susan cries out. "Oh God, please help!" she screams at the top of her lungs while painfully limping up and down the shoreline.

Suddenly, she does a double-take, zeroing right in on the crossbow hanging out of the top of the knapsack, several yards away. She limps as fast as she can towards the knapsack, grabs a hold of the crossbow, and frantically rips it out from its entanglement, unknowingly releasing the safety while doing so. Now full of adrenaline, she dashes right to the edge of the crashing shoreline, miraculously blanking out any pain associated with her twisted ankle. She nervously raises the crossbow and points it directly at the bandit. She turns her head, closes her eyes, scrunches up her face, and squeezes the trigger.

The arrow flies over the water in slow motion, striking the bandit right in the middle of his back. The bandit wobbles back and forth, shocked and stunned as he looks down to see the point of the arrow sticking a few inches out from his bloody chest.

Brad has been held under water for quite some time now and there are only a few bubbles rising from the water. The bandit unwillingly releases his death grip from around Brad's throat and slowly sinks into the blood-soaked water.

Brad instantly shoots up out of the water, gasping for some much-needed air, and sluggishly staggers towards the shore.

"Brad!" Susan cries out as she shuffles against the incoming waves towards him. They meet halfway and lovingly hold each other like they will never let go.

"We made it," Brad says softly as he leans back and gently cups her face in his hands.

"Yes, we made it," Susan whispers back as joyful tears roll down her face and they kiss.

* * *

Several days later, very early in the morning, the local paperboy nears the old gas station on his bicycle. He fires one of his many old-school folded newspapers right at the gas station door and flies on by.

Seconds later, Shawn arrives to work right on time. He exits his car, strolls towards the door, slips in the key, and pushes it open. The newspaper immediately springs open, revealing a recent photo of Brad and Susan plastered right across the front page.

"What the? Holy shit," Shawn shouts, crouching in for a closer look.

"Local Hero Rescues Local Girl from the Clutches of Notorious Bandits Deep in the Jungles of Mexico." Shawn whispers to himself. "What? Wow, just wow. Unbelievable," he expresses, fixed on the front page of the newspaper. The song "Under the Cancun Moon" begins playing over Grandpa's old-fashioned radio.

Printed in Canada